Seasons of Love: Book 3
Sweet Summertime Love

A Collection of Sweet & Sensual

Summer Themed Romances

by

KAREN SUE BURNS
KIM HORNSBY
LORI LEGER
CARMINE VALENTINE

Each story remains the copyright of its individual author, Karen Sue Burns, Kim Hornsby, Lori Leger and Carmine Valentine, 2013.

Seasons of Love: Book 3
SWEET SUMMERTIME LOVE
Compiled and arranged by:

CAJUNFLAIR PUBLISHING

These stories are works of fiction. Names, characters, places and incidents are either products of the author's imagination or used fictitiously. Any resemblance to actual events, locales, or persons, living or dead, is entirely coincidental.

All rights reserved.

No part of this publication can be reproduced or transmitted in any form or by any means, electronic or mechanical, without permission in writing from the authors.

ISBN-10: 1940305012

ISBN-13: 978-1-940305-01-1

TABLE OF CONTENT

Karen Sue Burns	SUMMER LOVIN'	1
	Other work by K. S. Burns	66
Kim Hornsby	DO-OVER SUMMER	87
	Other work by K. Hornsby	153
Lori Leger	*STILL* LOVING CAT	171
	Other work by Lori Leger	240
Carmine Valentine	THE LAST BLIND DATE	281
	Other work by C. Valentine	345

ACKNOWLEDGEMENTS

Cover art and interior formatting by
Lori Leger/Cajunflair Publishing
http://www.CajunflairPublishing.com

Edited by Lori Leger and Karen Sue Burns

SUMMER LOVIN'
By KAREN SUE BURNS

Chapter One

Were the parking gods on strike? Right then on a Saturday evening in early June, Ella Pace expected a thunderbolt to strike at any moment. She had circled the block for almost ten minutes going past balloons, a giant bouncy thing, and a huge "Happy Birthday" sign in the yard next door to Jenny and Mike's house. With every pass by the house, she prayed a parking spot would open.

Finally, a couple with a little blonde girl strolled out the front door and hurried to a luxury sedan. Ella stopped a space behind them and turned on her blinker. After an eternity, they pulled out and she snuck in behind. She grabbed her purse, the gift, a bottle of wine, and let herself in Jenny's front door. Walking down the familiar gallery hallway to the kitchen, she heard the head caterer's barked orders, along with the clang of metal pots and pans as the team worked. The granite counters were a sea of chaos with food, boxes, and serving trays covering every surface.

She hurried through the open patio door and stopped. The back yard teemed with people, which meant as usual, she was late. She surveyed the crowd, looking for Jenny. Instead, she made eye contact with Jenny's mother, Lori, who hurried over and surrounded her in a massive hug.

"Ella girl, finally you're here. Do I need to buy you another watch?" Lori drew back and looked at her, one corner of her mouth hitching down in a frown. She reached toward the gift bag in Ella's hand. "Didn't you hear this is a no gift party? But never mind, I'll put it with all the others. No one listens to directions these days."

"Thanks." Ella had never been able to figure out Jenny's mother, even though she'd known her over fifteen years. She was one of those women who rained fire or ice, and you never knew which was pouring when you encountered her. "Where's Jenny."

"Do I look like I'm able to follow her around these days? Lord, my arthritis will be the death of me." She walked off on her designer high-heeled sandals, hobbling first on one foot then the other.

Ella shook her head and shifted the wine bottle from one arm to another. She again scanned the crowd for Jenny or Mike. Instead, she saw Jim Campbell, Mike's best friend and a detective for the Houston Police Department, wrapping an arm around a tall redhead. Typical, that man attracted women like flooding in a hurricane—predictable and much too intense, at least for Ella's taste. A few months back when they'd been in Las Vegas, Jenny and Mike had unexpectedly re-married, and he'd stepped away from his smart-ass-detective veneer. She enjoyed a glimpse of the man behind the cocky exterior. It was a pleasant experience and they'd had a nice conversation over a casino buffet table.

It hadn't lasted long. He'd been back to his jerk-self at the airport for the flight back to Houston. She remembered how he'd called her "doll", which she hated. His condescending tone hadn't helped matters. From her vantage spot across the patio, she watched him canoodle with his sexy girlfriend. Damn him for—

"What are you glaring at? You look like you could spit nails."

She turned at Jenny's voice and threw an arm around her best friend. "It's nothing more than indigestion. Good to see you." The two had been friends since middle school and worked at the same Sugar Land hospital. They were as close as sisters and had made a blood vow in high school to never leave each other. So far, their friendship had endured the years.

Ella stepped back and offered the bottle of wine. "This is my contribution to your bar."

Jenny looked at the label and smiled. "Thank you for thinking of me."

"That's right girlfriend, and I expect you to save it for a night when I really need a glass of our favorite wine."

"I'll save it for a special occasion. Not saying that occasion will include you, though."

Ella placed her hands on her hips, enjoying the play. "It that right, little missy?"

"Is what right?"

Ella turned toward the masculine voice. Ah, geez, the devil had crawled over. "Jim, peachy, you're here, too."

"And don't you look like an exquisite rose, so delicate and sweet." Jim grinned, no doubt pleased with his ludicrous statement.

"Seriously?" Ella glared at him. She raised a hand, ready to throw out a smart retort, and stopped. He wasn't worth the trouble. "Seriously, you're impossible." She dismissed Jim, and then turned back to Jenny. "I'm going to stow my purse then get some food and a beverage. See you in a few minutes."

She retraced her steps into the house without looking back. Damn that Jim! Why did he continue to irritate her? Maybe she needed therapy. No, that was silly, too dramatic, and too expensive; she'd simply ignore him. He wasn't her type.

∽∽

"Man, I dig that girl, she's just my type." Jim took a pull on his beer and nodded at Mike.

"I've told you a million times, Ella's not into you. Give it up." Mike tapped his beer bottle against Jim's. "What about that redhead you were talking to? I think she works with Jenny."

"Nice looking, great rack, not so much on conversation." Jim was tired of dating great looking women who didn't know the name of the U.S. president or the purpose of an IRA. Yeah, sure, that had been his type for the past ten years. But he'd grown out of it. He wanted, no, he *needed*, a woman with substance. He needed a damned challenge and Ella was perfect.

"Whatever, scratch Ella off your list."

"We got along pretty good in Las Vegas."

"You-are-so-sad; that was pure accident. She was bored 'cause Jenny was with me." Mike drew a wide circle with his index finger. "This is real life. Ella thinks you're a player."

"A player? Where the hell did she get that idea?"

"Where'd she get it?" Mike repeated, pushing out his chin and leaning forward. "Are you freaking serious? Look at your dating history. Ella's not an idiot."

Jim raised his hands in mock surrender. "Okay, okay, I get it. I've dated my share the past few years. But I'm ready to settle down. I'd like to see a couple of my own kids graduate high school before I'm eligible for Medicare."

Mike placed the back of his hand on Jim's forehead. "Are you feverish? Do you feel sick?" Then he doubled over in a fit of laughter.

Jim couldn't believe his best friend would react like that—laughing at his admission he'd like to have kids. What was so damned humorous? "Not funny. Don't you plan on having kids?"

Mike wiped at his eyes. "Sure, but hell, I'm married, settled down, it's next on the agenda. But you—"

"Stop." Jim raised his beer bottle. "I need to get another one of these and something to eat. I'll catch you later."

The summer sun threw its last assault of heat on the flagstone patio as Jim strode across to the tiki bar. He grabbed a final Texas brew out of the ice chest and headed toward the food. He smiled at a few people as he walked but didn't stop. He wasn't in a mood for small talk right then. At the buffet table he loaded his plate with sliced brisket, ranch beans, and potato salad. He looked around, wondering where to sit, and settled for an empty table in a quiet section on the opposite side of the pool.

He walked around the rectangular pool. Most swimwear-clad attendees sat around the edges enjoying adult beverages, but a few splashed in the water. Jim smiled as a group of people exploded with raucous laughter. Mike and Jenny's parties had a reputation for being a good time. He approached the back expanse of grass and sat at the table.

About half way through his meal, Mike's father joined him.

"John, how's it going?" Jim wiped his mouth with a paper napkin. "I haven't seen you since the Rockets play-off game."

"Glad you could join us for it. I know you don't have much free time these days." John sat in the vacant folding chair, crossed one leg over, and looked as relaxed as a beaver in a woodpile of premium oak.

"Got that right. Between my day job and finishing my dissertation, life is hectic."

"I remember those days." John sipped his drink and looked toward the pool. After several minutes, he turned back to Jim "What are your plans after you get your doctorate?"

"Quit HPD after finding a teaching job, hopefully in Houston."

John leaned over the table and casually glanced from side to side. "You didn't hear this from me, but I've good reason to believe that Houston Cullen University is in the preliminary stage of starting a major in criminal justice. I think they'll need a program director soon."

Jim's heart started beating a bit faster at that piece of news. He settled into the idea, imagining himself at the helm of such a program—a dream come true. But seriously, what chance did he have of getting an interview, much less the position. "That sounds interesting." He sipped his beer, figuring John would know who to contact at the university. He'd retired a couple years ago after teaching there for forty years. "If I were interested in the job, who should I call?"

John smiled, tipped his glass at Jim. "First, I'd keep an eye on the employment section of their website. Once you see the job posted, give me a jingle and I can provide a name."

"Fair enough, I can do that." Jim nodded and tossed his wadded up napkin on the empty plate. This party had just turned from mindless fun to an opportunity for his future.

~∽

Ella sipped a glass of white wine and watched a game of water polo in the pool. Amazing how loud a group of adults became when beer and a ball were involved. She knew many of the people at the party, but sat alone at a table under a red umbrella, partially hidden by a large potted fern. Frankly, she enjoyed the time alone. Her life was beyond crazy with hardly a moment to herself unless she was sleeping, eating, or taking a shower.

But it would soon be over. At the end of the fall term, she would have her master's degree in nursing and she'd be able to breathe without a textbook or computer under her nose. Hopefully, all her hard work would result in a promotion at work, at least that was her plan.

"Watcha smiling at?" Jenny stood next to the table.

"Thinking about being done with school."

"You're so dedicated. I hope the hospital realizes you're the best pediatric nurse on staff."

Ella fidgeted in the chair. "Thanks. We're all pretty dedicated. Uh-oh, here comes Jim." She watched him thread his way through the crowd around the pool and knew the minute he spotted her with Jenny.

Jenny leaned over the chair and spoke near Ella's ear. "Play pretty if he comes over, and give him a chance. There's a nice guy under that tough-detective exterior." She rose and walked off in the opposite direction, throwing Jim a casual wave.

Ella scanned the area, wondering how to get out of a conversation with the one man who grated on her nerves. With no savior in sight, she braced for his approach.

"Mind if I join you?"

"Sure." She had no logical excuse to deny him. She pointed at a chair.

"I need to get a drink, would you like another wine?"

She nodded and he strolled toward the bar. He did look good in his jeans from the rear. Actually, he was quite handsome—blue eyes with dark brown hair, well-muscled, and six-feet tall. Combine that with his playboy reputation, and it meant trouble with a capital "T." She knew it was true, as Mike had mentioned it several times. How could she ever trust a man like that?

He soon returned with her wine and a bottle of water.

She watched him crack open his water bottle, somewhat surprised at his choice. "No alcohol?"

"Already had my two beer quota. Duty in a few hours."

With Jim sitting so close, Ella felt a twinge of guilt. "Hmm, I apologize for what I said before. It was rude."

He studied her for several moments before retrieving her hand from the table. "I'm not impossible then?"

Her breath hitched. He rubbed his thumb over the back of her hand then turned it over and kissed the palm. His eyes captured hers and held on as his thumb rubbed in the moisture from his kiss. She shook her head. "No, I guess you're not."

"Good." He squeezed her hand then let it go. "Are you enjoying the party? Seems like we've done this before."

"I guess we have." Since they were both Jenny and Jim's best friends, the four of them had been together many times over the past few years, except for the two years Mike and Jenny were divorced. Most of those times, Ella did her best to avoid him. The chance meeting in Las Vegas had been the one time they'd actually spent time alone. She'd enjoyed it in spite of herself.

"I'm glad Mike and Jenny are back together. They fit," Jim said.

"Fit?"

"Yeah, yin-yang, like that."

She put a hand over her mouth to hide a giggle. "You're right, they're soul mates."

"Uh-huh, it's cool." Jim drank some water, turned his head toward the pool. After a few moments he swung back to her, his mouth formed in a sexy smile. "Have dinner with me. I promise I won't bite and you might enjoy yourself."

"Oh." A dinner invitation was the last thing she'd expected. Oh hell, why not give him a chance? She needed to eat. "Sure, when?"

"I'm off on Monday. Would that work?"

She didn't have a class that night. "Sounds fine. Where should I meet you?"

"I'll pick you up. Hold on." He stood and a pulled a cell phone out of a pocket of his jeans. He turned away from her as he talked and shortly shoved the phone back in his pocket. "Gotta go."

"That was work?"

"Yeah," he said as he pulled out his wallet. He handed her a business card. "Email me your address. I'll pick you up at seven, Mexican food okay?" He brushed his lips across her temple then hurried to the patio doors and disappeared inside the house.

"How about that?" Ella muttered as she looked at his card. He really was a homicide detective for the Houston Police Department and he had left because of police business. She shivered, wondering how he'd spend the rest of his evening. She sipped her wine thinking that she didn't know Jim at all. Their dinner on Monday might very well turn out to be an enjoyable evening.

She hadn't had a date in over a year. Work and school took priority but she deserved a night off. Knowing the little bit she did about Jim; dinner was bound to be interesting. She could hardly wait to see which side of him turned up that night—would it be the charmer or the smart ass? At the very least, it would be entertaining. There was one issue—what to wear?

∽

What a mess. Ella looked in her bedroom closet trying to decide on an outfit and vowed to give the closet a good cleaning once her summer class ended. Jim had said Mexican food so that meant casual. She pulled out skinny black jeans, a white scooped neck top, and red sandals. After dressing, she spritzed her favorite perfume on her neck and added dangly earrings.

By the time the digital clock on the nightstand read 6:58, she was ready. Perfect.

In the living room she turned on a couple of lamps and the townhouse's front porch light. Since a scare two years ago when an unknown man appeared on her doorstep pounding on the door, she never left her house at night without the inside lights being on. The doorbell rang. After grabbing her purse and keys, she opened the front door.

Jim stood on her porch holding a large shopping bag in each hand and wearing a lopsided grin. He raised the bags. "May I come in? I can explain."

"Of course." Ella stepped to the side and caught a whiff of a musky scent as he passed by her. Oh dear, she loved the smell of a good cologne on a man. She pointed to the kitchen and followed him.

He set the bags on the dark granite counter. "Do you mind if we have dinner here?"

"Is something wrong?"

He sighed. "Nothing is wrong, I need to relax."

"What kind of relax?"

"The kind where I lean back, put up my feet, and enjoy the presence of a beautiful woman."

"Right. What's the real story?" Ella started to unload a bag, placing plastic containers on the counter.

"Remember when I left on Saturday night?" He pulled two bottles of wine from the second bag. "I didn't get home until around two this morning and then I had a good eight hours of work on my dissertation. Where's your cork screw?"

Ella retrieved it from a drawer and handed it to him. "Did you get any sleep?"

"Some, and then on my way over here I remembered I needed toilet paper and when I stopped I noticed the deli and here we are with a home-style dinner." He deftly removed the cork from the wine bottle.

"You're not too tired?"

"I'm fine." He lifted the bottle. "I don't mind chugging but you might want a wine glass."

She rolled her eyes and pulled two glasses from a cabinet along with plates. "Let's eat in the living room."

"Okay with me. I hope you like salads and pasta."

Jim poured the wine and Ella retrieved the final containers from the bag. She peeled off container lids and her stomach growled. Jim had a good eye for deli food.

In silence, they each loaded their plates with broccoli-bacon salad, pasta salad, boiled shrimp, and chicken with spicy noodles. Jim settled in the leather easy chair and Ella on the matching sofa.

"I promise I'll take you out for Mexican food," Jim said.

"Are you asking me out for a second date?"

"Absolutely."

"Uh-huh, let's see how the first one goes." Ella dived into her food and noticed Jim did the same. He looked right at home in her townhouse, and much too attractive in her easy chair. Jerk, or not, he was a man who had that aura of hunkiness that appealed to women.

After a few minutes, Jim rose from the chair. "You need anything else?"

Ella shook her head and watched as he filled his plate a second time. He came back with the wine bottle, topped off her glass, and returned to the chair. She appreciated anyone with a good appetite. Her preferred non-work activity was cooking.

"What's your favorite food?" Ella said.

Jim cocked his head. "Hmm, anything my mom cooks. She calls herself a gourmet cook. But I will admit I don't like snails, frog legs, or snake."

"You're safe with my cooking then."

"Good to know."

"You said you were working on your dissertation. What's the story with that?" Why was she only now discovering they were both pursuing graduate degrees?

They spent the next half-hour sharing stories about their programs. Ella was genuinely surprised by Jim's dedication to his doctoral program.

"I have a question," she said. "What is your goal once you're finished? Will you get a promotion at work?"

Jim chuckled. "No promotion. I hope to quit HPD."

"Quit and do what?"

"Teach. I enjoy my work but I can't see myself doing it for thirty years and having a regular life, you know, with a family and all."

"Really? I didn't realize things were so tough for cops."

"My dad was a detective in Dallas, where I grew up, and I hardly saw him as a kid. He was always on the job."

"I'm confused," Ella said. "Why did you join the police force?"

"I love being a cop. Every case is like solving a puzzle. I kind of have a knack for it." Jim finished his wine and went to the kitchen. He opened a cabinet door and pulled out dessert plates. "I figure I'll be more useful to the department by teaching what I know."

Ella joined him and looked in the last plastic containers. "That one looks like banana pudding. What's the other one?"

"Tiramisu. My mom makes it every Christmas."

"One of my favorites. Let's have some coffee."

Ella made them each a cup of house blend with her new single cup coffee maker while Jim scooped a portion of each dessert onto the plates.

"Jim, do you suppose your mother would give me her recipe for tiramisu? I haven't found one that I like."

"Don't know. I'll ask." He grinned over the top of the coffee cup. "Does this mean we can have a second date?"

Ella smiled and nodded. "I think it does."

"Good. Will this Saturday work?"

"Yes, I think it will." The first date was going so well Ella wanted to clap her hands like a school-girl.

They chitchatted for a several more minutes, and Jim rose. "I hate to cut the evening short but I have to work tomorrow and so do you." He gathered the plates and cups, and took them to the kitchen.

"This was fun." Ella smiled, somewhat surprised that she meant it. She walked Jim to the front door. "Thanks for bringing dinner."

"My pleasure," Jim said as he took her hand and kissed the palm. "You're so beautiful. I've wanted to go out with you for a long time."

Ella pulled back her hand and placed it on her hip. "Because I'm beautiful?"

"Uh, sure, but that's not all." Jim stepped back from her. "I think—"

"I guess you only consider dating women you think are good-looking." Ella couldn't believe she'd agreed to go out with this shallow, chauvinist of a man.

"Sure, I like good-looking women." He rubbed a hand over his forehead. "Not attracted to the other ones."

"The *other* ones? You mean normal, average women?" She gave her head a sad shake. "Thanks for letting me know I passed the test. See you later." She shut the door in his face. *Damn, he was a player.*

∽

"I'm going to cancel our date." Ella damn near stamped her foot. "Men are pigs!"

"Tell me what happened." Jenny had joined Ella for their regular Wednesday lunch time walk around the hospital grounds.

The helmet of gray clouds tamped down the sweltering temperature to a tolerable level. They strolled in silence along the wide walk, bordered with seasonal flowers and the occasional park bench. Live oaks provided a welcomed spattering of canopies over the manicured lawn. They stopped at a circular fountain in the middle of the grounds.

Ella watched the water pour from a large urn into the pool in the base and turned to her friend.

"Maybe I'm too sensitive." She relayed the conversation at the end of Saturday evening. "What do you think about what Jim said?"

"I can see why you've reacted as you have." Jenny sat on the base of the fountain. "But, it's Jim. He's always been attracted to the ladies."

"I know, but still . . . maybe I'm not ready to date again."

"That's silly, in my opinion, but it's your decision, your life." Jenny brushed a lock of stray hair out of her face. "Maybe you're stressed from too much going on—school, work, keeping up your house. You're a busy girl."

Ella knew that was true but it sounded lame. She had enough experience to stay organized and keep a busy schedule without excuses. "But that's not it."

"What is it then?"

Ella blew a long breath, thinking about how to best approach the complicated subject of Jim. This was going deep but she'd never lied or avoided the truth with Jenny. "I'm terrified. I devoted seven years to my last relationship and look how that turned out. What if Jim and I date and it happens again? I don't think I'm willing to put in the time to discover whether Jim's a decent guy."

"And me telling you he is a good person doesn't make it true."

"Exactly." Ella shook her head slowly. "I need more time to think about this."

Jenny rose and hugged her. "Come on, let's keep walking."

They walked past the fountain then turned and followed the pathway to the hospital's back door. Jenny's words "…it's your decision, your life," kept running through Ella's head. She did need time to think about seriously dating anyone. In the meantime, she knew the right thing to do.

"Once I get a free minute this afternoon, I'm sending Jim an email canceling dinner on Saturday."

"Okay."

"No, I'll say I'm postponing it."

"Okay."

"Hmm, maybe I better say cancel. I'll say something has come up."

"That should explain it."

Ella nodded and felt a small bubble of unease snake down her throat. Was she doing the right thing? Was she being silly by trapping herself in a box of loneliness? Worst of all, she didn't know her own mind.

∾

Damn, the meeting had started. Ella snuck into the back of her townhouse complex's clubroom, nodding at a neighbor or two. She ignored the disapproving looks. Most of the residents were retired and thought five in the evening was too late for a meeting. No argument there. She'd rather be at home on a Friday opening a bottle of wine than going to a homeowner's gathering with a bunch of her grumpy neighbors.

Mildred Pierce, president of the association and a lover of pink-hued hair, pointed a crooked finger at the front row of chairs. "Joyce, get up here and tell everyone what's going on."

Joyce hobbled to the front carrying a brown paper shopping bag. She plopped the bag on the table and faced the group. "Apparently, I've been elected to do the show and tell." She threw a go-to-hell look at Mildred, opened the sack, pulled out an object, and held it up in front of her chest. "This is what I found on my front porch yesterday morning."

Ella leaned forward and squinted to get a good look at it. How weird. It looked like a garden gnome. Joyce turned it around and Ella nearly laughed. The back of the gnome showed a bare over-sized butt. Based on the shouts of "disgusting" and "put it away" she surmised the retired crowd didn't find it funny. She shook her head and vowed she would not be so uptight when she retired.

"This is not the worst of the bunch," Mildred said as she waved her hand motioning Joyce to return to her seat. "Linda and Betty, stand up and show your stuff."

Joyce gathered the bag and gnome and moved slowly back to her chair. Ella studied her as she walked and noticed something—her derriere encased in lavender polyester slacks seemed a bit large based on the overall size of her body—uh-oh, inspiration! Her husband threw a skinny arm over her shoulder after she returned to her chair.

"Okay girls, hold 'em up," Mildred ordered as the two ladies stood in front of the table.

Linda held another gnome and moved her hands from side to side so everyone had a good look. This one looked like a witch with a broom between the legs, a black pointed hat, and a large hooked nose.

"Gawd, but that's ugly!" someone declared from the back of the room.

Thought-provoking, considering Linda usually dressed as a witch on Halloween and had a long, pointed nose.

Betty, who was six feet tall and very thin, raised her hands gripping another gnome. This one mimicked a skeleton with a clownish grin on the face. Ella shook her head, wondering who thought this was funny. Whoever deposited these trolls around the complex knew the residents.

"That's enough," Mildred said and shooed the two women back to their seats. "Now, it's obvious we have a problem. Someone has gotten through our security gate."

The residents started talking over each other and the noise level increased.

Mildred scowled before banging the gavel. "Quiet down." Before long, she had the room as quiet as school kids threatened by a teacher with a big stick. "We need to get to the bottom of this. Is there anyone present who hasn't received a surprise on their front porch?"

Ella raised her hand and quickly realized that of the dozen or so people there, she was the only one who hadn't. She lowered her arm, but not in time.

"It appears that only one resident didn't receive a gnome. Ella Pace, why do you suppose that's so?"

The residents turned as a group to stare suspiciously at her. Ella rose and waved a hand. "Hold on everyone. It's true a . . . a garden statue wasn't put on my porch, but I sure as heck didn't do this. I have no idea where they came from."

After a couple of sarcastic comments of "Right!" and "We don't believe you!" Mildred banged the gavel again. "Give her a chance to speak."

"Honestly, this is as much a mystery to me as it is to you." Ella prayed they'd believe her. She didn't want to get cross-wise with her neighbors.

"Then you figure out who did it," Joyce said.

"I agree," Linda chimed in.

"Yeah, you're the youngest resident and you have time," Betty said. "We're much too busy to solve a mystery."

Ella waved a fist above her head. "Hold on—"

Mildred cut her off. "I make a motion that Ella Pace figures out where the gnomes are coming from. All those in favor of this, raise a hand."

Every person in the room, other than Ella, raised their hands.

Mildred banged the gavel. "That concludes this meeting. Ella, give me a report in a week."

"But, I . . ." Panic filled Ella. She didn't have time to play sleuth for her neighbors, regardless of what they thought.

People shuffled out of the clubhouse while Ella waited for Mildred. After a minute or two, Betty walked past Ella without acknowledging her. Mildred was three steps behind and stopped after Ella said her name.

"What do you want?"

"I'm not sure this is a good idea. I work full-time and I'm not at home as much as the rest of you."

"Doesn't matter. You're the smartest of the bunch, so get it done." She winked and walked past Ella out the door.

Ella threw her hands up in the air. How the hell had this happened? She knew nothing about investigating an attack of garden gnomes, or whatever you'd call this. She had no choice but to figure it out or risk a mutiny by her neighbors.

An idea bubbled in her head. It might work if she was careful. She knew someone who was a professional at sleuthing and maybe he could give her some pointers. It was simple actually. All she had to do was muster the nerve to contact a particular HPD detective.

Chapter Two

Jim pushed his chair back from the ratty old desk in his studio apartment and stretched out his arms. Sitting for six hours with ass glued to the chair definitely cramped his style. However, the time and the effort to complete his dissertation on schedule justified a sore butt. He'd spent too much time selecting the topic and researching to screw it up in the end.

His goal of receiving his Ph.D. was the single most important one of the moment. Well, other than a beautiful blonde he couldn't seem to keep from his thoughts. He could do his job at the department in his sleep.

Ella had gotten under his skin. True, it was totally out of the box behavior for him, but he meant every word he'd confessed to Mike at the party last week. He wanted to settle down, and couldn't think of anyone he'd rather do that with than Ella. Unfortunately, she had a different opinion . . . so far. He needed a plan to woo her. Woo? He laughed at his word choice, even knowing in his gut she was The One. His mother didn't approve of his dating history and had never hesitated to give him her opinion on the subject. She'd always insisted he'd drop like a deflating balloon when he finally realized he'd found that one, all-important person.

He rose, grabbed a bottle of water out of the refrigerator, and stood at the one large window, staring at the busy street below. He loved living in downtown Houston. The station was close and so were plenty of bars and restaurants for extracurricular activities. The first time he'd met Ella was at Vic's Bar down the street, several years ago. She'd been with Mike and Jenny and he'd joined them for happy hour.

He'd never forget his first sight of Ella. Perched on a barstool next to Mike, she had been laughing with her head thrown back, her long, blonde hair streaming down her back. She looked like a goddess emerging from the sea. Once introduced, he got a good look at her. With pretty blue eyes and her cute as can be dimples, she looked like your typical, all-American girl with one sexy smile. Definitely not his type, or so he thought at the time.

He cringed at the shrill ring of his cell phone, praying it wasn't work. He really needed some time off.

"Jim, are you busy?"

It took him a couple of seconds to recognize Ella's voice. "Just taking a break. What's up?"

"I'm sorry I had to cancel dinner tonight. But . . . I was wondering, how about coming over for lunch tomorrow, my treat."

Oh man! How perfect was this? "Sure, what time?"

They agreed to a time, and clicked off as Jim performed a satisfying fist pump. "Yessss…that's what I'm talking about."

Only allowing a few moments of celebration time, he went back to the chair and resumed his position at the desk. He'd work another five hours then he'd reward himself with a burger and a beer. He tapped happy fingers on a stack of printed pages. His wooing strategy was off to a good start.

∽∽

Ella gave the salad one final check before stowing it in the refrigerator. She turned the shrimp in the marinade, then checked the table one last time. The red tulips in the center vase added a festive flair. She blew a breath and leaned against the kitchen counter. After she'd emailed Jim last week cancelling their dinner she'd felt silly and childish. Because of their differences, they had virtually no hope of making a relationship work. Once she'd accepted that, her anxiety had evaporated. She'd thought long and hard about his "good-looking women" remarks and decided it was his own player version of a compliment.

Her plan was to fill his belly with a delicious lunch, then ply him with questions on how to capture the neighborhood gnome deliverer. Hopefully, he wouldn't realize the only reason for her invitation was to solicit information on playing townhouse detective. The doorbell rang, introducing the arrival of her guest.

She opened the door and Jim walked in, giving her a light peck on the cheek. He straightened, handing her a bottle of wine. "I'm taking a break this afternoon so I thought we might enjoy a glass."

They entered the kitchen, opened the wine and filled the two glasses she provided. He grinned as they tapped glasses. "Did you have a good week?"

She nodded. "Busy as usual and a mid-term on Thursday for my advanced pediatrics class."

"Exams are the one thing I will never miss about college," he said. "Glad that part of my program is over."

"I'm looking forward to being exam-free myself." Ella rotated the shrimp again, turned the oven on, and retrieved garlic bread from the freezer. She stopped at the counter and tasted the wine. "This is good." Jim beamed, obviously pleased at her reaction, and a chill raced along her spine.

"Once I pass the defense of my dissertation I'm officially looking for that teaching job." Jim leaned against the counter and absent-mindedly stirred the shrimp in a glass dish.

"Is your plan to stay in Houston?"

"Yep." Jim cocked his head. "I plan to move as well. I've thought about Sugar Land. You like living here?"

"I've lived here all my life and Sugar Land keeps getting better. We have great shopping, restaurants, a minor league baseball team, and great medical facilities."

"You work for the chamber of commerce?" Jim asked.

"No." Ella glanced back at him as she put the bread in the oven. "I like living here. It's a great place to raise a family."

"You like kids?"

She stopped on her way to the pantry and swiveled to face him. "I'm a pediatric nurse at Sugar Land Presbyterian Hospital. Yep, I like kids."

He raised his glass, saluting her. "Sorry, dumb question."

She shrugged and set a broiler pan on the counter. "Would you mind putting the shrimp on the pan? One of these days I'm buying an outdoor grill."

Jim followed her instructions. "What else can I do to help?"

"If you'll watch the shrimp in the broiler I'll take care of everything else."

Within a few minutes, Ella had their lunch on the table. Jim played the gentleman and pulled out a chair for her before seating himself at the opposite end of her small table.

"I hope you like chunky salads." She spooned a portion on her plate.

"Chunky?" Jim looked at the salad bowl. "You mean with cut veggies and stuff? My favorite."

"Good to know." Ella saw a different side of Jim every time she was around him. The more she saw, the more she liked, but, whatever—it didn't matter how much she liked him, she wasn't in the market for a relationship. She didn't have the time, and she sure as hell wasn't ready to trust a man again. Case closed.

"You like living in a townhouse? I can't decide whether to buy one or a single family house."

"I guess it depends on how much time you have for lawn maintenance and major upkeep." She cut her shrimp into equal-sized bites. "Myself, I've no time for yard work or maintaining the common areas."

"Are your neighbors okay?"

She nearly choked on a bite of shrimp. Were her neighbors okay? How about cranky and crabby? Every once in a while they surprised the hell out of her—like when Mildred winked at her as she left the clubhouse after the co-owner meeting.

"Most of the residents here are older than me, lots of retired people."

He grunted. "There's nothing wrong with that. I'd expect both the crime level and the noise level are low."

"You're right." Ella knew this would be the perfect time to ask for his help with the gnome situation. Yet she hesitated.

"I'm ready for a house . . . I think, one thing at a time." He pointed at his plate with his fork. "This salad is good."

"Glad you like it." This was it, time to get it over with. "Could I ask you a question about investigating a crime?"

"Sure." Jim put his elbows on the table and leaned in. "What kind of crime?"

"Maybe crime isn't the correct word." She noticed Jim's eyes narrow, uh-oh. "Actually this is the situation." She took a healthy sip of wine then explained Friday's meeting and her assignment as the townhouse detective. During her little speech, she noticed Jim's eyes crinkling but the expression on his face never changed. The man had nerves of steel.

"Hmm, let me think about this," Jim settled back in the chair, his face toward the ceiling—no doubt deep in detective case analysis.

Right. He was probably working on the proper words to tell her she was nuts. Ella rose and retrieved the wine bottle. She refilled their glasses, and resumed her seat at the table.

"Any ideas?" she said. He looked at her and smiled—one of those lazy grins that could charm the spanks off a fifty-year-old virgin. She shivered and ran her hands over her arms. Her reaction to him was scary. This proved to her she'd made the right decision not to date him. Who knows what mayhem would ensue if she succumbed to her attraction to this charming detective.

Oh man, this was perfect. Jim took a sip of wine then causally pulled out his cell phone and acted as if he was studying it. "I do have an idea but it's going to take some work. I needed to check my calendar."

"You'll help me? I really have no idea what to do." Ella's eyes widened, big and round, and she looked so damned cute.

"I'll help you but it'll be an unofficial assignment. Okay?"

"I figured that. Where do we start?"

"I'll do some research and then we can get together again and decide on the next move."

"That sounds fair to me." Ella reached out and touched Jim's arm. "I do appreciate your help."

He shrugged. "It's nothing. We'll get to the bottom of these gnome appearances." He cocked his head, trying to keep a straight face. "Except, I don't know exactly what category of crime it would fall under."

"What do you mean?"

"Well, it's not exactly a misdemeanor, since nothing has been stolen or destroyed."

She shook her head. "No, not exactly."

He rubbed his hand over his face. "Maybe…it's a…wait for it…a mis-gnome-er."

She choked, coughing and snorting on a gulp of wine.

He laughed. "Pretty good, huh?"

"Pretty lame, I was about to say."

He chuckled and slid the phone back in a pocket of his jeans. "Are you free on Wednesday? I should have an investigative strategy developed by then."

Jim could barely keep from gloating. It was funny how the right situation appeared at the right time. In this case, garden gnomes mysteriously appearing on porches. Looking into this would be the perfect excuse to see Ella without calling it a date. He sensed she was hesitant to date him officially, so investigating the gnomes would allow him to spend time with her. Damn, he was a lucky son of a bitch, and Ella was so worth sacrificing a little time off.

"Wednesday should work," she said. "I don't have a class."

"My shift is over at six so I'll head over after that."

"Sounds good, is there anything I need to prepare?"

"Nah, let me take care of it." He already had an idea of what he'd do. In the meantime, he intended to take advantage of their time together.

She nodded and rose from the table. "I'll make some coffee to accompany our dessert."

"Dessert, too? I like eating here." He rose to stretch his legs and walked into the living room. A bookshelf in the corner caught his attention. One shelf held framed photos and he leaned in to get a better view. A beaming Ella stood in front of a white sand beach with a group of girls. She wore a pink bikini and looked good enough to eat. Uh-oh, none of that. "One thing at a time" was his new mantra.

His gaze latched on a pile of neatly stacked music CDs. He perused the titles and selected one, approving of her music library. He popped the disc in the player. "Sexual Healing" flooded the living room. He loved it, instant relaxation.

Ella walked into the room and stopped. "Not everyone likes Marvin Gaye music. I had no idea you did."

"I'm a man of many mysteries. Besides," he snorted. "Anyone who can't appreciate Marvin has no taste, whatsoever." He closed the space between them in three steps and wrapped one arm around her back, placed his hand in hers. "Dance with me."

Ella moved toward him, less than half a step. He felt a stillness in her, which pleased him. They began to move, slowly, a gentle rocking from side to side, with hands fully engaged. Jim's heart threatened to torpedo from his chest. He took a deep and silent breath, surrounded by a soothing melody and tempting lyrics of the song. He let the song guide his feet as he led her in slow loops and circles. His hands caressed her back, her fingers, the delicate palm of her hand. He enjoyed every damned second of that dance.

Ella finally spoke, her voice a hesitant whisper breaking the silence between them. "You . . . you surprise me."

Her hips pressing against him surprised the hell out of Jim, but he'd keep that revelation to himself. "How do I surprise you?"

She pulled her head back from his shoulder and gazed up at him. "You're different."

"Different? From what?'

"From who I . . . from . . . oh, never mind. You're just different." She stepped back and pulled her hand from his. "The coffee should be ready. I'll get the dessert."

He followed her to the kitchen, enjoying the view of her backside in tight jeans. This was truly a first, a good first. Most of the women he dated used the kitchen to open take-out containers, not to actually cook. Funny that had never bothered him before. He poured the coffee in mugs already set out while Ella retrieved a plate from the refrigerator.

"What's that?"

"Chocolate cheesecake." She sliced two servings and they moved back to the living room.

"You amaze me," Jim said.

"Why? Cheesecake isn't hard to make."

"You're complex." He began to explain by counting with his fingers. "You work full-time in a tough job, you're getting a master's degree, you take care of your home and your neighbors, and to top it off, you're a fantastic cook."

"If you hadn't been so busy dating Barbie and Victoria's Secret models all those years you'd know there's nothing special about me. This is how *normal* people live, Jim. Regular people, busy people." "You'll get no argument from me. Women like that are nice to look at, but most of them use the oven for storage. Some of them make it difficult to carry on an adult conversation."

After emptying her plate, she checked her watch. "I have homework to do this afternoon. What time again on Wednesday?"

"I should be here by seven. That will give you time to unwind after work." Jim stood and placed his dirty dishes on the kitchen counter. "I'll head out now. Thanks for lunch."

Ella rose and went to the front door. "Thanks for offering to help me with the gnome issue."

"My pleasure." He was hesitant to kiss her, but that had never stopped him before. He leaned towards her and pressed his lips to hers. He felt her surprise but she didn't pull back. He increased the pressure and stroked her arm. Their tongues touched and the kiss deepened. She seemed fully into it and that confused him. He squeezed her shoulders, pulled back, and stepped through the open door.

She followed him to the porch. He cast one backward glance her direction, and thought she looked like an angel with the sun shining on her golden hair. "I'll see you on Wednesday. Don't study too hard." He waved and headed to his SUV.

He felt that kiss all the way back to his place—thinking Wednesday couldn't get here fast enough. There's nothing quite like pursuing the one thing you want more than anything else in the world, until you get it. And he would get it.

~·~

Ella glanced at her watch; her Wednesday shift had been over three hours ago. She'd been waiting on a lab test for her new nephew. Her older brother's wife, Jackie, had given birth to little Alex four days ago and he had promptly developed hyperbilirubinemia. She explained to them it was a severe case of jaundice with high bilirubin levels.

After three days of treatment and careful watching, she hoped he'd be ready to go home. Jackie was going stir crazy staying extra days in the hospital but wouldn't leave since she was nursing. Ella had promised her brother she'd stay with his wife and child until the tests results were back. She hoped they'd be good. Poor little Alex had been poked too many times for blood tests.

She walked the hallway to Jackie's room to check on her. The quiet ward was a testimony that this particular mid-June wasn't a popular time for having babies. She knocked on the door then poked her head inside. "You busy?"

"Yes, ma'am, I'm packing my stuff. We're gonna blow this joint." Jackie had her suitcase on the bed along with a large tote bag. "Little "A" and I are ready to go home."

"I can see that. I'm still waiting on the last blood test." Ella stood on the other side of the bed from her sister-in-law. She'd been surprised when her brother, three years her senior, had married a woman ten years younger than himself. Jackie was young and feisty, and accustomed to getting her own way.

"Can't you tell them to hurry?"

"No," Ella said with a chuckle. "You have to be patient."

"Yeah, right, like patience is my middle name." Jackie zipped the suitcase and patted the top. "I'm ready to go home. I need to sleep in my own bed. Plus the food here sucks."

Ella stepped around the bed to look at Alex. He was sleeping soundly in the bassinet and his color looked good. She had a hunch he'd be approved to leave the hospital. The attending physician had earlier signed the release papers, contingent on the blood test results.

"Alex is adorable," she said, amazed at the child's resemblance to his father. The thought brought a tear to her eye. She brushed it away and perched on the guest chair. "Let's talk while we wait."

"Okay." Jackie plopped on the bed. "How's your love life? Spill it, chickie."

Her question shocked Ella at first, until she made the connection. Jenny had spoken to Mike, who had talked to her brother, who worked for the same law firm. Big brother had naturally spilled his guts to Jackie. The man was beyond besotted with his wife. "Are you—"

"Don't play coy with me. I've heard all about Jim the hunky-police-detective. Why haven't I met him before? Are you serious? Any plans down the road?"

"Whoa, hold on." Ella needed to set the record straight. "I don't know exactly what you've heard but there's nothing going on between Jim and me. No, we're not serious and no, there are no plans."

"Uh-huh, sure."

"No, really—" Ella's phone rang. She listened for a moment then smiled. "Okay, Jackie, the test results are in and y'all are good to go."

Jackie clapped her hands. "Yay! Hubs will be here any minute, because I've already called him." She sat on the bed and stared up at Ella. "But, look sis-in-law. Before you go, I want you to hear me out. I wasn't sure about marrying your brother. Not so much because of the age difference, but the fact that he was a lawyer, for chrissakes. I'd never been attracted to the type of man it takes to be an attorney. I figured if he was a lawyer, then naturally, he'd be all stuffy and arrogant."

She reached over to touch her newborn son and smiled the kind of blissful smile produced by extremely happy people. "But I was wrong about him. We both took a chance...and it paid off." Her gaze met Ella's again. "Hon, don't you think it's time you take a chance, too?"

∽

Ella was still smiling as her car crept through the townhouse gate. It had been such a thrill at the hospital to see her brother leave with his new son. Watching his big hands place little Alex so gently in the car seat nearly did her in. She'd nearly cried, but managed to maintain her composure in the end.

As she pulled into her driveway much later than she'd expected to be, Jim exited his SUV parked along the street. She stopped in the garage and met Jim on the front porch.

"I'm sorry I'm late. I stayed at the hospital with my sister-in-law."

"No problem. I heard you have a new nephew."

"You're kidding." Ella hadn't realized the reach of the gossip train was so wide. Not good. She unlocked the front door and turned on a light. "Let's sit at the kitchen table."

Once seated, Jim pulled a couple of papers from the pocket of his sport coat. "I've done some research."

"What have you learned?" Ella was eager to hear Jim's plan. Strangely enough, just sitting beside him gave her a sense of comfort and well-being.

"First I pulled a report of the home owners, twenty-four in total. That's a manageable number. Next, I looked at crime stats for the last year. Nothing—no break-ins, and no emergency calls. This is a safe complex."

"What does that mean?"

"Whoever is playing this little game has access to the front gate." He spread a paper in front of him. "I think we need to interview the other homeowners and see what we find."

"Where did you get this list?" Ella noted that it had home values on it. Geez, now he knew the value of her house—too much information.

"Property records," he said with a lopsided smile. "It's public information."

"Right, didn't think of that." Slapping her forehead would be too obvious so Ella stepped up her game. "I think we should start our interviews with the ladies who brought gnomes to the homeowners meeting."

"That's right, start with what we know." Jim pulled out a ballpoint pen from his jacket. "What are the names?"

"We should start with the association president, Mildred, and then add the three residents who spoke at the meeting, Joyce, Madeline, and Betty."

He shoved the paper toward her. "Mark them on the list of owners."

"Geez, you're bossy." Ella attempted a teasing tone, punched Jim on the arm.

"Just trying to help." Jim tapped the paper with an index finger.

She scanned the list, sorted by townhouse number, and placed a star next to the four names. "This is where we start."

Jim nudged her arm. "I agree. Call all of them to set a time. Will Saturday morning work?"

"Yes, I'll let them know and then we can go from there."

"What's the name of your management company?"

"Hmm . . . oh, that's who I make the maintenance check to, Crest Townhome Management." Another mental slap to her forehead. He must think she was a clueless nincompoop. "I suppose you'll look into the gate and the security system."

"Correct, but after we do these interviews."

"What questions will we ask the homeowners? Just so I can let them know if they ask when I call." She had a hunch she'd get pushback from everyone but Mildred.

"The usual—when and where the gnome was received, any problems with neighbors, witnessing any strangers around the complex, any problems with their security system—questions like that." He put the paper and pen back in his pocket and rose. "I better get going, more work to do at home."

Ella scrambled up from the table and retrieved a plastic container from the kitchen counter. "I made these yesterday and thought you might enjoy them."

Jim opened the container, smiled, and took a bite from a chocolate brownie, chewing slowly. "These are good, better than my mom's."

"Don't tell her that," she said, pleased that he liked her baking.

"Not to worry." He headed toward the door, opened it, and stepped to the porch. "I'll see you Saturday morning." He waved and walked to his car.

She shut the door once he started his vehicle. While turning the door lock she realized he hadn't kissed her goodnight like he did on Sunday. Why not?

The phone rang.

"Hey sis, how are you?"

"I'm fine. How's Alex doing?" What did her brother want? He never called, just texted.

"Great. Jackie is feeding him. I have a question about the guy you're dating—"

"Dating? What guy?"

"Mike's friend, the cop, I met him a couple of months ago. What's going on?"

"Nothing, nothing is going on and we're not dating. Geez, you and Mike gossip like school girls."

"I've heard this guy is a player. I'm looking out for my little sister."

"Not needed this time, not dating, no nothing is going on."

"Okay, but let me know when something is going on. Gotta go, Jackie is calling."

The gossip fest was worse than she thought. She'd talk to Jenny about keeping a lid on her seeing Jim. Mike had obviously jumped to a huge conclusion and passed it on. Men were the worst about spreading rumors.

Ella went to the front window to check the street. It was empty except for a sweet couple, Sadie and Max, taking their nightly walk. She wondered what kind of gnome they'd received. Maybe she should add them to the list for an interview, which reminded her, she had better start calling. She dug out the phone list from her desk and sat at the kitchen table with her cell.

As she flipped through the list for Mildred's number, she caught a whiff of Jim's cologne. She closed her eyes and took a deep breath. She loved that scent, always had. She hadn't seen his "player" mode at work other than the end of their first dinner at her townhouse. Except for that one comment, he'd been a gentleman and a regular guy. Hmm . . . maybe she *should* consider dating him.

∼∾

"This is Mildred's house." Ella spoke in low tones as she pushed the doorbell. The unit was at the front of the complex with a full view of the main gate. "She asked us to visit her first."

"No problem." Jim stood casually next to her, sexy as hell in a polo shirt the same shade of blue as his eyes. He filled out his crisply pressed jeans nicely, the police badge displayed at his hip, only adding to his masculine appearance. The man looked like the contemporary version of a Greek god . . . no, he looked like the hot man she longed to drag into the nearest cave and have her way with.

Mildred opened the door, saving Ella from rating Jim's hotness on a one-to-ten scale.

"Ella, finally, you're here," Mildred stepped to the side. "You and your friend can come in."

Ella did the introductions and they followed Mildred to the family room. Jim and Ella sat on a beige sofa and Mildred across from them. She wasted no time. "What have you learned?"

Jim glanced at Ella and spoke. "I reviewed crime statistics for the last year and there have been no reported incidents. That means that whoever is leaving the gnomes has access to the property and knows the security code for the main gate."

Mildred's eyes narrowed. "Oh no, who would do such a terrible thing? Everyone gets along here . . . well, for the most part."

"Who are you thinking of, who doesn't get along?" Ella had always thought all the residents were friendly with each other.

"Oh, phooey, it's nothing," Mildred fanned her face with a magazine. "Sadie and Max are standoffish at times but that's just them, they're Yankees." She put the magazine down and pointed with her index finger. "Now I expect the two of you to get to the bottom of this, and pronto. We can't have some maniac running around here scaring everyone."

Ella initially bristled at Mildred's tone then let it drop. She was only doing her best for the homeowners, which gave Ella an idea. "I was wondering, what do you think about forming a group to keep a watch on who goes in and out the gate? It would be a good way to see who else visits the complex besides residents."

Mildred clapped her hands and rose. "I like that idea. I'll take care of making a schedule and getting volunteers. You two get out of here and start those interviews." She ushered them to the door. "Nice to meet you, Jim."

"Yes, ma'am, the pleasure was all mine." He put his hand on Ella's back and guided her out the door. Once they were on the sidewalk, he grabbed her hand and led her to a bench in a sitting area that doubled as a community flower garden. "Let's go over the questions. We need to be in control of these interviews."

"What?" she said and giggled. "Surely you don't think a bunch of retired folks will get the best of the experienced police detective?" He sent her the sexiest smile she'd ever seen on a man. A swarm of butterflies made a pass through her stomach.

"That's exactly what I'm afraid of. These folks will eat my lunch."

She patted his knee in understanding and they spent the next five minutes agreeing on the questions. Joyce and her husband were next on the list.

Ella stood, "Come on, let's get this party started. Joyce and Ben live a couple doors away."

After introductions, Joyce took them to the living room where Ben watched the morning cable news blasting on a huge television set.

"Damn liberals, we should cut off their b—"

"Ben," Joyce shouted. "Turn off that damned TV and watch your language. Ella brought a police detective to talk with us."

Ben lowered the volume and half-heartedly raised a skinny arm. "Hi, Ella, Mr. Detective. Why the hell are you bothering me on a Saturday morning? I'm missing my market show."

"Damn it, Ben Rogers, you mind your manners and answer Ella's questions." Joyce grabbed the remote and turned off the TV.

"Ben, I promise we'll be quick," Ella said. "Have either of you noticed anyone around the complex lately who you don't recognize."

Ben shook his head and Joyce raised her hand, like in a classroom. "I can answer. It's the mailman, he's new."

"Okay." Jim scribbled in a small notebook. "Anyone else?"

"Bruno is here all the time. I think he's sneaky," Joyce said.

Jim shifted on his feet. "Can you tell me *why* you think he's sneaky?"

"Because he listens to that damned music too loud," Ben barked. "The man must be deaf."

"What time of day did you find the gnome on your porch?" Ella asked, looking first at Ben then Joyce.

"I found the damned thing when I went out to get the paper. Let me think." Ben rubbed his scruffy face and tapped a finger to the side of his nose. "That was the day I started the coffee, no, it was the day I went outside first. No . . . dammit Joyce, what day was it again?"

"It was a Wednesday," Joyce said.

Ben slapped the arm of his chair. "That's it. I found the stupid thing at five in the morning."

"You're certain of that?" Jim said.

"Young man, I'm sure. I always get the paper before making coffee on Monday, Wednesday, and Friday. I believe in adding a little spice to my life."

Jim clamped down on his jaw, clearly close to losing it. Ella decided it was time to finish the interview. "One last question—do you think one of the residents is responsible for these gnomes?"

Ben shook his head at his wife and looked up from his recliner. "Hell, no! Everyone here is too damned cheap to spend money on a joke. Don't you read the news? Things ain't like they used to be for retirees."

Jim and Ella thanked the older couple for their time while Ben ranted on about thieves in government making it hard for old folks.

"Worked hard all my damn life for the pansy assed liberals to give it to . . ."

The door shut behind them, effectively cutting off Ben's tirade of verbal abuses against whomever.

Jim hugged Ella tightly then looked at her. "Please don't let me get that old."

"It's all in your attitude. Exercising and eating right are important, too."

He threw an arm over her shoulder. "I know, I know. Where are we going next?"

"To Linda's house, her gnome was the one that looked like a witch. She's a very nice person, widowed I think, and she has several grandchildren who visit."

They strolled in silence to the next building. Clouds had rolled in so the summer temperature hadn't risen too much. It was actually pleasant walking outside. They approached Linda's door, but she pulled it open before they could ring the bell.

"Oh, my goodness, I've been waiting and waiting for y'all to get there." She motioned for them to enter. "Come in, come in, let's go to the kitchen. I have coffee and cinnamon rolls all ready for you hard working people."

Ella and Jim exchanged a mutual food-sounds-good-to-me look and followed her to the stainless steel kitchen with bright white cabinets, butcher-block countertops, and red accents. It was a cook's dream.

"Linda, I didn't know you liked to cook," Ella said.

"I know it's fashionable today for the young people with all the foodie shows on TV." Linda poured coffee and served up the rolls. "Now me, I'm just an old lady with some great recipes from my grandmother. Now y'all get a bite to eat then ask me any ole question that needs an answer. I'll go get Georgia the Gnome so the detective can get a looksee."

She must have noticed a look on Jim's face and patted his hand. "My granddaughter named the gnome. You know how girls are."

"Interesting group of residents here." Jim sipped the coffee then shoved the rest of a cinnamon roll in his mouth.

"But they're all good people." Ella licked topping from her lips, deciding it had to be possibly the best cinnamon roll she'd ever eaten. "Man, I wonder if she'd give me this recipe?" It would be a nice addition to her collection.

"Please do, and I'll let you bake them for me anytime," Jim groaned.

Linda returned with the gnome and placed it in front of Jim. "Isn't that the saddest thing you've ever seen? I know someone was trying to make a joke but seriously, y'all . . . this is more mean than funny."

"Any idea why this was given to you?" Jim said.

"Oh, sugar, look at me and my big old nose. I've played a witch on Halloween for years."

"And, that must be the good witch, right?" Jim said, and smiled at Linda who grinned back at him.

"Have you had an argument lately with anyone here at the complex?" Ella asked.

"Oh dear, no."

"Have you seen anyone who doesn't belong here?" Jim said.

"No, the visitors are pretty regular, family or friends." Linda ran a dishtowel over the counter. "The other day I saw one of them gals from the management company walking around, snooping most likely."

"Did you talk to her?" Jim said.

"Nope, I mind my own business."

Jim rose. "Okay, that's it. Thanks for answering our questions, and the coffee and rolls."

"Just holler if you need anything else." Linda walked them to the door.

As Ella walked past Linda, she whispered "Nice young fella you have there." Rather than correct her, Ella just nodded, then joined Jim on the sidewalk. They made the short walk back to her house and stood next to his SUV.

"I don't think we need to talk to any other residents," Jim said. "None of these people did this."

"I agree, what's next?"

"I need to talk to the maintenance guy, Bruno. When is he usually around?"

"He works Monday through Friday. I can try to find him after work on Monday."

"That'll work. Call me, I'll come out, we'll talk to Bruno, and afterwards I'll take you to dinner."

"Dinner? Like a date?" Ella shivered, this is what she had secretly hoped would happen.

"Yes, ma'am, like a date. I gotta go, stuff to do." He leaned in, kissed her cheek, and ran his hand over her head. "Great hair, by the way."

Ella watched him drive around the corner before strolling to her front door. She smiled as she touched her hair. Jim liked her hair. In spite of her initial misgivings, she liked him, too.

Chapter Three

Early Monday evening, Jim and Ella hurried to the townhouse community pool. They entered through a wrought iron gate and found Bruno emptying a trash can near the chaise lounges. His shiny brown skin seemed stretched over his thin frame, but he beamed at them with a wide smile.

"Hey there, Bruno. Are you staying cool?" Ella waved and hurried over. "This is Jim Campbell, my friend from Houston who I mentioned earlier."

"Nice to meet you, Mr. Campbell." Bruno nodded and planted the can back on the concrete deck. "You wanted to talk to me?"

"Sure did, we're looking into the garden gnome situation. You know about it, right?"

"Yeah, I heard a couple of the ladies talking about it the other day, doing their water exercise, ya know." Bruno grabbed a broom from his cleaning cart and stamped it on the ground. "Seems weird to me."

"I agree," Ella said. "Have you seen anyone around here lately that doesn't belong?"

He pushed the broom a couple of times. "Nah, no one much comes in here that don't belong. 'Course that new mailman, he's kinda strange—sings when he puts mail in the boxes."

"Have you noticed anyone sneak in the gate after a car drives through?" Jim said.

"Nah, but I don't watch the gate, too much work to do."

"Nothing around the complex seems unusual to you other than the mailman?" Jim said.

"That's right."

Ella figured that was enough since they kept hitting a wall of nothing unusual, except for a singing mailman. "Thanks, Bruno, have a good evening."

"Yes ma'am, you, too."

Ella and Jim walked in silence back to her house.

"Let's get to the restaurant and then we can discuss this." Jim opened the passenger door of his SUV and Ella climbed in.

After a short fifteen minutes, they entered a crowded seafood restaurant along the Southwest Freeway. Jim added their name to the table list and they headed to the bar area. A couple of stools opened at the ultra-modern concrete bar and Jim grabbed them. He helped Ella perch on one and sat next to her.

"We'll have to wait a while so we might as well get a drink. Wine?"

Ella nodded as she glanced around at the crowd. "This place is a zoo." She hadn't realized Monday night was so popular for eating out. Usually she was studying or doing her laundry.

Once Jim snagged the bartender and placed their order, they locked gazes.

Jim rubbed a hand through his hair, looking a little unsure of himself. "This isn't my normal investigation. You know that, right?"

"I had a hunch," Ella said, lightly touching his arm. "Seems to me we're basically nowhere."

"That's the gist of it, but those gnomes didn't walk in by themselves. Someone put them there."

"I have an idea. I watched a TV show last Christmas where the police looked at electronic records for an alarm system. Would the same thing be available for the gate? I think all the residents have different codes."

"Yeah, and then what?" His voice held a hint of teasing.

"Stop it, I'm serious."

Jim leaned toward her and cupped her face with his hands. "You are so cute." He then kissed her hard on the mouth, once then twice, and pulled back. "What's your theory?"

Ella tapped her fingertips on her lips. His out-of-the-blue kiss had rocked her all the way to her hot pink painted toenails. What did he ask? Oh, right, her theory.

"If we obtained a list of the codes used to open the gate we could identify everyone who visited the complex the night before the gnomes were found."

"Sounds good." He stroked his finger along the underside of her forearm. "Why don't you ask Mildred to call the management company? They should have that information."

"I'll call her tomorrow." Ella sipped the wine the bartender had delivered. "Hmm, I like this." She could barely concentrate on her words, Jim's fingers caressing her arm sent tremors spiraling across her shoulders.

He nodded as he drank his wine. "Tell me, what you do for fun when you're not working or studying."

"Fun?" Ella assumed window-shopping, reading, and cooking wouldn't seem all that intriguing to a police detective. "I haven't had much time the last couple of years. What about you?"

"Busted. I'm in the same boat as you. We'll both have time for enjoying life once our degrees are completed."

"I'm looking forward to getting up on a Saturday morning and not going to my laptop first thing."

He took her hand and rubbed his thumb over the palm. "Maybe you won't be alone on that Saturday morning."

"I'd like that." Ella nearly clapped a hand over her mouth. The words had just popped out.

"Me, too," Jim said. He leaned into her and this time he kissed her gently. "Ya know what? I like you."

"I like you, too." Her words slipped out so easily that panic welled in her chest and threatened to cut off her windpipe. She scooted off the stool. "Be right back, going to the ladies room."

Ella needed a minute by herself and headed straight to the restroom, breathing deeply as she hurried. She needed to gather her thoughts. She needed to be honest about Jim. As she washed her hands, a marvelous shudder swirled from her head to her toes as clarity filled her mind and her heart. Jenny was right, Jim was a good guy. Thank heavens for the garden gnomes.

She'd finally seen the real man and liked what she saw. After throwing the paper towel in the trashcan, she checked her face in the mirror. Her cheeks flushed as she remembered Jim's kisses. The man certainly knew how to kiss a woman. She brushed on lip-gloss and fluffed her hair. Excitement bubbled through her, excitement about the evening with Jim.

In a haze of anticipation, she strolled back to the bar and immediately saw a petite woman with a long ponytail standing close to Jim. What the hell? Ella slowed her pace and watched. Jim laughed and hugged the woman. She stepped closer, overhearing part of their conversation.

"She's not important to me," Jim said. "Just hanging out, nothing more."

Ella froze mid-step, as her heart pounded in her chest. *Not important? Just hanging out?* Damn him! He'd played her for a fool. Again. Just like in Las Vegas. She approached, teeth gritted with a smile plastered on her face. This night was over.

Jim noticed her and said something to the woman who patted his cheek and walked away.

"Our table is ready." Jim rose and grinned at her. "I'm starving."

"I'm not feeling well. You need to take me home."

"What's wrong?" He placed a hand on her shoulder. "What can I do to help?"

"Nothing but take me home." Ella walked past him to the restaurant's exit.

Jim caught up with her. "Are you okay?"

"I just want to go home." Ella didn't want to talk to him or look at him. They walked in silence to his SUV.

The drive to Sugar Land was quick and quiet. After a couple attempts at conversation, Jim stopped trying, which suited Ella just fine. Within minutes, he pulled into her driveway.

She opened the passenger door and jumped to the curb. "You don't need to get out." She hurried to her front door without looking back. After letting herself in, she went to the window and watched Jim back out of the driveway. He hesitated in the street before heading toward the exit.

She went to her bedroom, kicked off her shoes, and fell on the bed. Hugging a pillow to her chest, she launched into a major pity party. Tears trailed down her face as she considered what a fool she'd been in thinking Jim Campbell was a good guy. He had played her like.a damned guitar. That sounded so ridiculous.

A picture of him and his sexy smile came to mind and she hugged the pillow tighter. She *was* a fool, plain and simple.

Once she ran through every encounter with Jim that proved her point—that he was a jerk—Ella fell asleep. She woke after the pillow ended up on her face and she sat up, her mouth feeling like a dried up riverbed. Still fully dressed, she went to the kitchen for a glass of water. She wandered into the living room to turn off the lights and stopped to squint out the window at a lone figure directly across the street from her unit.

She turned off the lamp in her living room and watched as someone made their way along the sidewalk carrying a large bag. The person stopped under the streetlight and turned for a moment, illuminating her face. Definitely a woman, and though she didn't look familiar, Ella couldn't tell for certain. The woman hurried down the street and turned the corner.

It was weird seeing anyone walking around the complex so late at night. Yes, it was suspicious and maybe she should call the police or Mildred, but she was too tired. She'd think about it in the morning. Ella yawned and went back to her bedroom. Tomorrow was Sunday so she could sleep in before speaking to Mildred.

∽∾

Ella opened the door for Mildred as they entered the Houston office of Crest Townhouse Management in Greenway Plaza. The mission for this Tuesday morning was to retrieve records on the use of the front security gate. Every townhouse resident had woken up Sunday morning to a new batch of gnomes on their porches. Ella had found a pink ballerina with huge feet on her own porch. In addition, they'd discovered an elf-looking gnome with a noose around its neck hanging from a pink crepe myrtle near the front. That alone had created a huge tizzy among the residents, thus resulting in today's visit.

When they asked to see the complex's account representative, someone ushered them quickly to an office down the corridor.

Jill Monroe rose and walked around her glass desk with her hand out-stretched. "Mildred, it's so very good to see you again. And, who is this with you?"

"This is Ella Pace." Mildred plopped in a guest chair. "She's a homeowner and has done some research for the residents."

Ella shook Jill's hand and sat in the other chair. "That's right. A friend of mine with the Houston police has given me some help in looking into this gnome situation."

Jill returned to her desk chair and looked at the two of them, her large smile displaying straight, white teeth. "You mentioned that on the phone, truly distressful for senior citizens. How can I help you?"

"Ella, you tell her what we want," Mildred said firmly.

"We need the list of names and codes for the front security gate."

"That shouldn't be a problem," Jill said, still smiling.

"Along with a list of the codes entered during the last three weeks, by date and time, please," Ella said. She watched Jill's smile fade. "We'll wait while you print out the information."

"I'm not sure I can retrieve that data so quickly."

"We pay Crest Management every month for this service," Mildred stated. "We'll wait right here for you to get a move on."

"All right," Jill murmured, as she swiveled her chair to the adjacent computer. Ella held back a giggle, as she watched Jill's fingers punch the keyboard. Something about her side profile seemed familiar even though they'd never before met.

Mildred began to tap her foot as the minutes passed. Ella kept quiet and made a mental list of all the homework assignments she had to complete before the end of the summer term. She hoped they'd have the information before Mildred's obvious lack of patience hit the fan.

Finally, Jill's printer hummed and she handed several pages to Mildred. "This is a list of your main gate's security codes and the codes accessed during the last three weeks."

Mildred glanced at them before handing the papers to Ella. "You check these out. Your eyes are better than mine."

Ella first looked at the list of codes accessed for Saturday night and Sunday morning. Sure enough, it showed a code punched in at 1:17 a.m. She searched for the number on the code list and there it was. No wonder Jill Monroe looked so familiar.

"Jill, why were you at the townhouse complex this last Saturday night? It seems to me that one in the morning is after normal business hours."

"I . . . I wasn't there. Someone else must have used my code." Jill looked first at Ella then Mildred. "Really," she pleaded.

"I don't believe you," Ella said, concluding that Jill truly was the mysterious "Miss-gnome-er." Her code entry time sealed the deal. "Why were you there? I know you delivered all those nasty gnomes. Why would you do such a thing?"

"I didn't. Someone else used my code." Jill's face flushed a bright pink as she fanned her head with a yellow file folder.

Ella leaned forward on the glass-topped desk. "Jill, give it up. I saw you on the street outside my house holding a large bag."

"Tell us right now why you would do such a terrible thing," Mildred demanded. "These stupid gnomes have upset the residents terribly. This was plain mean."

No one said a word; Ella and Mildred continued to glare at Jill.

Finally, a tear ran down Jill's cheek. "All right, I did it. I know it was stupid. I'm sorry."

Mildred planted her hands on her knees, looking like she was about to pounce on the other woman. "But why would you do something so utterly ridiculous?"

Jill sniffed loudly, wiped her face with her fingers, and pushed her hair back. "I did it because of my grandmother. She mentioned that she'd love to live at your complex. Units don't often go on the market so I thought if I could scare someone they might decide to sell."

Mildred looked at Ella and smiled. She then rose and stepped toward the desk. "Miss Monroe, we will forget this happened because you obviously love your grandmother and I respect that. But do not try anything so ridiculous again or Ella will have you arrested."

Mildred took Ella's arm as they exited the office and walked down the hallway. She whispered in Ella's ear. "Good work, figuring this out. You should have been a detective."

∽

Ella performed a fist pump as she answered the final exam question, thereby ending her last summer class. She looked forward to a month off before the fall term began for her last master's course. Her plans included cleaning her closet and spending time with Jenny. They'd hardly seen each other the last month other than their regular Wednesday lunch. Jenny didn't know the truth about Ella's refusal to talk to Jim these past few weeks and she didn't plan to tell her. At least not until she understood why she so easily assumed Jim was a jerk.

She gathered her backpack, turned in the final exam, and exited the classroom. As she stepped onto the wide walk surrounding the academic mall at Houston Cullen University, the evening heat of late July hit her like a blast from a furnace. The sun filtered through the trees in the center of the mall. A few students sat on the grass celebrating the end of the summer session. Ella hurried to the parking garage and heard her name called. She stopped and turned.

Jim jogged over to her. "Hey, you just get out of class?"

"Just took the final." Ella couldn't image why he was on campus. Yet here he was, appearing just as her head filled with thoughts of him. "What are you doing here?"

"I had an interview for director of the criminal justice program HCU is starting."

"Good for you. I hope you get the job." Her pulse raced as she talked with him. This wasn't good. "I better get going, been a long day."

"Wait. Can we talk?" He smiled sweetly, his eyes wide and hopeful. "Maybe go somewhere for a drink?"

God, he looked so damned cute. She blurted out "yes" before she'd actually processed his question. "Do you mind if we go to my house? I'm tired and I'd like to change my clothes." She still had on her work scrubs and didn't want to go out in them.

"No problem. I'll head that way now." He touched her arm and headed in the opposite direction of the garage.

Ella walked to her car wondering why in the hell she'd agreed so quickly to see him. She was more tired than she thought. All the late hours studying had fogged her brain. Either that, or, she truly wanted to see him.

Thirty minutes later, she drove into her garage and shut the door. Jim's SUV was nowhere in sight so she had time to change clothes and shrug off her misgivings about inviting him to her house. Ella went directly to the bedroom and replaced the scrubs with a pair of black capris and a pink T-shirt. She brushed her hair into a loose ponytail and stroked on lip-gloss. That was the extent of her primping.

The doorbell rang. She gave herself one last look in the mirror—her eyes were bright and her cheeks flushed. Butterflies danced in her stomach.

Jim walked in carrying a shopping bag. "I made a stop. I thought we could celebrate the end of school, for both of us. Do you mind?"

"I never turn down wine. You finished your dissertation? I didn't realize you were so close." Ella was truly surprised.

"I haven't seen you in over a month. A lot's happened." He placed the bag on the kitchen counter. "I passed the defense. You are looking at a man with a Ph.D."

"I guess I should call you *Dr*. Campbell, then."

He took two steps, wrapped his arms around her, and whispered. "No, you can call me Jimmy, like my mom does." His lips touched hers lightly then he kissed her forehead and pulled back. "I brought you wine and chocolate cake."

She drew back from him, shaking her finger. "Hey, none of that. No touching." To keep busy, she pulled the bottle out of the bag and checked the label. "How did you know I like this wine?"

"I called Jenny."

How sweet that he'd go to the trouble of asking. So, he wasn't a total jerk. She watched Jim as he uncorked the wine and poured. He had such an ease about him no matter the setting. The man oozed confidence with a capital "C." Perhaps she'd confused confidence with . . .

with his ability to be larger than life. Did that even make sense?

Once again, they settled in the living room, both on the couch. After bland conversation about the weather and the Houston Astros baseball team, Jim changed the subject.

"I guess I should confess that I pumped Jenny for information—"

"Information on what?" Ella interrupted. That couldn't be good, considering how Jenny really liked Jim. Ella was close to admitting she liked him, too.

"Why you decided not to see me again." He placed the empty plate on the side table and shifted toward her. "Jenny said she had no idea. I've banged my head against a wall trying to figure out what happened. Things were going great, and then boom, you clamped it down. Why? What changed?"

She had two options for replying to his question—tell him the truth or tell him she wasn't interested. She circled her fork through the cake crumbs on her plate. The decision was easy; she'd never been a coward.

"When we were at the restaurant, I heard what you said to that woman when I came back from the ladies room."

"Woman?" he said, raising his eyebrows. "I remember now, that was Suzie, she's a friend of my sister's."

"I heard you say that a girl wasn't important to you, that you were only hanging out."

He frowned briefly. "I was talking about a girl I used to date. Suzie had met her at some party and asked if we were still going out. Did you think I was talking about you?"

"Yes." Heat spread from her chest to her face, painting her as a fool.

"Guess you jumped to a big conclusion." He rose and paced in front of her. "I guess I shouldn't be surprised. You automatically assumed that because I have a history of being a player, going from woman to woman without a care in the world. Right?"

She nodded, feeling even more foolish when he said it like that. "Yes, that's what I thought."

"I'm not going to apologize for my dating history. It is what it is. Everyone I dated wanted the same thing—no attachments and no hurt feelings."

"I'm sorry. I made a terrible mistake." She smiled, relieved that he didn't seem angry at her. In fact, he seemed happy to be with her. She patted the cushion next to her. "Just so you know, jumping to conclusions is my one fault, other than being late once in a while."

He sat next to her. "I accept your apology. I have one fault, too."

She scooted around to face him. "The police detective is admitting he has a fault. Let me guess . . . I bet you don't make your bed every morning."

"I don't but that's not a real fault." He played with a strand of Ella's hair that had escaped the ponytail.

She pressed her lips together, thinking, but nothing else came to mind. "I give up."

"My fault," he said, leaning closer and rubbing his thumb along the side of her chin, "is that I love kissing a beautiful woman named Ella Pace."

"Don't let me stop you," Ella teased as his lips touched hers. She met his kiss and hooked her arms around his neck. Their kiss deepened as he pulled her closer. She sucked in a breath, surprised at how comfortable this felt—how right it felt.

"My pleasure," he murmured, sliding a hand along her waist, inside her T-shirt.

The touch of his fingers sent heat swirling around her abdomen. She grabbed his shoulders as his mouth once again took hers. Their playful meeting of lips and tongues leapt from cool burn to hot sizzle in a matter of seconds. Ella sank into the luxury of the turmoil created by this man.

His hand moved higher and touched the satin of her bra. This was it, this was the moment.

Jim drew back, looked deep into her eyes, searching for a sign—a sign to stop or to give him the go-ahead. He prayed she'd let him love her. He'd known it for a while and it had happened, just as mom had said it would. The player had fallen, and fallen hard for the all American, girl next door . . .the pretty, blonde nurse. The nurse who'd captured his heart and made his life a living hell the last month. But everything had changed. His wooing had resulted in a home run.

Ella tugged at the shirt tucked into his jeans. She pulled it out and snaked it up his torso and over his head. It landed on the floor. He had his answer.

"I think we need to play fair." His voice was husky. In one motion his hands slid under her top, pushing it upward as he drew her arms over her head.

"Very clever," she said, as her tee dropped to the carpet. "What else have you got?"

He nuzzled her neck, spreading kisses under her jaw. "Lots. You wanna play?"

"Yes sir, detective."

Jim loved the sound of her voice—feisty and smoky, all bound together in one sexy package.

"Okay, then," he said as his thumbs brushed along the curve of her breasts. "But remember, I don't play fair." He stood quickly and scooped her into his arms. "Where's your bedroom?"

∽

Sitting on a picnic table in the shade of a majestic oak, Ella watched Jim and Mike play basketball on the court around the corner from Jenny and Mike's house. Both men were drenched in sweat and egging each other on under the late morning sun. The miserably hot days hadn't eased up yet, even though it was Labor Day weekend and the unofficial end of summer.

"Those two are such showoffs." Ella laughed at the playful antics of the men who were intent on one-upping each other in their game.

"I wish Mike had that much energy when I ask him to take out the garbage," Jenny said. She glanced at her friend and nudged her with an elbow. "I'm so happy you and Jim got together. I told you he's a good guy."

"I know I was slow to figure it out, but I did." Ella counted her blessings every day. Dating Jim was the smartest decision she'd ever made. She hadn't spoken the words out loud but she *knew* they had a future together. It was a knowing deep inside that she accepted as the truth.

Their relationship was night and day different from her last one that had ended with a sigh and a thud.

The two of them had zoomed from zero to sixty in no time and Jim had become a constant in her daily activities. Funny how simple it had been to incorporate him into her life after she'd resisted getting to know him for so long. She'd certainly learned a valuable lesson about jumping to conclusions.

"I figured you'd come to your senses eventually." Jenny sipped from a water bottle.

Ella playfully knocked her fist against her head. "Yes, I can be strong-willed at times. But, things are great between us."

"Who won?" Jenny yelled as Mike and Jim walked across the grass. She threw each a hand towel she'd pulled from a backpack on the table.

Jim wiped sweat off his face. "We don't keep score."

"That's what he thinks," Mike said, snapping his towel on Jim's arm. "I won."

Jim rolled his eyes. "Whatever. Are you ladies ready to get some Mexican food and a margarita?"

"I'm ready," Ella said and wrinkled her nose. "*After* y'all shower—you two are some kind of ripe!"

"Jenny can't have a margarita," Mike said.

"Why not?" Jim leveled a glare at Jenny. "Don't tell me you're on some dumb diet."

"No, it's nothing like that," Jenny said. She glanced at Mike and nodded.

Ella gasped suddenly and jumped off the table to hug Jenny hard. "This is so exciting. How long have you known? How are you feeling?"

"What the hell is she talking about?" Jim sent Ella a curious gaze. "Do you two always speak in code?"

"No, but we have news." Jenny rose and put her arm around Mike. "Mike and I are having a baby."

"What? A baby?" Jim said. Ella poked him in the side. "Oh, a baby . . . " He pumped Mike's hand and gave Jenny a gentle hug. "This is great news."

"Thanks. We're excited," Jenny said. "Let's go home so you guys can shower."

Jim high-fived Mike, and filled the area with robust laughter. "Yeah, man. You're having a kid! I sure hope he gets his mom's good looks."

Twenty minutes later, Ella waited alone in the family room reading a magazine. She put it aside as Jim walked in from his shower, all slicked-back wet hair and looking cute as a pickle in a green golf shirt and khaki shorts. He spread out on the couch next to her. Ella's toes curled as his musky scent floated around her.

She leaned into him and tucked her arms around his chest. "You smell good."

"Hmm, thanks."

"Isn't it exciting about Mike and Jenny's baby?" She laid her head against his shoulder, enjoying the masculine feel of him.

"Uh-huh." He patted her thigh and swiveled to meet her gaze. "I've been thinking about something. Actually, I have an idea."

"Really?" She nipped at his chin.

"I'm serious. Let's move in together."

"What?" Ella pulled back and studied his face. He looked serious enough. She'd never considered the idea herself. "You mean that?"

"Yes. We spend almost every night together at your place. Let's make it official. I don't think either of us is going anywhere."

"Let me think about this." Ella rose and walked to the window overlooking the patio and pool. She stared at the pool without seeing it. Could she live with a man?

Living with anyone would impact her independence and cramp her style. What would Jim think about her wearing her pajamas until noon or eating ice cream out of the carton? Would he help with the laundry, vacuum, or take out the trash? Would he love her when she wasn't at the top of her game?

Would she love Jim regardless? Yes.

She turned from the window and faced him. He sat at the edge of the sofa, forearms on his thighs, and hands clasped together. She wanted to whoop and holler, shout to everyone. She was lost—one hundred percent, bonafide and certified, over the moon in love with this man.

"I have one condition," she purred as she walked back to the sofa and kneeled in front of him.

"What's your condition?"

"We buy an outdoor barbeque. No more grilling in the kitchen." The look on his face was priceless. The sparkle in his eyes and raised brow were evidence that she had scored a homerun.

"Oh baby," he said as he wrapped his arms around her. He kissed her firmly and ruffled her hair. "I'll even wear one of those dorky 'kiss the cook' aprons."

"Now you're talking."

Ella pulled Jim to his feet and patted his butt. "I have the perfect apron at home."

"Oh yeah?"

"Yep, it says 'kiss Ella.'"

And, he did just that . . . a lot.

It's worth the risk to find out who you are when you're in love.

Summer Lovin' Yummy Brownies

Ingredients

- ½ teaspoon salt
- ½ cup plus 2 tablespoons all-purpose flour
- 1/3 cup cocoa
- 2/3 cup granulated sugar
- 2/3 cup brown sugar
- ½ cup semi-sweet chocolate chips
- ½ cup chopped pecans or walnuts
- ½ cup white chocolate or butterscotch chips
- 1 teaspoon vanilla
- 2/3 cup vegetable oil
- 3 eggs

Directions

- Preheat oven to 350 degrees and grease a 9X9 inch pan
- Combine all of the dry ingredients in a mixing bowl
- Add the vanilla, oil, and eggs, and mix well
- Pour batter into the prepared pan
- Bake for 30 minutes
- Let the brownies cool a bit before cutting

Seriously, these brownies are fabulous!

If you enjoyed this story, please leave a review on Amazon, or on Goodreads, if you are a member.

Other Works by Karen Sue Burns

Excerpt from
IN HOT PURSUIT

Chapter One

Friday, 2:54 P.M.

The life path for Quinn Wells encountered a major detour on an afternoon in mid-May — one of those close to scorching afternoons when office workers shuffled paper or checked movie times, waiting for the clock to tick-tick to going-home time. She considered herself productive that afternoon, color-coding her accounting files for the upcoming fiscal year end.

Then her office phone rang.

It was an outside call, from First National Bank. Her hand hesitated over the receiver, but she was a sucker for a ringing phone.

"It's Lynne Jenkins."

"How are you?" Quinn said.

"Confused. We haven't received the wire yet."

"What wire?"

"The wire for the twenty-five million dollars from the Bridge Foundation. Can you check on it?"

Quinn had no idea what Lynne was talking about — and no way would she let her know that. It was embarrassing, once again, not knowing about a major gift before it arrived.

"Give me a few minutes and I'll get back to you."

Quinn replaced the phone, shook her fists at the ceiling. A twenty-five million gift was being wired today? What the hell? She jumped out of her chair and headed for the office of her boss, the vice president of finance. Surely, he knew about the wire. She rushed down the long hallway and found his assistant, Ellie, at her desk.

"Is Scooter here?"

Ellie looked up from a paperback novel. "No. I came back from lunch and he was gone. Calendar says he's at a meeting and should return in half an hour."

Quinn blew a slow breath, worked at calming her frustration. "Let him know I need to talk to him as soon as he returns."

She debated what to do next. Should she wait for Scooter or should she call Development, the department responsible for soliciting gifts? Would Scooter be upset if she didn't wait for him?

Back in her office, she turned her chair away from the desk and her eyes moved to the CPA certificate on the wall. She'd worked her ass off to pass the exam and earn that credential. Ten years ago, she hadn't worried about making the wrong decision, she simply went with her instincts. She picked up the phone to call the executive director of development.

"Rebecca, I need to ask you about a gift that was wired today."

"You mean the one from the Bridge Foundation?"

"That's the one. The bank called and the funds haven't arrived."

"That's strange. The wire should have been sent first thing this morning. We sent the wire instructions two days ago." Rebecca's voice was calming. "Let me contact the donor and I'll call you back. I'm sure it's a simple mistake."

While Quinn waited for the return call, she shuffled files on her desk, then dug an antacid tablet out of her purse. The taco she had for lunch was talking to her. She chewed the tablet and stared out the office window. Friday classes at Houston Cullen University were over and students rushed toward the parking garage down the street. The weekend would officially begin at five o'clock.

The phone rang. Rebecca's name appeared on the digital read out.

"I called the director of the Foundation. He said he talked with their brokerage firm this morning and the wire was sent as planned." Rebecca was still calm.

"Something is wrong." Why wasn't she freaking out like Quinn was about to do?

"Don't worry," Rebecca said soothingly. "I'm sure it's some glitch within the bank. They're all having problems these days."

"Right, thanks for the information."

Something was definitely wrong. How did twenty-five million dollars disappear? Quinn's head was hot. Where was Scooter? He should be the one calling the bank. But Lynne from the bank had called Quinn, so she'd do her duty and follow up. She punched in the number and Lynne answered on the first ring.

"The Bridge Foundation says the wire was sent this morning," Quinn said.

"You're sure?"

"That's what our Development Office told me." She wiped sweat off the back of her neck. "What should we do to find the funds? This can't happen every day."

"No, it doesn't, and not with such a large sum. I'll call the brokerage firm and get their transaction number for the transfer so we can trace it through the Federal Reserve System. Should I follow up with you or Scooter?"

"Would you mind calling Scooter?" Quinn knew he'd want to hear it from Lynne himself.

"No problem, I'll call him as soon as I have an update."

Quinn next called Ellie to find out if Scooter had come back to the office ... not yet. Now what?

She stacked the color-coded file folders on the credenza adjacent to her desk, then decided to clean out her email. The distraction of busy work kept her from imagining why the gift might be missing. She glanced at the time in the corner of the monitor — 3:27. Surely Scooter would return any minute.

She first went through her inbox and deleted messages she'd already read, jotting reminder notes on a yellow pad. She clicked through the list and checked the time again — 3:51.

Where was Scooter? This would be the day he was late coming back from a meeting.

Quinn next focused on the spam folder, a total of 112 messages. She worked her way through it to those dated today, then she stopped, her fingers clutching the mouse. This was strange, a message from Gregory James, Inc., the brokerage firm used by the Bridge Foundation. Why would they send her an email? She double-clicked and read the message. Her throat squeezed shut, and she couldn't catch a breath.

Holy shit. The message confirmed a change, her change, to the wire instructions for the Bridge Foundation's gift. The receiving bank and the associated account number had been updated as instructed ... by the controller of Houston Cullen University. She swallowed, then sucked air in her lungs. What?

She jumped out of her chair and rushed to the office door, closed it quietly. Then the shaking started, from her elbows to her knees. She began to pace her office from the small window to the door, ten steps, back and forward. As she walked, the shaking lessened. Although her brain spiraled around in a state of shock, her limbs began to regain their memory of function.

After a few minutes, she stopped pacing and sat back at her desk, ready to deal with the message, still open on her monitor.

The email was an error. She had made no change to the wire instructions. How could she since she didn't even know about the gift until two hours ago? The message implied she stole the twenty-five million by changing the HCU wire instructions. It was a mistake or a joke. Someone had a sick sense of humor.

She took a deep breath and printed the email. She debated telling Scooter about the message but decided to keep it to herself for now. She grabbed the paper off the printer and folded it in half, then half again, small enough to slide into her wallet. She tossed the wallet back into her purse. She'd analyze this later and then determine the right thing to do.

Even a lousy plan was better than no plan at all.

$ $ $

"Quinn, this is your fault," Scooter Taylor said through thin lips an hour later. He sat at his huge oak desk. Late afternoon sunlight filtered through the window blinds, creating prison-bar stripes on the honey-toned wall behind him.

He'd finally returned and told her he'd already called the police, not wanting to waste time or HCU resources.

"What? My fault?"

"Yes." He squeezed the bridge of his nose with two fingers. "You should have verified the wire was received this morning. But you didn't and now the funds are missing."

"I didn't even know about the gift." She blew a slow breath. The Gregory James email popped in her head and she pushed it quickly to a back corner.

"You would have known about the wire if you were on better terms with Development. But, oh no, you're always picking at them." He lowered his voice. "They don't like you, so they don't talk to you."

Of course, Development didn't like her. The by-the-book procedures she insisted on routinely placed them on opposite sides of an issue. How did that relate to a missing gift? She crossed her arms over her chest. "Maybe we're not all best friends, but that doesn't mean this is my fault."

"It doesn't matter now. Finding twenty-five million dollars is what's important." He glared at her again, shook his head. "I expect you to be a team player."

"I am a team player," Quinn reminded him, on the edge of pleading, even though they were in familiar territory. He reminded her every few months to get along with Development.

"Damn it, you better be."

"I'll do whatever I can to help. Just tell me what to do."

"Good. I — "

A campus security officer knocked on the door. "Mr. Taylor, Houston PD is here." She nodded at Scooter, then left.

Quinn took another slow breath. The police had arrived so quickly. The situation was now a bona fide disaster.

A tall man wearing jeans and cowboy boots entered Scooter's office. He surveyed the room with a calm face. He had that ruggedly appealing look that screamed *don't tangle with me*.

"Good evening, I'm Roddy Phillips from the Burglary and Theft Division, HPD's Financial Crimes Unit." He pulled a small notebook from his jacket pocket and flipped it open. "We received a call from a Mr. Taylor reporting missing funds."

"Yes, detective, I'm Scooter Taylor, vice president for finance here at HCU." He walked around his desk and shook the cop's hand, then turned toward Quinn. "This is Quinn Wells, our controller."

"Good to meet you, Mr. Phillips," Quinn said. He nodded in reply.

Scooter directed the detective to the round conference table across from the desk and waved a hand to Quinn to join them. Rebecca Holland from the development office, accompanied by a man who looked like he stepped off a New York runway, hastened into the office.

"Rebecca, you're here," Scooter said, smiling.

"Looks like we made it in time." She pointed to the man beside her. "This is Logan Rice, the executive director at the Bridge Foundation."

Scooter made the introductions and hustled everyone to sit at the table. Quinn turned her chair around to join the group. She had a good view of both Logan Rice and the detective, each a good-looking man. But looks were often deceptive.

"Mr. Taylor, tell me about the missing funds," the detective said.

"A twenty-five million dollar gift to the university is missing," Scooter explained. He waved a hand toward Logan. "The Bridge Foundation, one of our most prominent donors, electronically transferred the funds to a HCU bank account this morning. They used wire instructions faxed to their office by Rebecca's assistant."

"I can verify our brokerage firm used those instructions," Logan added.

Quinn's stomach performed a loop-da-loop. How could Mr. Rice be certain the correct wire instructions were used?

"The problem is that the wire was sent but the funds never arrived in our bank account," Scooter said.

"Okay," the detective said. "Why was the transfer made today?"

"The date has been set for two weeks," Scooter explained. "HCU is in the middle of a six-year capital campaign to raise 100 million dollars. The foundation's cash donation was the premier gift for the campaign."

Quinn's breathing hitched. This could prove to be a nightmare for HCU. She wished she had worked harder at getting Development to understand the importance of her accounting procedures. Maybe then she wouldn't have received a mysterious message. Would the detective suspect her? Her face was hot and her left leg tapped a steady rhythm on the carpet.

"This is terrible," Rebecca said. "What are we going to do?" She ran a hand through her blonde hair, mussing her perfect bob.

"Our bank officer told me she would put a trace on the wire using the transaction number from the brokerage firm," Quinn said.

"That's good. But, Detective, Rebecca is right, this is terrible for the university. What do we do now?" Scooter said. "My God, twenty-five million dollars gone ... like that." He snapped his fingers.

"This is ridiculous." Logan spat out, glaring at Scooter. "How in the hell, in this electronic age, does your bank lose our gift?"

Scooter's eyes widened at the outburst. "Mr. Rice, please, we need to stay calm. Like Quinn said, First National is tracing the wire."

Logan glanced at Quinn and their eyes locked. In that instant, she felt her heart flutter in her chest. Then he broke his gaze and dismissed her with a curt nod. What was that? He pulled a business card from a pocket of his suit jacket and slid it across the table to the detective. He rose. "I have to go. My grandmother needs to hear about this before it hits the local news. Please contact me with any updates."

Detective Phillips jotted in his notebook. "Thanks, Mr. Taylor. Before I leave, I'll need a copy of the wire instructions, all the contact names at the Bridge Foundation, their brokerage firm, and your bank."

Scooter nodded, his face a grim mask.

Quinn felt the tension in the room crawl along her arms. She knew Scooter worried about the potential negative impact on donors. Would this mess cause them to reduce their giving to HCU?

To make matters worse, neither the university president nor Rebecca's boss, the development VP, were even on campus. They were traveling somewhere together, trying to raise more money. Neither executive would be happy when they heard about the theft and the possibility that the Bridge Foundation might publicly blame HCU.

"Also, I'll also need a list of names, work locations, and phone numbers for employees in the development and finance offices." The detective's eyes focused on each of them, one at a time. "There'll be additional requests if we get into an investigation. I hope that won't create any difficulty for y'all."

"Not at all," Scooter said, glancing at his watch. "We'll do everything we can to help with your investigation. I'm sure our president will want to talk with you as soon as his plane lands. I'll leave a message for him"

"Good." Detective Phillips handed out business cards. "We'll put a trace on the wire transfer to verify it's not a bank error. You'll hear from me once I know something."

"I realize we don't know if there has been a crime," Scooter explained. "But I wanted to alert you as to our concern."

The detective nodded. "We'll see."

"Scooter, can I help you get anything?" Quinn asked.

"No, both you and Rebecca can head on home," he said. "I'll give you a call tomorrow since I know you're scheduled for vacation next week."

"My vacation can wait," Quinn said quickly.

"Let's see what happens." Scooter rose and went to his desk. They were dismissed.

Rebecca and Quinn left quietly and walked down the hall to the front of the Finance Office.

"This is like a freaking nightmare," Quinn said.

"Or a really bad horror movie," Rebecca replied. "I hope the police find whoever did this."

"Me, too." Quinn also hoped they didn't consider her the number one suspect once they started the investigation.

$$\$\ \$\ \$$

Logan parked in the circular driveway in front of the Rice family home. No doubt about it, he'd rather be drinking a beer at his favorite neighborhood bar. Telling his grandmother about the loss of the gift would not be easy. She'd probably blame it on him.

He found her in the study, watching some reality show on television. He hated the stupid shows.

"Good evening, Gram." He bent down and kissed her cheek.

Sarah Rice, the regal matriarch of the Rice family, beamed at her grandson from her seat on the luxurious leather sofa. "Logan, what a surprise," she said, lowering the television's volume. "What brings you here? No date tonight?"

He sat across from her. He knew she wouldn't appreciate any hedging at his reason for visiting her unannounced on a Friday evening. He got right to the point.

"I had a meeting at Houston Cullen University thirty minutes ago. There's a problem."

"A problem?"

"The Foundation's gift didn't make it to the University's bank."

"What in the world do you mean?"

"The money is gone, possibly stolen.

"How could someone steal a wire transfer?" She rose, anger flashing across her normally composed features. She walked to the fireplace with a slight limp, her back to her grandson. After a long minute, she turned. "How could you let this happen?"

He ignored her question. "I don't know how a wire transfer gets stolen."

"We need to call the police."

"Taken care of. Remember Roddy Phillips? The guy I trained with for the Houston Marathon a couple years ago."

"Yes, of course, a nice young man."

Logan nearly rolled his eyes at the "nice young man" comment. Roddy was tough as nails with a wicked sense of humor.

"He's the detective working on the case. I just met with him."

"I need to talk with him. This situation is totally unacceptable." She returned to the sofa. "Logan, the Rice family does not have this type of thing happen to them." She punched a small pillow, her lips a thin line. "I expect you to find the bastard who stole our money. Then bring him to me. I'll make sure he pays for his crime."

"Gram, please, the police will take care of this."

She looked at him with steel in her eyes. "They damn well better do their job, then. The Rice family will not tolerate anyone taking advantage of us."

Logan changed the subject and asked his grandmother about her spring garden. She loved planning the colors every year. The change in conversation helped to keep her blood pressure in check. At least he hoped it did.

He left an hour later, after assuring his grandmother that he'd provide updates on the police investigation. As he drove away, he congratulated himself on convincing her he'd deal with the theft and that she didn't need to be hands on. After all, she had a full schedule running the family and he did have some experience with police matters.

He called Roddy on his cell phone.

"Man, what a surprise to see you at HCU. I thought you were working homicide."

"Switched a few months ago," Roddy said with a chuckle. "Sorry this happened to your family. You guys have been good to Houston over the years."

"Whatever. Do you have any suspects yet?"

"Hell, no, we don't even know if there's been a theft. We're starting with a bank trace and we'll go from there. But ... if it is a theft, who would be on your suspect list?"

"I don't know. How about everyone working at the school?"

"We'll start with the ones who knew about the transfer."

"I'd start with that controller, Quinn something," Logan said. "Rebecca told me she said she didn't know about the transfer. That doesn't make sense considering her position."

"I agree."

"There was something strange about her, too, like she was nervous or on edge. What could be the reason for that?"

$ $ $

Quinn started her ten-year-old Volvo wagon, adjusting the air-conditioning to neutralize the heat of the day. She dug her cell phone out of her purse and called her best friend, Ruthie.

"Something awful happened at work and I'm not in the mood for a noisy bar."

"We can do happy hour next week."

"No, come to my house," Quinn said. "I have alcohol and I'll make you dinner."

"You are so predictable. You always cook when you're stressed."

"And lucky for you, I'm a good cook."

"All right, I'll be there in a thirty minutes."

Quinn drove on autopilot down Highway 59 to Sugar Land, an upscale community southwest of Houston, her thoughts on the Gregory James email. She didn't know what to do. The obvious answer was to show the email to the police. Of course, they would then consider her the thief. Whoever had changed the wire instructions and sent the fake email had probably covered their tracks and all guilty roads would then lead to Quinn. She was better off keeping her mouth shut and pretending she'd never received the damned email.

Although staying quiet didn't feel right, it felt dishonest. She'd see how things went with the police. That was the best she could do for now.

She turned in the driveway of her townhouse and hit the button to open the garage. Once inside, she shed a layer of stress and turned on the lights. She headed up the stairs to her bedroom, threw her purse and tote on the bed, then went into the closet, pulling off her summer suit.

After donning a T-shirt and shorts, the doorbell rang and Quinn hurried down the stairs. She swung open the front door and enveloped Ruthie in a fierce hug.

"I'm so glad you're here."

"You really did have a bad day."

"You have no idea. Come in the kitchen and I'll give you all the details."

Ruthie sat at the granite island, in her favorite leather stool, while Quinn retrieved a bottle of wine from the under-counter cooler. She held it up. "Cabernet okay?"

"You bet."

Quinn uncorked the wine, then poured two glasses, handing one to Ruthie. "How about pasta and a salad for dinner? I made pesto sauce last night."

"Sounds great. What can I do to help?"

"Nothing right now, this won't take long."

"Tell me what happened. I'm dying to hear."

As she cooked, Quinn explained everything from the phone call from Lynne Jenkins to walking out of Scooter's office with Rebecca, everything minus the Gregory James email. She ignored the guilt battering her heart.

"I thought you didn't care much for Rebecca?" Ruthie said.

"I don't. She seems fake to me but everyone at HCU loves her." Quinn sipped her wine and thought about that. "Maybe I'm a bitch."

"That's not it. You're just prickly at times." Ruthie smiled, eyes crinkling.

"You're right. But this is awful for the university. That Logan Rice was a real piece of work, leaving in a huff. The police detective was so calm it was eerie."

"You can't blame Mr. Rice for being upset. That's a lot of money to lose."

"Of course it is. I'm not thinking straight. Scooter wasn't thinking straight either, saying it's my fault."

"You two have had a bit of a love-hate relationship the last ten years."

Quinn dropped linguini in a pot of boiling water and stirred the noodles. "He's just so unpredictable. I've always wondered if his marriage is good. He never talks about his family."

"Neither does my boss. Maybe Scooter is simply a moody guy."

Ruthie always made good sense. "You're probably right. Would you mind putting the salad together? I'll put garlic bread in the oven."

Ten minutes later, the dinner was served and the wine glasses refilled.

Ruthie waved her fork in the air. "I was thinking. What if Scooter meant it, that he thinks the theft is your fault?"

"Why would he seriously think that?"

"You're the only one who claims she didn't know about the wire transfer. You know that old saying, she who protests too much is guilty."

"That's ridiculous."

"Just playing devil's advocate. If I thought it, you can bet the police will as well."

"Like I said, that's ridiculous." Quinn wanted to shout the words but kept her voice low. She couldn't forget the email. "This is a terrible blow to HCU but I didn't cause it. Scooter said he'd call me tomorrow. I figure my vacation next week is history."

"Do you suppose the police will want you to stay in town?" Ruthie's lip twitched, then she burst out laughing.

"Stop that," Quinn said. "This is a horrible situation."

"Sorry, trying to keep your spirits up. I realize HCU has a rough road ahead."

"You can say that again. I'll do whatever I can to help Scooter. He may not be boss of the year but he deserves my support."

"Good for you," Ruthie said.

"I wonder who really did it. The thief had to know a wire transfer was ordered along with all its details." Quinn drummed her fingers on the granite counter.

"Exactly, and you know what?"

"What?" Quinn said.

"The thief had to know how to change those details."

"Damn, we're smart … unless some hacker in cyber space got lucky."

"Not likely," Ruthie said.

"Okay then, that means everyone at HCU, First National, the Bridge Foundation and their brokerage firm is a suspect."

Ruthie finished off her wine. "Look at it from the bright side. The more suspects there are, the less chance of the thief being you."

Quinn threw a dishtowel at her.

Ruthie left after a cup of coffee, a brownie, and a good laugh. Then Quinn turned on the dishwasher then headed upstairs to bed. After washing her face and donning a cotton nightgown, she climbed in bed and clicked on the television. The glare of the local news cast shadows across the bed and she snuggled in a pillow. A story about the upcoming hurricane season nearly put her to sleep. Then she heard "Houston Cullen University" and rolled back toward the screen.

The newscaster stood in front of Brennan Hall on campus and provided the bare essentials of the theft. No one on campus was interviewed. Quinn didn't know if that was a good thing or a bad thing. Sure seemed like the theft of $25 million from a local institution would generate more interest from the media.

She clicked off the TV, rolled over, and punched the pillow. Damn, what a lousy day. Would the police eventually find the Gregory James email? Would Scooter or the police actually consider her a suspect? Well, hell, she'd prove them all wrong.

$ $ $

Scooter called mid-morning on Saturday. And bless him, he didn't mention yesterday's chewing out but he did say the Detective Phillips had contacted him and the police now considered the loss of the $25 million a crime. Quinn agreed to meet him at the office on Monday morning. He would need her around for moral support.

After loading the dryer with towels, she left for a noon kickboxing class at the local Sugar Land fitness club. The club bordered the Southwest Freeway on the edge of the Sienna Colony Shopping Center. She parked on the freeway side, a minor miracle for a Saturday, then stepped on the sidewalk and stopped. What the hell was this? Exiting through the mall doors were Bill Jenkins, the VP of development at HCU and Rebecca Holland, holding hands. He must have returned to Houston last night.

Bill disengaged his hand when he noticed Quinn.

Rebecca spoke first. "Hi, how are you?"

"Hey y'all, didn't expect to see you in the suburbs." Her curiosity was sparked instantly as neither Bill nor Rebecca lived in Sugar Land.

Bill lifted a shopping bag. "We picked up some donor gifts from a specialty shop in the mall. Looks like you're on your way to the fitness club we passed."

"Kickboxing." She glanced at her watch. "I'm late. I'll see you on Monday."

"Enjoy your class." Bill pulled Rebecca's elbow and they moved to the parking lot.

Rebecca turned to look Quinn as she walked away. Their eyes met, then Rebecca grinned.

What was that about?

∽

Info for IN HOT PURSUIT
Genre: Romantic Suspense
Publisher: Crimson Romance/Adams Media
Length in words: 72,100
Heat rating: PG13

Available at:
- Amazon: http://amzn.com/B008195ACU
- Barnes & Noble: http://tinyurl.com/9ksmmfl

- Kobo: http://tinyurl.com/8uoj33z
- Sony: http://tinyurl.com/9pwrrd4

Karen Sue Burns also contributed to Book 1 of the Seasons of Love series, HEARTS, HEARTHS & HOLIDAYS: http://amzn.com/B009ZP5R86
As well as Book 2, of the same series,
SPRING PROMISE: http://amzn.com/B00C4O8KFM

ABOUT THE AUTHOR

Karen Sue Burns writes romantic suspense and mystery featuring feisty heroines who find themselves embroiled in risky situations full of adventure and sexy heroes.

Karen Sue Burns has worked as a CPA for over 25 years. She's traveled to Rio de Janeiro, London and Oslo, audited glass molds for wine bottles in California, and taken a helicopter to a drillship off the Gulf Coast—all in the name of accounting. For the last 16 years she's been controller at a liberal arts university in Houston, Texas handling the financial statements, the annual audit, and preparing IRS Form 990. Accounting has been good to her, but writing romance novels is her passion. *In Hot Pursuit* is her debut romantic suspense novel. She is a contributor to the sweet and sensual romance anthology series *Seasons of Love* with the books *Hearts, Hearths and Holidays* and *Spring Promise*.

Find Karen Here:

Website: www.karensueburns.com
Facebook: http://facebook.com/KarenSueBurns
Twitter: http://twitter.com/karensueburns
Blog: http://karensueburns.com/blog
Pinterest: http://pinterest.com/KarenSueBurns

DEDICATION

This story is for all the romance readers who love a happy ending. I do as well! A special thanks to Carolyn and Ellen for being such good friends and for loving a good story.

DO-OVER SUMMER
By KIM HORNSBY

Chapter One

From what Jewell Price could see while standing at the kitchen window, the man kayaking by her aunt's dock was maybe in his fifty's. Grey hair. Today he wore a lifejacket, a Mariner's cap, and was bare armed. She imagined he led an athletic life with such a strong stroke. The slim boat sliced through the quiet morning water and passed the dock at a good clip. He was too old for her. Not that she was looking. She'd seen him paddle by every morning this week, that's all.

Jewell drained the dishwater in the porcelain sink, silently thanking Aunt Queenie for offering this cottage to live in. Island life wasn't so bad, once you got used to it. A little restricting, but she loved living on the water. Aunt Queenie hadn't used the place in years. "It's just a ramshackle, old hut, but if you and Joey want to hide out from whatshisname, it's yours." Her father's only sibling had a way with words.

"We aren't hiding from Warren. He moved to California without us." It was hard to not sound bitter about a man who'd chosen an acting career over his son. Especially when he had based his decision on one small speaking part in an indie movie. "We'll take it." Jewell had given her favorite aunt a big hug and moved in last May, just in time to find a rental space near the ferry dock on Daniels Island and open a bookstore. One year later, Pages was still open and showing a small profit. She wanted to keep it that way, since her mission was to provide for her ten year-old son. It wasn't that she hadn't always had to work to keep money in the bank, but this time it was all on her shoulders with no one to blame except herself.

After feeding her son a bowl of granola and making sure he brushed his teeth and wetted down his too-long, messy curls, she put him on the school bus at the end of their driveway. Back inside the cottage she changed from her sweats into a pair of tan capris, and threw a striped T-shirt over her cami. She'd read somewhere that stripes were in this summer, not that she bothered with trends on Daniels Island where Eddie Bauer clothes ruled. Even eight miles to the southeast, Seattle residents didn't seem to bother much with fashion unless it involved Gortex and toggles. Seattleites were a sporty bunch.

Even though it was unusually warm for May, layers were a must in a climate that could change 30 degrees in five hours and she added a jacket as the final layer. At the last minute, she dragged a brush through her wavy blonde hair. Along with their dog, Tie Dye, Jewell set out down the gravel driveway. This would be Tie Dye's first summer on the island and so far, he seemed to love the absence of the long, rainy days. He hated the rain. They'd adopted the Jack Russell Terrier mix at Christmas time, near her parent's house in North Bend, Washington. Jewell's brother's family had been fostering him for a rescue organization and Joey fell in love with the mutt at first sight. Realizing that this was the happiest she'd seen her son since Warren left them, Jewell secretly applied to adopt him and two weeks later, he was theirs. So far, Tie Dye had been one royal pain in the patootie but he couldn't help it. Terriers had a lot to live up to in the barking and scallywag department. Besides, Tie Dye had kept his end of the deal as Joey's saving grace and cuddle partner on days when the absence of a father got him down.

The two-mile walk to the ferry landing gave Tie Dye a chance to get some ya ya's out before he sat in a store all day long. It also gave Jewell a chance to change from the mom of a ten year old boy, to a Daniels Island business owner. The transition was a good one, remembering she was a person and not just a mother. Twelve years ago, before she was a mother, or even a wife, she'd been a singer at coffee houses and bookstores, not unlike Pages.

Long ago. She'd sold the guitar years ago for rent money when Joey was a baby, and she rarely sang anymore.

Opening the glass and wood-framed door, Jewell took in the musty scent of the old building. She swore each book had its own unique scent—a combination of paper, ink, binding glue, along with the addition of dust. She inhaled the welcomed aroma and smiled. Being surrounded by books was about as perfect a career as she could've ever imagined. Always a reader, Jewell had collected boxes of books as a child, never throwing anything out, and when the family home burnt to the ground and destroyed everything, a nine-year old Jewell had cried mostly for her books.

All three of her employees were serving coffee from behind the old counter she'd found at a flea market in Seattle. Cam and Brenna manned the coffee shop side during the nine a.m. morning rush, and Jill did the book store. They were college students, hired for the Island's summer season, the four months when Jewell would make most of her money for the year. The three greeted her and Tie Dye with various hello's, and before she went to check her computer for messages, Jewell made sure she wasn't needed out front.

Sunshine streamed in from the east windows. It would be another gorgeous day on the picturesque island in the San Juan's. She opened the door to let the fresh air and briny ocean smell into the shop. A ferry had just docked and foot traffic already marched up the hill from the landing. Soon they'd walk right by her door. Many would come in. "Ferry's here." She motioned to Brenna that more customers were coming.

Jewell was deep in discussion with a woman about the merits of printed books when a man walked into the bookstore, his presence blocking out the morning sun briefly. Looking up, Jewell instantly recognized the Kayaker. Bigger than she'd imagined, he was probably 6'3", and also younger. But she'd know those arms anywhere. And the baseball hat. Same one he always wore. The Mariners. He walked straight to the window display and picked up the featured book.

"Hi, how are you today?" Cam walked by him with a box full of books. He set them down by the display.

"Good. You?" The man nodded at Cam who opened the box and pulled the books out.

"Good too. You just come in on that ferry?"

"Nope."

Jewell's conversation partner turned to look at the man and did a double take, suddenly turning her back to him. Her face slowly took on a shade of red. "Oh my God!" she whispered.

"What's the matter?" Jewell touched the woman's arm.

"That's Matt Cross!" she hissed. "I'm sure it is. I heard he was here."

"Really?" Jewell's first emotion was relief that she stocked the famous author's bestsellers, but her second thought was that he was at the huge display she'd made for another thriller writer. Probably his competition.

"Where's his section? I want autographs," the customer whispered.

Jewell led her to a shelf dedicated to Matt Cross's bestselling novels. "Take your pick." There were probably eight different titles on the shelf, even though he'd undoubtedly written more than twenty bestsellers in his career.

Grabbing an assortment of the books, the woman plucked a pen from the counter and headed for the man by the window. "Mr. Cross?"

He turned.

Wow! It really was Matt Cross. Jewell positioned herself behind the counter and watched as the author realized the woman's mission.

"Are those my books?"

"Would you sign them for me?"

"Of course I will." He flashed a grin her way.

Jewell had no idea that the author Matt Cross was such a looker. Hell, she'd just come to terms with the fact that the kayaker was blonde, not grey.

It didn't take long for another customer to realize what was going on. Soon people were lined up to get books signed, until the store ran out of Matt Cross thrillers. In a matter of ten minutes, Jewell had sold thirty-two novels.

When the fans finally left the store, she approached the author. "Thanks for doing an impromptu signing." His gorgeous green eyes sparkled in a classically handsome face.

"Hey, we're both in the business of selling books, right?"

He still had on his promo smile and Jewell was strangely disappointed, then realized that perfect smile might be genuine. What did she know? She hadn't even recognized him. "That's true," she said. "I'm really sorry I don't have a huge Matt Cross section. Now, I have *no* Matt Cross section. I just sold every one of your books I had in stock." She smiled at him and his expression changed in that instant. He looked almost shocked.

"Time to reorder." He looked around the store. "This is a nice place. Are you the manager?"

"Owner." She formulated a question in her mind like "What are you doing on Daniels?' but didn't have time to voice it before he spoke.

"I'll take this while I'm here." He handed her a copy of the thriller from the window display. "He's a good writer." He followed her to the cash register.

"Yes, he is. This book just hit number one on the New York Times Bestseller List."

"I saw that. Good for him. My next book is out in a few weeks. Maybe you'll save some window room for me, then." He gave her an American Express card that said his name was Matthew Crosston.

She nodded. "I'll make it a point to clear this guy out and make room for you." She made a sweeping motion with her hand and grinned, then handed back the card. Not wanting to appear star struck, Jewell tried to hide the fact that she was wildly impressed that Matt Cross was in her store. But her nervousness was double-fold. The famous author was also alarmingly attractive. "The window's yours for the next one. What's it called?"

"Killer Intuition." He took the book from her. "I don't need a bag. Thanks..." He stared at her name badge and suddenly she wished she hadn't put it so close to her left breast. "...Jewell." His eyes met hers. "Nice name."

"Thanks. Come back anytime."

"I'll be back when you get more of my books," he flashed another one of those gorgeous smiles her way, and walked out the door into the sunshine.

Jewell stood on the dock, staring out at the morning mist hovering over the ocean. She hadn't made the coffee strong enough today but it was hot. Wrapped in a blanket to cover her flimsy nightgown, she contemplated going back in the house to wake Joey for school, then decided to let him sleep for ten more minutes. She'd finish her coffee. Have just a little more time to herself before beginning the usual morning fight to drag her son out of bed. He'd been moody lately and wanting to spend less time with her and more with his friends. Soon he'd be eleven and then twelve and then a teenager. What was she going to do about a moody teenage boy then? The lack of a father figure weighed heavily in her heart these days. At least his friends had fathers who were good to him.

With the visibility down to thirty feet off the dock, the morning mist contributed to the quiet eeriness.

Jewell loved living in Aunt Queenie's run-down cottage. It was just the right size for a mom and her son. Even though it didn't have internet access, it was close to the store, on the ocean, and free. Just far enough away from her parents in North Bend. They hadn't been thrilled that she'd taken their grandchild far from them and gone to live on an island. Jewell loved her parents, but being in the same town with them was not always good, especially when they had strong opinions on how to raise Joey.

When she heard the drip, swoosh, drip, swoosh, she turned to see the kayak slicing through the water, only twenty feet off the end of her dock. Matt stopped paddling, obviously startled to see a dock, or a woman wrapped in a blanket.

"Hi." He nodded. "Sorry, I couldn't see I was so close to shore here."

As he turned the red kayak, she passed her hand self-consciously over her hair. It usually stood up in the mornings and today was no exception. "How's that book?" she called.

He looked back, frowning slightly in obvious confusion. He must not have recognized her as the bookstore owner.

"The one you bought in my store," she explained. "Is it a good book?" Why was she prolonging this conversation? Here she stood wrapped in an old blanket with messy hair—not exactly man bait.

Matt turned the boat with one slight dip of the paddle then set it down across the cockpit. "It is, as a matter of fact. It deserves the window display."

"That's good to hear." They smiled at each other for an awkward moment and Jewell took a sip of coffee.

"My book is better. Get that window ready."

She smiled. "I will." Why couldn't she think of something witty or intelligent to say?

"You have any more coffee?" He nodded to the house.

What? Oh shit, he wanted to come in. "You want a cup?" She didn't mean to sound so surprised.

"I'd love a cup. My coffee maker broke and I'm going through withdrawal." He waited for the invitation.

"Can't have that. Come on in." Even to her own ears, her voice sounded shaky.

Matt paddled to the sandy part of the beach and exited the kayak to pull it up on shore. Jewell used that time to pat her hair into place, wipe the crust from her eyes and lick around her lips just in case she'd been drooling in her sleep.

"Where are you staying?"

He did a quick head to toe assessment of her and laughed. "Did you just wake up?"

"Yes," she said defensively. "It's only seven am."

His smile made her feel exposed, and she hoped he realized he was only coming in for coffee. They made the trek back to her place in silence.

At the kitchen table in the cottage's main room, her guest stretched out his legs and leaned back in the chair while she made fresh coffee. Joey didn't need to get up until 7:30 at the latest to catch his school bus at 7:45. She had at least ten minutes before waking him.

"I like this place. It has character. Is it yours?" Her guest looked around at the saggy couch, small TV, printed armchair and various other pieces of run down furniture.

"My aunt owns it." Having Matt Cross in her kitchen wasn't something that happened every day, and she realized that as a business owner, she had to take advantage of this opportunity. "Will you be here when the new book comes out? Can you do an author signing? I'll pre-order hundreds, if you say yes."

He looked over, smirking. "Is that the price of the coffee?"

"No, but if you're here, it would be nice." The blanket fell off one shoulder and she pulled it around her again and then placed the mug of strong, fresh coffee in front of the stranger at her table.

"I'll be here. Order those books." His tone held a hint of challenge.

"Thanks." After a few minutes of talking about how the bookstore limped along in the off-season, she noticed movement by the hall. Tie Dye came around the corner, Joey following. When the small dog saw Matt, he barked and ran towards him, wagging his tail, but snarling.

"Tie-Dye, stop!" Jewell scooped up the dog, the blanket dropping in the effort. "Joey, this is our neighbor, Matt Cross." She held Tie Dye in front of her braless chest.

Joey stood at the door wiping his eyes, his camouflage PJ's still twisted and wrinkled from slumber. "Hi. Mom, is it time to get up?"

"Sure is. Get dressed first and come on out here. I bought Captain Crunch for a treat." She set the dog down and he ran after Joey.

"You're a mother." Matt's voice held a note of surprise.

"Yes, I am." She grabbed the blanket from the floor and swept it around herself.

"But you don't wear a ring, so I assume you're single."

"Divorced." Why was she telling him this? If he wasn't so gorgeous to look at, would she even stand for this conversation? *Heck no!* How shallow was that?

"Let's see what I know so far. Your name is Jewell, you own the bookstore in town, stay in your aunt's cottage with your..." he paused here to contemplate something, "...*nine* year old son..."

"Ten."

"Ten year old son, and a dog named after a sixties fashion trend..."

"Oh, but Tie Dying is back again with a vengeance."

"I'll take your word for that." He smiled. "You drink coffee, don't get up with the sun, and you wear little nightgowns to bed." He gestured towards her, his expression making her blush.

"And you're a thriller writer who kayaks every morning, and invites himself into women's houses for free coffee so he can analyze them."

"Touché. I didn't mean to be rude."

When he held his palms up in surrender, she noticed he didn't wear a wedding ring.

"Are you renting near here?"

He nodded to indicate a house behind him. "I'm at an ungodly-sized, modern home around the bend. When I see how homey this place is, I'm wondering what I was thinking."

"The Markson place? It's the biggest one on this stretch. I've heard it's all glass and chrome." She set the box of cereal on the table and got the milk out of the fridge for Joey.

"I like this place better. Wanna switch?" His expression was playful.

She laughed. "Sorry, we kind of like this little place too." He was so damned handsome with his dirty blonde hair and twinkly green eyes. She took a deep breath and tried not to stare. What was wrong with her, letting a stranger into the house like this? Even if he was a famous author.

Joey arrived and plunked down at the table, his face still masked with sleepiness. Jewell reached over to push the hair out of his eyes. "Sleep okay?"

The boy nodded. "I need to take an extra snack today."

"Oh fudge, I forgot to make your lunch." She jumped up, looked at her watch and grabbed Joey's lunch box from the counter.

"I'll get going now." Matt stood. "Nice to meet you, Joey." He leaned down to pet the dog. "You too, Tie Dye," he chuckled as the dog growled and jumped away. "Thanks for the coffee."

Jewell looked up from the pantry where she was grabbing a drink box, crackers, a package of cookies and some beef jerky sticks. "Sure."

He put his cup in the sink and headed to the ocean-side door they'd come in through. "See you around," he called back to them. When he stepped through, he turned to look back at Jewell, his expression slightly wistful. "I have two kayaks." With that declaration, he turned and went down to the beach.

∞

Country music blared from the DJ's speakers into the May night at the Daniels Island Hoe Down Barn Dance. It was the last day before the official kick off to the summer season and tradition dictated that the island businesses have one final hurrah before the tourist season take-over. Jewell had organized the food, and with her helpers, was setting out the berry pies with the carrot cakes and plates of homemade cookies. Thankfully, the bugs had held off and she hadn't needed the fly screens for the desserts.

"Did you make all these?" She turned at the now-familiar voice, seeing Matt Cross with a beer in hand, his cap pulled low, the last orange glow of the setting sun illuminating his handsome, tanned face. *God, he must have been one drool-worthy teenager.* "Yes, I did. Each and every one. From scratch. I even milked the cow and churned the butter for the pastry." She blew a strand of hair from her eyes and straightened, her hands on her hips. "You enjoying our shindig?"

He looked around, observing everyone enjoying themselves. The entire area was crowded with people either dancing or eating, and the sound of laughter filled the air. "This beats all hell out of a Hollywood party."

His mention of Hollywood made her think of Warren and she cringed inwardly. "Do you live in Los Angeles?" *Please say no.*

He shook his head. "No, but I spend time there. I live in New York, but I'm relocating this fall." He took a swig of his Stella Artois.

"To Washington?"

"I haven't figured out where yet."

With a gesture from Jewell, he put his beer down and helped her move two tables together.

"Is Daniels Island a possibility?" Did she want him to say yes?

"Maybe. It definitely has advantages." The way he looked at her made her slightly uncomfortable. But then, she was terrible at flirting, having done so little of it in her life. She'd married Warren when she was twenty-one.

Just then, someone called her name for instructions on what to do with some dishes. "I have to go. Are you sticking around?"

When he nodded, Jewell realized she'd just told him she was interested in his whereabouts. Her words sounded like she cared. She did. Kind of. She was intrigued. "See you later then." As she walked to one of the outbuildings where they'd set up their kitchen, she felt Matt's eyes on her, and with that in mind, she made sure she didn't trip, or wiggle. Just before she turned the corner, Jewell purposely ran a hand through her long blonde hair and flipped it to one side in a gesture she hoped he'd think was sexy. Was it obvious she did that for him? She regretted it as soon as she got around the corner.

Joey was playing soccer with some boys in the upper field, and once she got the desserts placed, she'd be done with her hoe down duties. People were still eating, but someone else had signed up for clean-up duty. Grabbing a drink ticket from her apron pocket, she picked up a beer at the makeshift bar. "Thanks Scott." The town veterinarian in charge of the bar smiled at her. She downed the beer in a matter of five minutes while she watched the couples on the dance floor kicking up their heels to the country music. She couldn't remember the last time she'd danced. It had been too many years.

Once she'd procured someone's promise to take any leftover food to a shelter in Seattle, Jewell was done for the night. Mary Ellen Brady had agreed to take it over on the last ferry and stay over at her sister's in Issaquah. Island life was like that, with everyone pitching in to help each other, and reaching out to contribute to the less fortunate.

Jewell removed her apron and bagged up the last of the supplies she'd brought from her store. By the time she joined a group of locals by the coffee pot, darkness had set in, and the frogs were competing for air space with the band. The coffee pot lurkers talked animatedly about Matt Cross being on the island to write a book.

"He's renting the big house at Cliff edge," Jeff Lundstrom, the owner of the village hardware store told the group.

"Maybe he's going to put us in one of his books," Bobbie Sue, a recently transplanted teacher from Kentucky, contributed.

"Kill one of us off," Libby York added. "In his story, I mean."

Libby, who co-owned the ice cream parlor with three other ladies, was Jewell's closest friend on the island. Her business depended on summer traffic too, and once the September business died off last year, they'd passed a long, rainy winter making quilts at Libby's house. The two friends spent many an afternoon singing along to Pandora selections, talking about their sons, and piecing together their hand-crafted quilts for those boys.

Joey ran up and asked to go home with a friend for the night, begging to sleepover even though it was a school night. "Remember we said we'd have a do-over when Max got sick the last time? This'll be our do-over." The other mother promised not to let them stay up too late and would get them to school the next morning on time. "If you listen to Mrs. Prendergast, you can."

Once Joey left with Max and his family, Jewell was off duty as a mom. She found herself searching the crowd for signs of Matt. After an hour, she still hadn't seen him. Concluding that he went home, she danced with several of the island's single men, and then decided to call it a day. As she scanned the grass parking lot full of cars, trying to remember where she'd parked, she heard someone running up behind her. She turned, seeing Matt heading right for her.

"Wait!" he called out to her. "Are you leaving? We didn't have a dance yet."

"Yea, I'm going. I'm tired." They stood facing each other. "I have to open the store early."

He'd taken off his hat and looked just about perfect standing there with his beer in one hand and his other hand in his pocket, obviously trying not to look disappointed, but failing.

"Sorry," she muttered, feeling a little overwhelmed by the effect he had on her. Something about this guy hit her smack in the heart. She had to wonder if all women felt this way around him.

"I was looking for you when I got cornered by some readers." He shrugged, as though this was his life.

She sent him a sympathetic smile.

"Can I ask a favor before you go?"

"Sure."

"One dance." He put his beer down on the closest car's hood and held out his arms for her to walk into.

The band played a sweet, slow ballad and her heart jumped into her throat. Knowing there was no way out of this, her face heated with embarrassment while Matt wore an expression she couldn't quite place. Stepping into him, she placed one hand on his shoulder and took his other hand. He pulled her in close, and she couldn't help notice his delectable smell. She couldn't quite place his cologne but the combination of him and the scent took the attraction factor to an entirely higher level. She'd always been a sucker for really good men's cologne. They danced in silence and Jewell closed her eyes, feeling his body next to hers as they swayed.

"I haven't danced with a woman in a while," he whispered.

"Sounds like you usually dance with men."

He chuckled. "Like you made all the desserts tonight." He pulled her closer and she somehow knew he was breathing in the scent of her freshly shampooed hair.

When the song ended, he didn't let her go. Instead he pulled back only enough to stare into her eyes. "May I?" he whispered. When his lips touched hers, so softly, her first thought was that she was married, and then she remembered that both Warren and her marriage were long gone. It was a solid, nice kiss, no tongue, just lips, a little push but not too much, and when they drew apart, she had an overwhelming urge to go in for a real kiss.

"Nice lips." His breath was sweet, his eyes searching.

With their faces mere inches apart, she found herself leaning in for more. As their lips made contact again, she reached her hands behind his neck and threaded her fingers through his hair. It began as chaste as the first kiss, but deepened. And deepened some more, as her lips parted and he followed her lead. She hadn't kissed like this in such a long time. Their tongues tangled in the kiss, both wanting more, and things escalated quickly. His hands ran up her back to her hair and then around to cup her face. He pulled back slightly, said her name against her lips and nipped at her bottom lip.

Weak in the knees, she hung on to his shoulders as their kissing headed toward something much, much more. Suddenly, she stopped and pulled back, her hands now against Matt's chest, her tattered breaths breaking through the moment. She took a step back, away from Matt. "I need to go home."

He looked shocked. "What's the matter?" His voice was husky, full of want.

"I can't do this. I'm a mother." She placed both hands on her heated face and took a deep breath.

"But Joey left already."

"Oh, you saw that?" She looked around to see that no one was close by. "I just think that was too much, too fast, don't you?" Suddenly she felt like a prudish school marm, and shook her head. "Don't get me wrong, it was nice, but I don't know you well enough to be doing…" she waved her arms between them "that, with you, like that. So much." Oh, Fudge, she was tongue-tied. The music ended and suddenly people came pouring out of the barn. "I kind of started it, like that, and now I'm finishing it."

"If you're worried about someone coming by—"

"No!" No way she could take this any farther, could she? Joey was gone, and it was true she'd been looking for Matt, and had been disappointed when she thought he'd left. But out here, alone with this man in the darkness of a field parking lot, she wasn't brave enough to do anything with him. He'd want to go home with her, and even though that might be fun for tonight, did she want to sleep with the celebrity author who was only here for a few months? Soon he'd be gone to God knows where, while she stayed back on Daniels Island pining away for him? Oh *hell* no.

A grin tugged at Matt's lips. "You're wrong about one thing though. I officially started it, but you made it what it was. Which was a damned fine kiss, Jewell." He still held her and she wriggled free. "Sorry that it freaked you out. Or that you thought it was too much."

She looked around for her car. Shit! Where did she park? "No. No, it was fine. Just enough." She looked over at him to see him grinning at her awkwardness. "I mean…it was great but I have to go home."

"I'll walk you to your car. Where is it?"

"If I knew I'd be in it already."

Matt took the keys from her hand and pressed the unlock button several times until they found her car three rows over, hiding behind a Hummer.

The walk to her car was heavy with expectation and awkwardness. She had to get out of there. He took her hand and she let him, fighting the urge to snatch it back. When they reached her Honda, Matt opened the door for her.

"Drive safely, Jewell."

Why did it sound so sexy when he said her name like that? "You too. Goodnight." Just as she grabbed the car door, she felt his hand on her bare arm. She turned around.

"See you on the dock at seven. Wear that nightgown." He squeezed her upper arm and kissed her cheek before he walked away.

Oh, he was a bold man. What must he think of her? Did he do this everywhere he went? Single out a woman and dive in for the seduction? Jewell drove straight to Pages where she had a computer and internet access. She had to know more about this man who obviously had some interest in her. She didn't just go around kissing men without knowing who they were. The farther she got from their kiss, the better she felt about ditching him. Clearly he wanted sex, and she'd done the right thing by stopping it from happening.

Settling in at her desk, she typed in 'Matt Cross' and spent the next ten minutes sorting through the sites dedicated to the handsome author. She scrolled through head shots of him, stopping to scan an interview with Time Magazine. She stopped suddenly when the interviewer asked about Matt's wife, Celeste. "Does she inspire you to write more romance in your thrillers?"

"She's my muse, but she doesn't like me to talk about our private life so I guess I'll just have to plead the 5th on that one."

Matt Cross was married! Where was Celeste while he was gallivanting around the islands in the Pacific Northwest? *Isn't that just like a celebrity to sleep with any girl they could when their wife wasn't looking?* Jewell scrolled to the top of the interview to discover it had been published nearly two years ago. Maybe they were divorced. He didn't wear a ring. She poured over articles, Wikipedia descriptions and photos of Matt but saw nothing more about a wife. Her heart beat firmly against her chest, as her face again filled with heat. Celeste Cross. She typed the name into the browser box and clicked on the first article that appeared. Dead, 2011, at the age of thirty-seven, Celeste Cross had 'succumbed to uterine cancer' it read.

Jewell scrolled down, and what she saw at the bottom of the page, robbed her of breath. She froze, looking at the photo of Celeste Cross. With a beach and palm trees in the background, her hair blew to one side in a breeze. She stood by a restaurant table in this particular photo, wearing a silver evening dress and clutching a small purse. Nothing horrifying about that image at all, unless she considered the fact that Celeste Cross, the woman staring into the camera, looked just like her.

∽∾

The alarm clock was set for 6:30 but Jewell was awake long before the buzzer went off. It had been a restless night. She'd tossed in her bed, wondering what Matt must've thought when he first saw her at Pages. More than likely, that accounted for the strange look he'd given her. It had to be. She and Celeste Cross looked enough alike to be twins, or at least sisters. Same hair, same eye shape, same full mouth. No wonder she'd detected a hint of sadness in his stares.

After making coffee, she pulled on sweat pants, a hoody, and took two cups of coffee in travel mugs to the dock. Would he come? She had to tell him that she knew about her resemblance to his wife. Should she tell him how she understood that he'd kissed his dead wife last night, and not her? The thought made her heart heavy. She'd only had twenty minutes to believe that Matt Cross was interested in her. Twenty glorious minutes until her joy came crashing into a cement wall at sixty miles per hour.

Sitting cross-legged on the dock, Jewell sipped her coffee and tried not to look off to the left, the direction of the Markson house. It was 7am. Tie-Dye danced around the beach area, digging for clams in the sand. If Matt didn't come soon, the coffee would be too cold to be enjoyed. Last night, that kiss had just about done her in, resurrecting feelings that she hadn't experienced in a long time. As a woman of only thirty-two years old, she still had needs—strong needs that longed to be satisfied.

A raven called from the trees on the beach and startled her. Then she saw him. The red kayak stood out amongst the greys and muted greens of the morning as it came around the last corner and headed straight for her dock. Jewell's heart sped up, and she reminded herself that he'd probably just come over to tell her that he'd made a big mistake by kissing her. He might even be relieved she hadn't brought him home last night.

When the kayak got closer, Matt stopped paddling and drifted towards Aunt Queenie's dock. "Ahoy, pretty lady," he sounded so normal, like they hadn't gotten all hot and heavy last night in the parking lot.

"Ahoy, Sailor." She held up the covered cup. "I brought you coffee."

He tilted his head, as if he was measuring something and nodded slowly. "That was nice of you. Here, grab the end of this thing and I'll slip out on the dock. Probably go in the ocean doing it."

Bracing a blade against the dock, he carefully slipped out of the kayak and tied it to a ring on the end. He took the coffee from her and sat down close, a little too close for her comfort. "Sleep well?"

This would be the time to tell him that she knew about her resemblance to Celeste Cross, but she couldn't do it. All she wanted from the man beside her was to have a normal conversation, keep things light, not mention the other thing, and then let him go on his happy way. "Turned out I had some research to do online so I went to the store for an hour. I don't have internet here." She nodded back to the cottage while Matt took off his lifejacket. "But I made it to the dock at seven am." She stuck her finger in the air as if her presence was a major accomplishment.

He laughed. "Congratulations."

Holding her cup to his, they toasted and took a drink. How did he look so refreshed and bright- eyed this early?

"You knew I'd come?" he asked.

"I thought maybe. After all, I'm a pretty good kisser." She looked sideways to see his reaction.

The grin on his face said he remembered every moment of their parking lot kiss. "That you are." He gazed into her eyes, seeming to search for something. "You were doing some major back paddling, last I saw you."

"I hardly know you." She scrunched her brows.

"I'd say after that kiss, you know me pretty well."

Heat rose from her neck to her face, forcing her to remember the kiss and the passion between them. How sexy he smelled.

"I wanted to come home with you last night." He looked out at the island across the way and took a sip of his coffee.

Her heart skipped a beat. "Did you?" Not far off, an eagle dove into the water and flew away with a small fish in its claws. "I'm not ready for that, Matt."

"Understood." He chuckled. "But, if we'd spent last night together, we'd know each other pretty well, by now."

She gulped at the thought. Should she ask him about his wife? "Yes, we would, but I have a child and I don't do things like that anymore."

He was silent for too long. "Why don't you and Joey have dinner at my place tonight? I'm the world's best steak barbequeist, and this house has the most gorgeous grill I've ever seen in my life."

His green-eyed gaze had her melting into a pool of submissiveness. *Damn him!*

"I haven't fired it up yet because I don't want to cook for one," he added, throwing the match-winning blow.

"Really? That's sad. To put you out of your misery, I'll say yes to the world's best steak." She and Joey could drive over after his soccer practice. She'd get her employee, Jill to close Pages at nine. God knows she owed her one. "Joey has soccer this evening. Can we come at seven?" It was Friday. No school the next day.

"I'll get steaks."

∿

All that day, Jewell tried to ignore her fear that Matt Cross was only interested in her because of her resemblance to Celeste. She attempted to avoid the internet, but did not win that battle. Several times, she Googled the name 'Celeste Cross' and found sites that featured photos of the former editor at Random House. Some pictures did not resemble her as much, but still plenty close enough. Celeste and Matt had met when she edited his series about a serial killer. Shortly after he released the second novel in the trilogy, they were married. Matt Cross had no children, lived in New York City, and was an avid rock climber and outdoorsman. Jewell shuddered with pleasure at the memory of his hard body against hers during that kiss. At forty-two, he was ten years older than her, and one publication estimated that he was one of the world's most successful thriller authors. When he wasn't writing, he worked with his foundation that battled illiteracy in under-privileged areas of America. He promoted fundraisers and donated his time and money to a cause that taught reading all over the country. It touched Jewell that a wealthy man like Matt would work so hard to bring education to people who didn't know how to read. He clearly didn't have to do anything benevolent to sell more books.

When Jewell and Joey drove down the long driveway to the Markson house, she explained that their host would be the same guy who'd graced their breakfast table a week earlier. "He's a famous writer who's going to do a book signing at the store in a few weeks.

"Why do we have to eat with him?" Joey was annoyed that they'd had to leave Tie Dye at home.

"We don't have to eat with him," she mimicked the whine of his voice. "I thought it would be kind of fun. If we weren't doing this, you'd be at the store with me on a busy Friday night, and I know you'd rather do this." She ruffled her son's brown hair and he swatted playfully at her hand.

The house, perched on a rocky cliff and overlooking other islands in the distance, was an architectural dream. With the setting sun casting its golden glow against it, the structure resembled something out of a movie scene. The sheer size and opulence of the place astounded Jewell.

"I had no idea it was this grand!" she said, in awe as Matt lead them in to the vast main room. The floor-to-ceiling three-story high windows, different levels, and modern design looked out of place in the coniferous forest, but extremely impressive.

Joey went straight for the elliptical trainer by the windows. "Can I try this?"

"Sure." Matt led Jewell out to a deck the same square footage of her cottage.

She dropped her purse on a chair and went over to the railing to stare down at the water. The deck hung over the edge of the cliff, supported by pylons anchored into the rock below. "It must've cost a fortune to build here."

"Probably did. But after seeing your place, I wish I'd found myself a modest hang-out to finish writing my book." He held up a beer and a coke and she nodded at the beer.

"I have wine too, if you prefer."

She shook her head and took the chilled Stella from him, their fingers touching, lingering. "This is perfect. I've been at the soccer field and I'm parched."

Joey ran out to the deck and Matt offered him a drink from the cooler. He took a Sprite. "This is a cool house!"

"There's a trampoline just below us. Enclosed in a safety net." He looked over at Jewell. "You might have to sweep off the pine needles. I haven't been on it."

"Mom, can I?" His eyes were wide.

She laughed and nodded. "Just don't ask me to jump with you."

"Do you like steak, Joey?" Matt called to the boy's back.

Joey flew down the stairs, calling back a barely decipherable "Ya."

"He does," Jewell added. "I hope you didn't go to a lot of trouble for us. We're pretty easy to please."

Matt set his beer down on the table and rubbed his chin. "I have a confession."

Ah, here it comes. '*You look like my dead wife...*'

"I own this house. I bought it a few months ago, thinking it would be the perfect place to write." He looked apologetic. "I needed someplace to finish this book I'm having trouble writing. I can't seem to come up with a great ending. So I figured I needed someplace with few distractions."

"And is it?" She tried to hold back her initial excitement that Matt was a resident, not a renter.

He chuckled and flashed her a grin. "Well, aside from you, there aren't a lot of distractions, so I guess you could say it's working out well."

Flirting with him was irresistible. "I've become a distraction for your work?"

"You have." His piercing eyes were almost too much for her and a thrilling jolt shot through her body. "I find myself wanting to add a beautiful single mom/book store owner to my novel, have her fall for the recluse hero and see where their relationship goes."

Jewell laughed. "Now I've heard everything. How often have you used that line?" He wasn't laughing with her.

"Never." He stood and turned on the grill and she followed, touching his arm.

"I'm kidding, sorry."

"I guess it did sound like a pickup line." He checked to see that no one was coming up the stairs and gave her a little peck on the lips. "I like you, Jewell." He ran the back of his hand down the length of her cheek to her neck and tilted his head, studying her. "I'm not sure if I'm too old for you, or not your type, but on my part, there is genuine interest.

She took a deep breath and resisted the urge to lean in to his touch.

"And unless I'm wrong, I think I feel something from you." His voice was low and he looked like he needed some affirmation of her feelings, but she wasn't ready to ruin the evening by bringing up his dead wife.

"I'm thirty-two, and no, you are not too old for me. Aside from the fact that you are a famous author who'll be gone when summer ends, and the fact that I don't know you very well, you seem perfect for me." She walked away to check on Joey down at the trampoline, not wanting to witness his reaction.

After steak, grilled veggies and fresh bread from the bakery in town, Jewell was stuffed and liking Matt more and more with each hour that passed. Joey was enthralled by Matt, listening as he talked about his stint as a Black Hawk helicopter pilot in Afghanistan. Apparently, Matt had a high-risk military career before writing thrillers, and to Joey that made him more mysterious. To Jewell, too.

"My first series, set in Afghanistan was very successful, but I wanted to move on from that setting and write urban thrillers," he explained. Since meeting Matt, two weeks earlier, she'd read five of his books and wondered why she'd never tried the novels before. The writing was fast-paced, meticulous, compelling, and he wrote love scenes that were gritty and desperate. It was thrilling to think that knowledge came from experience. She watched her son and the man who was 'interested in her' talk about the danger of his former missions to rescue soldiers, and sexual interest invaded her body. There was no doubt about her attraction to Matt.

When asked how they came to the island, Jewell told him the abbreviated version of how she and Joey had few choices of where to go when Warren moved to Hollywood. "I didn't want to stay in my home town the rest of my life, but still wanted to be close to family."

"You didn't want to go to L.A.?"

"No." She wanted to say this so it put Warren in the best light possible in front of Joey. "He said it's just too big and noisy for us. And besides, Warren is very busy with his acting career."

"They got a divorce," Joey added. "Now, I never see Dad."

Matt took a deep breath and exhaled. She wondered what comments he withheld about how a man could choose an acting career over fatherhood.

"But someday he's gonna be a famous movie star," Joey added, matter of factly.

Jewell couldn't help but notice the clench of Matt's jaw, then smiled at her son like this would be very exciting for everyone. "Joey's dad is a very good actor and very believable in any part he plays."

The look Matt sent her said he'd received her hidden innuendo loud and clear, but he nodded anyway and directed his comment to her son. "Sometimes you just have to let the ones you love chase their dreams."

"Are you a Dad?" Joey looked interested.

"Nope." Matt said. "Never had the pleasure."

Joey finished off his last bite of dinner. "It's hard to be a dad."

Jewell's heart clenched and she thought about what she might have said to her son to make him think this. Before she could add anything, Matt interrupted.

"It must be very hard, Joey. I'm sure your Dad loves you a lot and would prefer to be here with you if he could work at the same time. Men have a great need to do their work. It's what makes us feel fulfilled."

The boy shrugged and looked out at a little sailboat drifting by the dock in the twilight.

"We need to get home," Jewell announced. "This has been so much fun and I really appreciate the invitation. Right Joey?"

He nodded. "Ya, awesome steak."

"We need to go let out Tie Dye who is probably dancing on the spot, having to pee-pee." Jewell stood and assembled their plates to carry in to the kitchen.

"Don't bother," Matt gestured. "I'll clear the plates, Jewell. Next time bring Tie Dye."

"Mom, we need to come back sometime," Joey said.

"Anytime," Matt followed them into the house. "You're both welcome here, anytime."

∽

Tourist season was in full swing on Daniels Island and Jewell didn't have time to think about Matt, let alone go for dinner to anyone's house. She hadn't seen him kayak by the cottage since their dinner and she wondered if he was paddling the other way, maybe avoiding her for some reason. When Cam announced at the store that he was house-sitting for Matt Cross for a few weeks while he was in New York, Jewell's heart jumped into her throat. "You're what?"

"I'm staying at his house for at least two weeks. He left a few days ago for New York." Cam had no idea how his announcement effected Jewell. "You should see his house! It's fricking awesome." His eyes widened as he shook his head.

Why hadn't Matt called to tell her this? She knew him well enough that it would have been common courtesy. Hadn't he told her that he was interested? If that was true, why was he gone two days later without a call? Jewell felt let down all day and moped around the bookstore, vowing not to let herself get so carried away with a man again.

She buried herself with work, and when Joey's school year wrapped up for the summer, Jewell juggled the business side of things with driving her son back and forth to soccer practices and a sports day camp he'd been dying to attend with his friends from school. Business was crazy good and the day she got an email from Matt, she'd just about forgotten about his effect on her.

"Sorry to leave suddenly last week without saying goodbye, but my publisher suddenly requested my presence to promote the release of *Killer Intuition*. I had three hours to get off Daniels and to the airport for a flight. I wanted to call you, then realized we hadn't exchanged numbers. In all the craziness here, I finally realized Cam might have your email address, seeing as my house sitter works for you. Don't be mad at the kid for giving it out. I told him it was business. I'm pretty sure you're not as interested in me as I am in you, but maybe when I get back, that will change. I can't stop thinking about our parking lot encounter, our coffee on the dock the next morning, and what a great mom you are to Joey. I have to admit, I'm intrigued. I'll be back on Daniels next week. Let me know if you care. If not, I'll understand and won't bother you, Jewell. I Promise.   Matt."

Jewell sat back in her office chair, smiling. He liked her. She couldn't pretend that it didn't make her happy to have his attention. She liked him too, but worried that he'd based his interest on some strange desire to date his dead wife. At least initially. She couldn't have the same personality, could she? Printing his email, she folded it to put in her purse and take home. It felt like a high school move, but she wanted to be able to read it later, alone, and without all the interruptions of the busy store.

Hours later, just as she was about to leave the store for the day, she wrote a reply and sent it off. Having resisted writing a reply all day in an effort to appear casual, the battle was lost when someone bought a Matt Cross book and she saw his picture on the back cover.

"Hi Matt: I wondered where you went. I haven't seen the lone kayaker for a while and thought maybe you decided to finish your book in NYC. Or were sequestered in that big house trying to avoid the island distractions. You know where to find me when you return. Jewell"

Still, she wasn't able to address her doubts about him in case for some creepy reason, he hadn't realized the physical similarities. She wouldn't do it by email. She wanted to show him she cared, but didn't want him thinking she was *too* interested. One of the mistakes she'd made in her marriage with Warren was not holding back anything. She'd married a handsome man, adored him, and expected him to behave like a standup guy with her, even though she coddled him and continually made excuses for his selfish behavior. When he'd taken acting classes, she'd supported him. When he'd gotten a part in a play, she'd secured a babysitter for Joey and sat in the front row more nights than she now wanted to admit. And when he was offered a part in a very low budget movie, Jewell encouraged him to chase his dream, even though it seemed like it didn't include her and Joey anymore. She'd been a fool. He'd left for L.A. promising to send for them once he found a place and steady work to support his acting dreams. But six months later, he asked for a divorce and assumed that Skype calls to his son were good enough. He'd always been the type of father who couldn't figure out what to do with a son.

If Matt came back, called her, wanted to see her again, kissed her, wanted to sleep with her, she would not let her libido call the shots. This time, she'd hold back something, not give up too much, too fast. If he wanted any more of those hot and heavy kisses, she'd need to know he was not just looking for a summer sex partner. He'd probably be leaving when the book was finished at the end of the summer. Earlier in the day, she tried to find out the length of time between Matt Cross novels. According to what she'd calculated, he wrote two a year, but that information could be wrong. As an avid reader, Jewell knew that he might secretly write under another name. It could take him two months to perfect a thriller but then he might take two months off to play. After all, if he was an outdoorsman, when did he find time to rock climb? Taking time out of her day to calculate this made her feel too desperate.

Scott Jansen, the island's veterinarian asked Jewell to dinner, and although he was nice looking, gentle with Tie Dye, and a divorced dad, she didn't exactly feel available to date. It had been two weeks since the email from Matt and she was half expecting him to come through the bookstore door any day. Good sense told her not to wait, to stop watching the ferry traffic, to accept the invitation to dinner. All weekend, she'd put off Scott by telling him she needed to do the late shift at the store, and that had worked.

Jewell was making lattes for a couple from Seattle waiting for the ferry out. When she handed the to-go cups to the man, she saw Scott come through the door with a pizza box. "I hope it isn't bad manners to bring food into a coffee shop," he grinned.

"Only if you're not going to share," Jewell said. "Cam." She called her employee to take over as she wiped her hands on her apron and stepped out from the coffee counter. Earlier, Cam had said he hadn't heard when Matt Cross was coming back.

"I brought dinner to the hard working lady." Scott held out the pizza box, his eyebrows raised, possibly wondering how to proceed.

This is awkward. Jewell motioned to one of the four tables outside the café's door. "What a nice surprise. Thanks Scott. How did you know I'm really hungry?" They sat at a small iron table, the box between them as Scott opened it to reveal a cheese pizza. "I couldn't guess what you like on pizza so I played it safe." He looked at her apologetically.

"I like cheese pizza!" The absence of toppings didn't matter to her when she'd spent the last two hours trying to figure out how to eat something before the next ferry arrived and the store got busy again. His 'playing it safe' comment stuck in her mind. Scott was the type of guy who always took the middle of the road, never straying too close to either edge. He was attractive, in a studious, *vet* sort of way, with his meticulous haircut, wire-rimmed glasses and button down shirt. She guessed he was early forties, and wondered where his wife lived with their two teenage kids who came over for visits.

The conversation was limited to unanimated, boring talking about their respective businesses. Once the ferry arrived, Jewell saw pedestrians approaching, walking up the incline towards her store, and the town. Wolfing down a second piece, she nodded at Scott. "I have to get in there. Cam is off work in a minute."

Cars passed the store on their way from the ferry, a long line of vacation vehicles, lumbering by. Jewell waved at her quilting friend, Susan Smart, who'd been on the mainland visiting her grandkids. Some pedestrians would stop in and several cars would probably circle around back to park. Lots of visitors stopped for a coffee, tea, or cold drink to sustain them during their drive.

"Showtime," she said.

Scott continued to eat. "Okay." He reached across the table and wiped the corner of her mouth. "Sauce," he explained.

"Thanks." Jewell's eyes drifted to the road just in time to see the back of Matt's Land Rover heading towards town. She knew the car by the 'Support your Troops' yellow ribbon on the back window. Dammit. Did Matt see Scott wipe her face? His intimate gesture had left her feeling awkward. "Thanks for the pizza, Scott." She didn't want him to do this again but how could she tell him that even without Matt on the island again, dating her wasn't an option. She just didn't see any type of future in the vet no matter how nice he was. Jewell hurried inside the store and dismissed Cam, her heart racing in hopes of Matt making the turn at the lights to come back to say hello. Had he looked over? Especially now that she'd made one of the front windows a gorgeous display of his latest release—*Killer Intuition*. Maybe he'd been busy looking at the display and not who was letting a strange man wipe her face outside the store.

But his car didn't return and the next morning he didn't kayak by, even though Jewell sat at the end of the dock at 7 a.m. with two cups of hot coffee. The following day, she simply watched from the couch, inside her house, but no one kayaked by between the times of 6:45 and 7:30. She told herself that he might be in writing mode, too engrossed in his story for her, or that he'd misread her email to sound too disinterested. Joey spent a lot of time with Libby's son Garrett, and between swimming at the local beach and riding their bikes around the island, Jewell felt lonely. Her son was getting older and needed her supervision less and less. And now, Matt, a man who'd passionately kissed her, invited her to his house for dinner and emailed about his interest, was nowhere to be seen.

Later that day, while Jewell busied herself unpacking books, her son came in through the back door. "Is Garrett here yet? Mom, I need money for ice cream."

She opened her purse to grab a fiver. "No, he's not. Are you meeting him here?"

Joey nodded. "He's watching a plane land near his house or something. A float plane." Joey took the money.

Libby's voice called from the doorway as she hurried inside. "I'm here to buy some books, Shop Lady."

Garrett walked in with his mother, waving his money at Joey and they took off for Libby's ice cream shop a few blocks down. "Hi Lib. What's this I hear about a float plane?"

Libby picked up a copy of *Killer Instincts* and held it up for Jewell to see. "Matt Cross just landed a float plane in the bay and motored it to his place. Guess Mr. Rich Man has his own plane." She grinned and grabbed a few more books off the display. "Have you ever met him? I hear he's approachable."

Jewell hadn't told her friend anything about her and Matt, not that there was much to tell beyond her own fantasy. "He signed some books here, one day. I'm going to do a 'meet the author' night, if he still agrees." She nodded, avoiding eye contact with her fiend for fear of giving away her secret. "He flew in on a float plane?" Libby's house was in the same bay as Matt's and even though she couldn't see the house amongst the trees, Jewell knew her friend had a good view of his dock.

"Yup. Just now. Those suckers are noisy too." She put her books on the counter. "You didn't tell me that you met him. Holding out on me?" she teased.

"No. He seems nice though. I need to get him to commit to a night for the event and put an announcement in the Daniels directory."

"Looked like he was the pilot. Two people got out. One was Mary Ann Cobble." Libby's eyebrows arched for affect. MaryAnn Cobble was a local real estate agent who was divorced, hot to trot, and beautiful. "She had an overnight bag with her."

Jewell's heart felt like a lead weight in her chest. "Oh. She'd just love Matt Cross, wouldn't she?"

When Libby left to grocery shop, Jewell stood at the window and thought about Matt Cross. Had he taken up with Mary Ann? Maybe they'd gone to New York together. The thought made her feel nauseous and she took a deep breath. Had he finally decided it was creepy to try to date a woman who looked like his dead wife? Mary Ann had spiky black hair and looked like a well-dressed rock star. Nothing like Jewell or Celeste. There was nothing Jewell was willing to do to look differently though. Why would she want to? Matt was obviously done with their flirtatious relationship and she needed to get on with her life.

∽∾

The next morning, Jewell woke to a bird calling from the beach. Over and over, it hooted and cawed. Like a crow, but more desperate. Wondering if it was in trouble, Jewell rolled out of bed and walked outside to the beach path, wondering if it wasn't the heron that had been hanging out on the dock. It was warm already and she guessed today would be another scorcher. The night before, she'd gone to sleep in a short nightdress with her hair pinned up. As she neared the bird's call, it sounded even worse. Stepping gingerly over the rocks, Jewell rounded the corner to see a flash of red showing through the bushes. Then Matt came into full view, seated on her dock and calling from cupped hands. His bird-call halted mid crow. "There you are! Hey, it's 7 am, time for coffee."

Her heart jumped and she reminded herself to go slowly with this man. "What the heck? You sounded like a deranged Dodo bird." She stood with her hands on her hips.

"I don't have your phone number." He threw his arms in the air. "How is a guy supposed to find you?" He wore only nylon shorts.

She tiptoed across the path to the dock. "I'd say this worked."

He laughed. "Were you asleep? I'm sorry. But you have to get up soon with Joey."

"He's on summer vacation and we sleep later now." She patted down her hair and then shaded her eyes from the morning sun as he approached.

"Well, it's gonna be a hot one. Let's have iced coffee today." He motioned for her to turn around. They were going to the cottage.

"Haven't you got a shirt somewhere in that thing?" She gestured to the kayak tied to her dock.

"Why do I need a shirt when you're wearing a see through thing like that?" Matt pointed to her nightgown.

She gasped, realizing that the morning sun lit her up from behind. "Oh Fudge! Stop looking." She bunched it up and threw an arm across her chest.

"Stop looking at me without a shirt," he grinned.

She had to admit that Matt had a great body, finely haired chest, with just enough muscle to look like he worked out, but not quite enough to pose as a cover model for romance novels. How could she not look? "Well stop walking around without a shirt," she said, as laughter bubbled up from her.

At the cottage, she grabbed an old sweater of Aunt Queenie's by the door, and put it on to hide her near nakedness. She ground some coffee beans and filled the pot with fresh water, before flipping the switch. The sounds and aroma of fresh coffee brewing filled the kitchen as she leaned against the cabinet to face him. "I hear you came in on a float plane. I'm surprised you didn't drive that thing over."

Matt playfully took her bib apron from a kitchen wall hook and put it on. "Wow! News gets around fast on an island. I wonder if they know I'm over here visiting you right now." He tied a bow around his waist and Jewell laughed. "Better?"

"Moderately. That thing highlights your pecs." He looked down to where the bib did not cover his nipples. He flexed his chest muscles and raised one eyebrow.

"Do you really want iced coffee?"

Matt picked up a book from the table and read the back cover. "Yes please. Remember, I've been exercising while you've been sleeping. Do you like this author?"

"I do. She really makes me think for my entertainment."

"Read any of mine?" He squinted looking like the answer might be painful.

"A few."

"And?"

She was intrigued that her answer seemed to matter so much. "And I love your writing. You *are* the master of thrillers."

He took a deep breath and held it in.

"I didn't know what to expect when I read the first one but you are one amazing story teller." She got a mug and a tall glass from the cupboard.

He laughed. "Whew! That's a relief. Thanks for reading them."

Jewell crossed her arms, her brows knitted. "Why? Why would you care what I think? You are world renowned."

"Sometimes that matters only so much." He ran a hand absently through his longer blonde hair. "I wanted to impress you."

He had to be kidding. She pondered that while waiting for the coffee to finish dripping. She poured them each some coffee, added ice cubes and milk to Matt's along with two teaspoons of sugar. She remembered how he liked his coffee. "Why have you been here for a week and not contacted me? Are you avoiding me?" She set the tall glass of iced coffee in front of him, then decided to make hers cold too. Not wanting to see him scramble for an explanation, she busied herself with the drink.

"I got here yesterday. I haven't been on the island for a week."

"I saw your car drive off the ferry a week ago." She sat down at the table across from him and hoped she hadn't sounded accusatory.

He nodded like he'd figured it out. "I hired someone to bring my car over from the airport when I knew I'd be flying in, instead of driving." He took a sip and grinned. "Aha, you do care."

"I thought you might be avoiding me."

"Why?"

"I couldn't imagine why."

"I'm not. As a matter of fact, I'm breaking all rules of writing by thinking about you way too much."

Her face felt hot as she stirred sugar into her coffee. "Really?"

"Really." His gaze locked on hers, penetrating her shield, and seeing things she wanted to keep hidden. "Come flying with me today, Jewell."

"You know, it's hard to take you seriously with that apron on," she said, buying herself a moment to think about his offer. She was extremely fearful of small planes. Would she … could she do this for him?

He removed the apron and set the thing on the chair beside him. "I promise I'll wear a shirt. Come flying this afternoon. Can you leave the store?"

"What about Mary Ann Cobble? What's the story with her?"

"Holy Cow! The trees have eyes! Did one of your spies see me with Mary Ann?"

She nodded and waited for the perfectly good explanation.

"She's my realtor. I gave her a ride back to the island after we finished all the paperwork yesterday." He shook his head. "You really don't trust me, do you?"

"I trust you enough to allow you to sit at my kitchen table while my son sleeps." She gestured to the two rooms at the back of the house."

"I have to say this is a little disconcerting. I wish you trusted me more."

"I just wondered what the deal was. Mary Ann Cobble is a beautiful woman." Jewell stared hard into those emerald green eyes.

"I suppose so but then I've never been interested in that type."

The type who don't look like Celeste? Jewell kept her mouth shut.

He stared back, just as hard. "Come flying with me this afternoon."

"What time?"

"Three."

"Fine. See? I trust you." With her fear of small planes, she wondered how she'd ever get her body inside a float plane in eight hours to show Matt that she wanted to trust him. How she wanted.

During the drive to Matt's house, Jewell felt less brave by the minute. The last time she'd been in a small plane, she'd freaked out and ordered the pilot, who was her cousin, to "take this sucker down. NOW!" Panic had overtaken manners, and logic, and when her impulse had been to jump out the window, she knew she couldn't handle being up so high. Big planes were fine, as long as she sat in the middle or on the aisle, but something about small planes turned Jewell Price into a screaming, unreasonable maniac. She'd contemplated taking one of Tie Dye's tranquilizers from when he'd last had his nails cut, something he hated as much as his owner hated small planes. But she didn't want to risk being a droopy, sleepy mess, just in case the meds worked their magic too effectively.

Matt was outside the house when she stopped her car in front of the massive garage and parked behind his Land Rover. "He wore khaki shorts and a tee-shirt that read *Read, Write, Live* with a picture of Liberace playing the guitar. She didn't get it.

"You ready?"

He had no idea she might panic and ruin everything. "I am a little nervous." *Like the Pope is a little religious*.

His expression turned to concern as he embraced her in a hug. "Don't worry, Baby. I'm a good pilot. We'll have fun." He kissed the side of her head, released her, and took her hand. "Trust me."

She so wanted this. For his sake. For their sake. He obviously wanted her to like flying and she would make a big effort, if that's what it took to make Matt happy.

Once strapped in, Matt told her he'd been flying for twenty years and had pretty much always owned a plane. That was good news to her rattled psyche, and as they took off across the water, Jewell reminded herself to take even, calming breaths. It was useless to anticipate fear.

Once in the air, he took her hand, pulled it over to his lips and kissed it. "You're doing great. How do you feel?"

"Surprisingly fine," she said into the headset microphone. She almost believed it. The roar of the engine was deafening. She swiveled in her seat to see everything below and everything beyond. There was plenty to look at. Islands dotted the scene, mountains in the background and white sails skimmed across the water below. It was absolutely gorgeous, like a virtual map. And she wasn't frightened to be up so high. For some reason, she had no fear of dropping from the sky. Matt knew what he was doing. He wouldn't be up here if it wasn't safe. When her usual trigger showed its ugly head—the question of how the little plane stayed in the air—she just turned to Matt and smiled. Each time she did that, he squeezed her hand and commented on something in the scenery around them.

"Isn't this something?" he asked her.

"It really is." Joey would love this and Jewell wondered if he'd ever get the chance. She looked down at Matt's strong, tanned hands and suddenly wanted them on her body. She wanted to feel his excitement over her. If he was so jazzed on flying, would he be this excited to make love to her? Her curiosity bred need, and need bred distraction. Distraction kept her fear at bay. Staying horny helped her get through twenty minutes of potential hell.

Eventually, they landed off Daniels and motored in to Matt's bay.

"That was incredible!" She felt pride in herself, excited, and sexually stimulated. Did Matt feel it too?

He glanced over at her, then did a double take. "You look… happy." He smiled big and reached to her lap to pat her thigh, an intimate gesture, especially considering how she felt, which was amorous … very, very amorous.

For the first time in a long time, Jewell wanted to get naked with someone, make love, and feel like a woman again. Her senses fired on all cylinders, every square inch of her skin tingled. She couldn't seem to stop herself from thinking about going up to that big house on the hill and falling into bed with Matt. A couple of hours stretched in front of her before she had to pick up a carload of boys at the soccer field. Would they? Seducing Matt might be a bit premature in their relationship, seeing they hadn't even talked about her resemblance to Celeste. But Jewell couldn't think of anything else as they tied the plane to the dock.

"Were you scared? You did great!" He hugged her innocently and Jewell refrained from pushing her pelvis into him, running her hands up under his T-shirt.

"You're a good pilot. Thanks for taking me."

He pulled back to look at her. "What's wrong? You look different."

Oh my god. Could he *see* she was horny as hell? "I am different, I'm a flyer now." She smiled at him proudly and when he moved in to give her a kiss, she told herself to hold back. It started as a nice little kiss but when she deepened it, he was right there, ready. Their tongues mingled, he moaned and cupped her buttocks with his hands as she threaded her fingers through his hair, pulling him to her possessively. A full minute later, he slowed it down and pulled back. "I'd say you like flying."

"I do, and I like you." Her throaty chuckle sounded like it came from someone else entirely. Someone sexual. Not a mother. Or a cautious divorcee. She kissed him again and his hands pulled her in to his groin to feel his readiness. When she remembered that Libby and all the other neighbors could see them, she quickly broke away from him. "Neighbors!"

Matt's eyes darkened, his face full of sexual longing. Jewell knew he wanted her as badly as she wanted him. "Let's go to the house." They practically ran up the steep path, only stopping once in the cover of the trees to kiss, tease each other, thereby sustaining the excitement.

Once they reached the house, he pressed numbers on the security pad, opened the door, and they ran to the bedroom. Matt stopped them at the bed and turned to her, cupping her face in his hands. "You sure?"

"Yes," she grinned. "I am so sure." She ripped off her tee shirt to reveal a lacy pink bra beneath. Her only pretty piece of lingerie, left over from an anniversary years before. Matt undid the bra, letting it fall to the floor and cupped her breasts in his tanned hands. Jewell thought she'd never seen anything more beautiful than his fingers surrounding her small, white breasts. His eyes were full of yearning and they kissed, devouring each other's mouths. He moved on to her neck, leaving a trail of gentle kisses. "Oh that feels nice," she said, in a low groan.

Moving to her breast, his tongue flicked a ready nipple.

"Oh, that too," she murmured.

But he didn't stay. Next, he kissed her abdomen, holding her with his strong hands round the waist.

"Oh, Matt."

He moved up to her neck again.

"You feel so good. I love when you kiss me there," she whispered.

"You love it everywhere." He ran his tongue along her shoulder, and moved to her neck, His breath whispered in her hair. "Celeste."

She froze, and he stopped.

Matt pulled back, his forehead creased. "What's the matter, Jewell?"

Horrified, she broke from him, grabbed her bra and T-shirt from the floor. She quickly pulled on her shirt and stuffed her bra in the pocket of her shorts, shooting him a look of betrayal. "You said your wife's name." She had to get out of there. Panic was on the edge waiting to take over. Matt might not even know that he said that, but she would not stay and make love with a man who was thinking about his wife.

"I didn't."

She laughed without smiling. "Oh you did. You most certainly did." She shook her head, left the room, and on her way out the door, grabbed her purse. "This was a mistake. A huge mistake." Running up the walk to her car, she heard the back door slam.

"Jewell, wait!"

She opened the car door, slipped inside, and once the car was running, she jammed the car in reverse.

"Jewell, please. Hear me out. At least let me defend myself." He'd reached the car and knocked on her window.

Against her better judgment, she rolled it down. "Look Matt. I can't make love with a man who thinks I'm his..." She didn't want to say 'dead wife'.

"I don't think that." He shook his head.

"I know I look like her and I was prepared to ignore that, but now I see that I shouldn't have."

Matt's eyes widened in surprise, as though he hadn't realized there was a resemblance. In that moment, when he had nothing to say, she knew it was over. The look on his face broke her heart, but she drove away, leaving him to contemplate the fact that he was interested in someone who looked just like his dead wife.

∽∾

Every morning for the next week, Jewell got up before seven, tried not to look out the cottage front window for a kayaker, and made coffee for one. She'd enrolled Joey in yet another sports camp and after she drove him to the field for the day, she continued on to work. Her three employees were doing a standup job of running the early morning coffee rush and it relieved Jewell to know that she didn't have to be at the store from 6:30 a.m. to 9:30 p.m. every day. The display of Matt Cross books was dwindling in size at a rapid pace and Jewell wondered if she should still ask him to do the author night. She hadn't seen him for six days but the talk around the island was that he was holed up in the house. According to Libby, who seemed to watch his dock religiously, the plane hadn't gone out, and no one had seen him all week. Probably writing, Jewell thought, as she entered the store and reminded herself to order more copies of *Killer Intuition*.

Libby had left a message reminding her to come to dinner that night. Her friend was having people over for a summer barbeque and even though you could see Matt's dock from the house, she figured she'd take Joey over. He'd be ready for a swim in the ocean after camp and Libby had a slide off her dock that the boys loved. Jewell left a message on Libby's voicemail. "I'm looking forward to it. Bringing a bottle of vino and maybe a dessert from the cafe. Let me know. We have a fresh German Chocolate cake that just came in this morning and I'm happy to snag that thing for us. Oh, and please tell me you haven't invited the vet for me. He's been calling lately."

Jewell didn't know how to tell Scott that she just wasn't interested. She may never be interested in men again after her almost love affair with Matt Cross. Her logical side told her that she'd dodged a bullet by leaving his house before they'd done the dirty deed, but her emotional side hurt. Burying her fear that he was only interested in her because of her similarity to Celeste had worked fine, until he'd called her by his wife's name. That moment brought the concern to the front of her mind, and threw a pail of freezing water on her interest in Matt Cross. It would take the rest of the summer to get over him, but she'd do it.

He'd leave in the fall and she'd go back to quilting and reading and living her life through Joey and his activities. It had been a pipe dream anyhow. The possibility of ending up with a man like Matt was such a longshot. Jewell was proud of herself for getting out before anything happened that made her fall in love with him.

Joey shot from the car in Libby's driveway like a Nerf bullet and Jewell carried the chocolate cake down the stairs and into Libby's kitchen. "Hello!' she called to the hostess who had her head in the fridge.

"Hi! Oh, look at that lovely, lovely, chocolate cake." Libby took it from Jewell and carried it reverently to the counter. "This should feed us all, and then some."

Libby wore a flowered sundress and a necklace. Jewell only had on shorts and a tank top with flip flops. "I didn't dress up. You look so pretty." She hugged her friend.

"No worries. I've been in a bathing suit all day and needed to make an effort. You always look good. You've got the legs for short shorts, not me. Let's open the wine, shall we?"

Out on the deck, Jewell recognized most of the guests, including several women from their off-season quilting group and their husbands. Scott stood talking to Libby's husband, Steven, and Jewell groaned inwardly. On a high note, there were at least twenty people milling about. It didn't look like Scott had been invited specifically as her date.

Libby went to the water to check on one of the boys whose nerf gun had malfunctioned. "Do-Over. Do-Over," Jewell heard the boy yell, as she poured herself a glass of Pinot Grigio. She leaned against the deck railings and watched as the guests circulated about, talking, eating Libby's crab dip and homemade rosemary crackers. She wondered how long she'd have to stay to satisfy Libby. And Joey. Attending a party so close to heartbreak was difficult.

"Come on up. We have so much food," Libby called from down at the dock.

The sun was in Jewell's eyes but she knew who Libby spoke to as soon as she saw the kayak fifty feet off the end of the dock. Her heart squeezed into a dry squeegie ball. Matt Cross was coming to the party. She had to stay cool about this. He wouldn't know she was here. As her heart rate jumped to see Matt pull in to the beach and slide his kayak out of the water, Scott moved in beside her.

"Hey Stranger," he said. "Haven't seen you in while." He looked desperately interested and she smiled at him, sympathetically. She knew what desperate interest felt like.

"How are you, Scott?" Matt and Libby laughed on the beach. From the corner of her eye, she saw him take off his life jacket and put on a white T-shirt.

"I'm thinking if you can get away for a party like this, we can try to have dinner again sometime," Scott said.

His face was too close to hers. She couldn't see Libby and Matt without looking around Scott. "How's the vet business these days?" Would he notice she changed the subject? Libby was still laughing at something Matt said as they disappeared around the corner to come up the stairs. When they came into view again, Jewell thought she'd never seen a more handsome man. His blonde hair had lightened with all the sunshine of late and his eyes sparkled with carefree pleasure in the afternoon light. Until he saw her. Their eyes locked and Jewell took a deep breath and pushed away from the rail. "Excuse me, Scott." She walked over to Libby and Matt, hoping to face her fears and get on with the party.

"Look who I found coming in with the tide," Libby joked. "Jewell have you met our artist in residence Matt Cross?" The hostess's tone was out and out saturated with "I brought you a man!"

"I have," Jewell smiled at Matt and tried to hide the fact that her pulse was racing. "Hi, Matt."

Matt nodded and explained to Libby, "I'm going to do an author night at Pages. Next week work for you, Jewell?"

She nodded. "Next week is perfect. Just give me a day and I'll promote it."

"Tuesday."

Libby watched them, wearing a curious expression.

Before anything more could be said, Steven walked over, shook Matt's hand and pulled him away. "Glad you could come. Let's get you a beer."

Libby slid in beside Jewell and whispered. "Steven desperately wants a ride in the float plane."

Jewell smile hopefully at her friend. As in hopefully Libby had no idea that she'd gone flying with Matt only a week earlier. Surely, if Libby had seen them groping each other on Matt's dock, she wouldn't be looking so strangely at her now. And if Libby knew that they'd almost fallen in to bed until he spoke his wife's name in a heated moment, she'd never have invited the artist in residence to this party.

It wasn't until the sun set, and the last guests remained at the beach fire pit, watching the kids roast marshmallows, that Jewell and Matt had a chance to speak again.

Finding herself suddenly alone with Matt at the table used as a bar, she spoke. "I don't think Tuesday works."

"How 'bout Monday?"

"I need time to promote it. How about Thursday?"

"Thursday it is. I have nothing but time." He sounded bitter.

She put the cork back in the bottle of wine and set it in the ice bucket. Joey and his friends were roasting marshmallows at the fire pit, yelling about the Nerf gun fight scores. "My gun jammed. I want a do-over!" Joey's favorite expression crept into everything these days.

Matt moved in closer. "I'd like a chance to talk to you alone, tonight." He handed her the glass of wine. Their fingers touched and Jewell could've sworn she felt a jolt from the feel of his skin.

"It's not necessary, Matt." Her words felt a little slurry, but she continued. "I get it. You were attracted to me because of how I look."

"Absolutely." His face was stoic. "And I'm sorry I'm attracted to blondes. I've tried to give the brunettes a chance but dammit, they just don't do it for me."

She didn't smile at his joke. "You know that's not what I meant, Matt. I look like her. I've seen pictures. I look a lot like her."

Matt took a deep breath and let it out slowly. "You look nothing like her except maybe for your hair. You have—" A shrill scream cut him off abruptly.

Jewell looked over to see the edge of Joey's sleeve on fire. Before she could react, Matt was already there, patting out the fire with the bottom of his shirt.

"Oh my God! Sweetie, are you alright? Did it burn you?" Jewell lifted up the charred sleeve and someone shone a flashlight on the child's arm.

"WHOA!" Joey said, his eyes wide with wonder. "I caught fire!"

Jewell pulled off Joey's shirt to see that his skin hadn't been affected underneath the blackened cotton sleeve. "Thanks Matt." She shot an appreciative look his way but Matt stared off after Joey, who was running around with his shirt off, pretending he was on fire, much to the delighted entertainment of the other kids.

He shook his head. "No problem."

"You reacted so quickly," she said.

"I used to be a soccer goalkeeper." He turned to look at her and must've seen something in her fearful face. "You okay?" He pulled her into a side hug and kissed the top of her head. "Poor Mom.

Libby stood fifteen feet away, watching, with her mouth open.

Jewell's biggest problem wasn't Matt's affection, but what had almost happened to her son. She broke away from the hug. "Libby can Joey borrow a shirt?" she said, and called out to her son. After thoroughly examining the boy's arm and telling him to stay away from the fire, Jewell was ready for a glass of wine. She'd dropped her first one in all the excitement.

Settling into a camp chair beside Mary Ellen Brady, she hugged her plastic cup of chardonnay to her. Suddenly, she realized how terrible that accident could have been. If Matt hadn't gotten there so quickly, they'd be on their way to the clinic. Maybe even to the hospital on the mainland, with Joey in horrible pain.

The conversations moved to other topics, but Libby continued to shoot her friend *the* look. The one that said she couldn't wait to get her alone for an interrogation about Matt Cross. By the time Steven pulled out his guitar and the sing along started, Jewell was a little tipsy. She'd been too nervous about Matt's presence to eat much dinner, and two glasses of wine had gone straight to her head. Vowing to sit quietly until the wine's affect died off, Jewell didn't sing along with everyone else to *Margaritaville*. Nor did she sing I *Wanna Hold Your Hand* when Steven started it just for her, but when Libby called out their anthem, "Girls Just Wanna Have Fun", Jewell had to stand up with her friend and sing, bouncing around to the old tune. Jewell assumed Libby was a little on the tipsy side, as well. They finished with a grand finale, and bowed to everyone's delighted applause. Steven handed Jewell the guitar and the crowd seemed to quiet immediately.

"Please Jewell, sing us just one song," Libby said.

Jewell loved to sing and had taken guitar lessons for years. She hadn't sung solo in front of people in a while. It had been even longer since she'd played the guitar. Not since she'd sold her own beautiful guitar four years earlier for rent money. That was the time Warren had single-handedly decided their family needed a motorcycle more than a roof over their heads.

Steven's guitar felt familiar under her arm as she feathered the strings and then played a few chords for practice. "Maybe just one." Knowing she was a little drunk, she chose a song that would be easy to play and sing. Matt's gaze was glued to her. Each and every time she looked in his direction he locked eyes with her. Did Celeste play the guitar too? Oh hell. Who cared?

The opening chords to Desperado, a classic by the Eagles, were standard, easy, and before she thought about the song's meaning, she'd sung the first line. Her voice drifted in and out of the melody, as she put her own spin on the tune and when she reached the bridge, even the kids had stopped to listen. By the time she sang the last word and played the final few chords, Jewell wondered why she didn't just buy a cheap guitar and play again.

Her reward came as roaring applause from everyone around the campfire. She handed the guitar back to Steven. "Thanks everyone." She smiled big and winked at Joey who beamed at his mother. After talking about her short career as a singer, Jewell got up and headed to the house for a drink of water before her drive home. She climbed the wooden stairs to Libby's kitchen and poured herself a glass. Before she could finish the water, Matt entered the kitchen, a sloppy grin on his face. She knew a fan when she saw one.

"Oh Jewell, you are killing me. I swear."

She set the tall glass on the counter and burped. "Excuse me. And what's this about killing you?" Although still a little fuzzy, she felt confident enough to have this conversation with him now.

"You have the voice of an angel. That's what this is about, and you're driving me crazy." He looked at her purse on the counter. "Are you and Joey leaving now?"

"Joey's staying here for the night and I'm trying to sober up enough to drive two miles down the road." They stared at each other.

"I s'pose you won't take a ride from me." He looked at her with such sadness, she felt badly for him. And attracted to him. He was one super-sexy man. Even more so because she'd been drinking. Jewell weighed out the possibility of jumping him in the car.

"I probably shouldn't be alone in a car with you." She tried to say this with a straight face, all business-like.

"I promise to just drive you home." He didn't realize it wasn't him she was worried about. "Then I will pick you up tomorrow morning to bring you back here to get Joey. How does that sound?" He was patronizing her. She hated that, but it was a good plan.

"Okay, let me say adios to Libby and Steven and Joey and Dr. Scott," she giggled. "Just kidding about Scott." Heading out the door, she almost ran in to Libby, who'd brought in a tray of s'more fixings.

"I'm putting the kids in the rec room now. Bedtime. They are too pooped to pop. Why don't you stay over, sweetie?" Libby's gaze landed on Matt, leaning against the kitchen counter, his arms folded across his chest. "Oh, am I interrupting something?" She set the tray down and looked at Jewell.

"No, Matt is going to drive me home because I've had too much to drink." She hugged her friend. "Thanks so much for a great night. You throw a fabulous party Lib. Watch my kid around the fire, will you?"

Matt held out his hand to Jewell. "I'll get your car turned around if you give me the keys." He smiled at Libby. "Thanks for having me, Libby, and you can stop giving her the evil eye now. I promise I'm only driving your friend here home, then driving myself home. I'll be back in the morning for my kayak."

Libby looked flustered. "Something is going on, and I'm amazed I don't know what it is."

Jewell grabbed her purse and smiled sympathetically at her friend. "Nothing is going on. It almost did, but I'm too smart for that." She held her pointer finger in the air and turned to go out the front door.

"Thanks for a lovely dinner Libby," Matt followed Jewell out the door and took her arm when they reached the stairs to the driveway. Only two cars remained. Hers and Scott's.

When she reached to open the driver side door, Matt spoke. "Hold on Desperado. You're a passenger, remember?"

Why did he call her that? "I'm not desperate and don't say I am." She crawled over the stick shift into the passenger seat and watched Matt move the driver seat back and get in behind the wheel. "And stop looking at my butt."

"Stop sticking it up in the air like that." He turned the key in the ignition and backed up to head out the long driveway. "And for your information, the song is about someone too scared to love."

"That's not me."

"Like hell it isn't."

"I don't want to fall for you because I look like Celeste and I know that's why you are trying to go to bed with me."

He looked over at her incredulously. "You are inventing any excuse you can think of why we can't be together." He turned left at the end of the driveway, and pulled onto the main road. "And just to make this clear, Jewell, you don't look that much like her." He sighed. "Your personality is nothing like hers, that's for sure. She was extremely confidant, almost arrogant." He let out a long breath. "You may not remember this in the morning but..."

"I'm not that drunk."

"Then good. I hope you remember this conversation tomorrow because if you do, you'll know that no one, and I repeat, no one called my wife Celeste. She hated her given name and everyone who knew her called her Cellie. And if I was calling out her name with you, and I'm saying 'if', I would never have said the name Celeste. Never." His lips were a hard thin line and he looked straight ahead. I called her Cellie. Always. Except when I called her 'Honey'."

Jewell had nothing else to say. Her insecurities over Matt were kind of shot out of the water now. "Oh."

"If you recall, we were talking about where you like to be kissed. Why would I say another woman's name when you'd just told me that you liked it on your neck and your breasts and on your shoulders?"

"I said I have a lot of favorite places. Neck, shoulders, breasts, tummy, legs."

An oncoming car's headlights lit the interior of Jewell's car. His face had softened. "I remember. And I said 'let's make a list.'"

"Make a list," she whispered.

Matt pulled the car into her driveway and stopped. "Make a list." He said it quickly and it sounded a bit like the name Celeste. "Is that what this is about? You mistook those silly words for the name Celeste?" The frustration on his face was back.

"I guess." Suddenly Jewell felt sober. Stupid. Foolish. She looked out the window at the dark forest. "I'm sorry, Matt." They sat in silence for a full minute. "I kept thinking you were interested in me because of my resemblance to Celeste, Cellie."

He rubbed his chin. "Just your smile a bit. Not much. At first it reminded me of her, but not now. Now that I know you, the resemblance is gone. And Cellie looked a bit like my girlfriend before her and the one before her. I have a strange interest in blondes with long legs. Is that a crime? I've dated red heads with short legs and thin lips but I just don't have the same attraction."

She almost laughed at the image of Matt with a severely short legged, frizzy haired red head with no noticeable lips. She covered her mouth so he wouldn't know she was stifling a giggle.

"For crying out loud, Jewell. Are you ever going to get over this insecurity?"

Jewell couldn't hold her giggle any longer. When she burst into laughter, Matt looked horrified. "I'm sorry, but I'm thinking of you with a short-legged red head with no lips and it's funny." She hardly got out the last word before he started up the car.

"I'm glad you think this is so funny." They drove down her driveway the rest of the way to Aunt Queenie's cottage. He didn't turn off the car, but put it in park. "I'll pick you up in the morning to go get your car. How about ten?" His voice was devoid of emotion. Flat.

She felt stupid about their misunderstanding but didn't know what to do next. She'd blown it with Matt Cross. She was too young for him. Too immature and inexperienced about love. All she could do now was try to avoid him on the island. "I'll be at the shop at ten. Pick me up there please." She opened the door, illuminating the car's interior. She cringed, knowing Matt would see the tears in her eyes. By the time she got out of the car and closed the door, his door opened.

"Ah shit, Jewell. Are you crying?" He walked around the front of the car and took her in his arms. "Why the tears, Baby?"

She melted in to him and let go of her emotions. "I blew it, Matt. I didn't think I was good enough for a man like you and I blew it." She sobbed into his shoulder, hanging on to him by fists full of his shirt.

He rubbed her back, tenderly. "I wouldn't have called out anyone's name when I was concentrating so hard not to blurt out that I was falling in love with you."

"It's just that when Warren left, I figured I wasn't good enough." She pulled back, letting his last words sink in. "What?"

"The one thing I do remember thinking when we were in my bedroom was that I was trying to not say the word 'love' and scare you away. But, honestly Jewell…" His eyes were dark green in the light from the car's headlights. "I'm crazy about you." He took her face in his hands and kissed her tenderly. "And I want you to be crazy about me, and for all the right reasons. Not because I'm rich or famous or because you like my float plane." He tried to coax a smile from her. "But because we are really good together."

A tentative smile crept to her lips. "Really?"

"Are you kidding me? I have been head over heels for you since that first cup of coffee at your kitchen table."

"That's because I was wearing a see-through nightgown." She remembered his almost predatory glare that morning.

"Well, I have to admit, that got things started, but the more I get to know you, the more I want to know you. I have a big ole crush on you, Jewell."

"Me too. But for Joey's sake, I have to be careful with my heart." She sent him what she hoped he'd take as a look of apology.

"I know that, and I think Joey is a fantastic kid, because of you. I appreciate that motherhood comes first for you." He kissed the tip of her nose. "When I went to New York I knew you weren't ready for us. I hoped my absence would give you time to think about us. I wanted to come back here and find you crazy about me. And, I wanted time to think about moving to Daniels. I didn't want my reason for re-locating to be you." He pushed a strand of stray hair from her face. "I wanted to move here because I love living on this island, the small-town life, the lack of distractions. Before I met you, I was headed this way—buying the house, moving in. I can write here. It's the perfect place for me. I sublet my house in New York, so I'm here, on Daniels, for a while."

She smiled and sniffed.

"You need to get to bed now." He kissed her forehead. "God, I hope you remember this conversation in the morning. I'd hate to start back at where you hate me for saying something I didn't really say." He shook his head.

"I'll remember." She didn't feel tipsy anymore. Not after this sobering conversation.

"Dream about you and me, and Joey." He lifted her chin with his finger and smiled at her. "I'll see you at the store at ten."

She moved in for a kiss. Just a sweet, good night kiss. Nothing fancy or overly passionate. When they parted, he headed for the car. "Matt?"

He turned around.

"Can we start again? A do-over?"

He smiled slyly. "Sure. See you at ten tomorrow."

∽

The store was crazy-busy when Matt walked through Pages' front door. The lineup for coffee was six people deep and several more looked ready to ring out on the store side. Jewell was making lattes while Cam took orders and Jill handed out scone samples to the lineup. When Jewell looked up to see the handsome author walk through the open doorway, her heart did a flip. She'd remembered every word of their conversation the night before, and hoped Matt did too. He was crazy about her. They were having a do-over on their relationship. Today was the first day in their new relationship. The one where they didn't hold back anything.

She nodded to him and wondered how a man could look so crazy sexy in just faded jeans and a T-shirt. He sent her a secretive smile that weakened her knees, and heated up a few other places. This was actually going to happen with Matt Cross. She would not let herself ruin it with 'what if's' before they even got started. She handed off the lattes, gestured to Jill to take over for her, and stepped into the bookstore side. "Can you give me a few minutes? I don't know why I said ten o'clock when the ferry comes in at 9:45."

He moved in, so only she could hear. "Because you were drunk." He smirked.

"I remember everything, including the fact that you are crazy about me." She lightly poked his ribs and moved to the cash register where a customer was ready to ring out.

Matt followed her behind the counter and got a small bag ready for the customer's books. "Thanks for coming in today. See you again soon," he said when the man turned to go. Another customer leafed through *Killer Intuition* and glanced over at Matt.

"I feel an autograph coming on," Jewell whispered, nodding to the woman at the window display.

"I like my display. You made it way better than that other guy."

"I did. But then I've never kissed that other guy." She trailed a finger down the length of his back. "You can thank me later, when I get you alone."

"If this is a do-over, then technically, we haven't met yet, whateveryournameis." Stepping out from behind the counter, he advanced to the customer with a pen in his hand.

Jewell smiled to herself and realized that it was her lucky day to have a celebrity author walk into her bookstore.

She hoped he was approachable.

If you enjoyed this story, please leave a review on the Amazon page or Goodreads, if you are a member.

DO-OVER SUMMER
By Kim Hornsby
PG 13
17,800 words
Contemporary romance

Other Works by Kim Hornsby

Blurb from
NECESSARY DETOUR
AN AMAZON BESTSELLER

After a stalker's attack, rock star Goldy Crossland flees L.A. for her secluded lake house in Northern Washington. Retired from the music business, she hopes to avoid both the press and her psychotic fan. But obscurity leaves her restless, and when a mysterious--and disturbingly handsome--new neighbor moves in, she can't resist spying.

Pete Bayer is undeniably attractive, but Goldy quickly realizes there's something strange going on in the log house across the bay. Is he a member of the paparazzi? Or a much more sinister threat? Despite her suspicions, Goldy can't deny her fascination with him.

When the press discovers her hideout, it's Pete who offers an escape route, but it comes with a price. Unwillingly drawn into his dangerous world, Goldy soon learns the reason behind Pete's secrecy--and her crush on her charming neighbor takes a deadly turn.

Excerpt from
NECESSARY DETOUR

Chapter One

Goldy ran onstage to the thunderous screaming of the Los Angeles crowd. The explosion of applause inside the Staple Center was the tangible evidence of their love for her; love that had fueled her drive over the years to get to this point. Soon she would desert them.

"Necessary Detour," she mouthed to the band, not waiting for her ex-husband, Burn's reaction to the song choice. It hadn't been played since she vowed to never give it credit again. Written about a female stalker, the hit song had been dropped from their repertoire when the stalker slit her wrists in the front row of a Goldy concert.

Tonight, for personal reasons, Goldy wanted it to be the final song. A new crazed fan, code-named Shakespeare by the FBI, had threatened to kill her at the end of the concert, and, if he was successful, she was damned well going to have the last word.

The opening chords filled the cavernous arena and, recognizing the long lost hit, the crowd cheered to barely tolerable decibels.

"You think you got me. You think we're done. You think it's over. You haven't won."

Burn's guitar screamed with the intensity of a locomotive as Goldy scanned the crowd, not knowing if she was staring into the face of the demon. Tonight she dared any one of them to take her on. The FBI had insisted on a bullet proof skin under her costume, and she could only hope that if it came to that, the material would save her life even if a quick bullet to the chest wasn't Shakespeare's style.

A dozen FBI agents peppered the audience looking for anyone who might have written six months' of heinous letters that threatened to torture Goldy with unimaginable creativity. Trickling acid along her face, then watching her melt was Shakespeare's style, to capture, torture, then relish in the hours, possibly days, that it took him to claim her life. That was his "fondest wish." He'd been code-named Shakespeare because he quoted the bard, but there was nothing poetic about his twisted mind.

Getting closer to the end of the song, Goldy moved to stage-left where a stray bullet wouldn't hit anyone else. With only two lines left, she pulled the microphone away from her lips to make a powerful run to the end and, as she did so, a shot of electricity pierced her hand and domino'ed along her arm to her shoulder, hitting her torso like a jack hammer. The pain was formidable. When her brain got the message, the hand flew open and the microphone dropped with a thud to the stage floor. *Pretend nothing is wrong. Finish the song.*

Goldy danced ran over to Burn's microphone, acutely aware of the one lying behind her, like the pariah it was. Agent Gateman looked worried in the wings, two seconds from shutting everything down. She shook her head emphatically, her steely gaze calling one last shot.

Her left arm hung limp as she reached for Burn's microphone with the right. What if this was the plan? Toy with her knowing she would persist? Then finish the kill with Burn's microphone. Leaving it on the stand, she moved in and, hearing the approaching notes, took a deep breath to make the final run to the end. This time she was careful to keep her lips off the metal.

It's a Necessary Detour

This detour's ……..Necessary!"

She punched the air with her good arm, stepped wide and threw her head back--Goldy's trademark pose. It punctuated the final moment of any Goldy concert.

The applause was deafening. She'd survived the final song, despite what Shakespeare said. *"I shall end it all with your final note, my love."*

The six band members laid their instruments on the stage and moved downstage, applauding along with the audience in their adoration of the international rock legend--Goldy. What they didn't know was that this was not only the last song of the tour, but the final tour in a twenty year career. No more CD's, touring, concerts. No more Goldy.

"Goodnight everyone!" she shouted above the din. "I – HAVE – LOVED – YOU!" Gold confetti rained over the masses as she spun a sparkly Frisbee into the crowd that promised one family a vacation to Hawaii.

Applause filled the arena's rafters. "Goldy! Goldy! Goldy!" Searing pain in her left arm reminded her that she'd just been electrocuted. She needed to get offstage. Taking a final bow with her partner and ex-husband, she hugged him with one arm and turned to her audience. The mass of people in her field of vision had been her reason for almost everything in the last twenty years. A wave to them, a bow to her band, and then Goldy left the party while she was still having fun.

Paramedics waited just out of sight, their dark blue uniforms a comfort to her worry. But it was her bodyguard, Dwayne, who lunged to catch her multi-million dollar backside before it hit the floor in a faint.

Faces were fuzzy, then clear, like focusing a camera. How long had she been out? Quinn was positioned at her left elbow, her tears dropping onto her mother's sparkly costume. "Mom! Mom! Wake up." Her voice gained volume with every second. No seventeen year old kid should have to endure as much as Quinn had in the last year.

"I'm okay, Sweetie." Goldy tried to sit but one of the paramedics asked her to wait. "Almost done, Ms. Burnside. Just let me finish checking your stats."

Ha! She wasn't a Burnside anymore. Just then, the crowd parted and the real Burnside burst through to kneel at her feet. "Nikki!" He used her real name. "What the fuck?" Burn was eloquent in any situation.

Looking worse than her, she wasn't surprised. He'd always needed more coddling than anyone. "I got a shock from the microphone, but I'm fine." She'd hold to the story that it was simply an accident and Burn would believe it. "I'm still on the floor to let the paramedics do their job, nothing more."

Burn had been an unintentionally horrible husband – negligent and unfaithful but never malicious. And everything they'd been through in their marriage had been necessary to achieve this end result which she wouldn't have traded for the world. Her career and her beloved Quinn meant everything.

"Give her room." One of the paramedics waved his arms to part the crowd, while the other helped her to stand.

"Thanks for your concern." she said. Being Goldy had been a sweet ride for a very long time and seeing their worried faces, she was reminded of how much her staff counted on her. For years, she'd signed their pay checks, put food on their tables, financed college for their kids and, knowing all that was going to end for them wasn't a pleasant thought. But it was a necessary detour.

"Enough." She waved away the paramedics. Goldy looked to the two bodyguards who rarely left her side. "Help me stand on this chair. I have an announcement to make."

∽

Also Check out Kim's Novel
(Which happens to be nominated for BEST INDIE FIRST BOOK by Indie Rom/Con)

Blurb from
THE DREAM JUMPER'S PROMISE

Tina Greene can't accept that her husband's body simply disappeared the day he went surfing off Maui and never returned. Struggling to pull her Lahaina SCUBA shop from bankruptcy, she is haunted by the idea he didn't die. When Jamey Dunn, an old boyfriend, walks back into her life and offers to help, things change. Inconvenient feelings for Jamey surface and Tina tries to ignore her attraction to him. Lifelike dreams of her husband have the dive instructor questioning her sanity and leaning heavily on Hank's best friend, Noble. At every turn, Jamey and Noble clash, both desperate to help Tina. When Jamey discovers her dreams hold clues to Hank's disappearance, he reveals his strange ability to enter dreams. Trusting him to enter her subconscious doesn't come easily, and as Tina, Noble and Jamey decipher the mystery of Hank's disappearance, danger sets in to reveal that one person is flirting with insanity, one is a traitor, and one is an imposter.

Excerpt from
THE DREAM JUMPER'S PROMISE

Chapter One

A shadow moved past the front window of Tina and Hank's Dive Shop and a Maui cop opened the door, the overhead bell announcing his arrival. The uniform, gun at the hip, even his downcast eyes were all familiar sights. In the last ten months, Tina had seen more than she wanted of Maui's finest, and they hadn't come through when she most needed them.

"The sharks will get the body," they'd said.

Everyone believed Hank was dead, but she wasn't convinced. Not yet, even though the search had been abandoned after only one hundred and sixty-eight hours— ten thousand and eighty excruciatingly long minutes of hoping.

Obi trotted over to the policeman, as if the man wasn't seconds away from pounding another nail in Hank's empty coffin.

"We found your husband's wallet." The leather in the policeman's outstretched hand was a small but powerful reminder of him. Memories meteored towards her— Hank's gypsy-black hair and twinkling eyes at the beach, driving his truck, smiling from their bed.

She cupped the wallet and closed her fingers around its edges. For all that remained of a dynamic man, it was surprisingly light.

"Where?" She tucked a wayward strand of hair behind her ear.

"Off the path, above Honolua."

No one takes a wallet surfing. "Thanks." It would hold his credit cards, medical insurance card, driver's license, dive instructor card, all part of Hank's life on Maui. A life he'd cherished. *Married only sixteen months, would a man simply abandon his wife and a charmed life in Hawaii without a word?*

The faint chugging of the air compressor in the shop's back alley broke through her thoughts. Katie had opened the shop for the morning boat dive and was now in the back alley filling scuba tanks. The policeman had gone. Tina pulled the driver's license from its slot and grains of sand fell, sand that Hank might have touched before he went into the water that day.

Katie popped in from the back room, her blond hair swinging. "Did I hear you talking to someone?"

"Police." Tina held up the wallet. "Hank's."

Katie froze.

Someone barely of drinking age would know little of consoling a thirty-four-year-old widow. "Katie, can you do the coffee run now? I'll finish filling the tanks." Tina needed something and she hoped it was just coffee.

In the back alley, she lowered herself to sit on an overturned milk crate. Leaning against the wall, her gaze drifted towards the sky. The gray clouds held in the humidity like a wool blanket, and sweat trickled down the small of her back into the waistband of her board shorts.

This new turn of events didn't completely eliminate the possibility that Hank might have faked his own death. He was smart enough to know credit cards were useless to someone who wanted to disappear. Still.

She extracted a picture tucked into a fold of the wallet and a stab of loneliness shot through her. In the photo she and Hank were smiling from a sun-drenched, black-sand beach in Hana. She fit perfectly into the curve of his long, lean body. Like phantom pain in an amputated leg, the memory lingered of how it felt to tuck in under his shoulder. That day, they'd driven to the sleepy town of Hana with their best friend Noble and his latest girlfriend, hoping to take a break from the craziness of the Lahaina scene. Back when she knew he loved her, beyond any doubt.

Days before his death, he'd said, "No matter what, always remember how much I love you." She'd thought he was worried about how their relationship would change when she got pregnant, a plan they were working on with feverish diligence.

Tina tucked the photo back in the wallet. Memories would drive her crazy if she didn't get a grip soon. A deep breath revealed the scent of plumeria flowers from the tree across the laneway at Mr. Takeshimi's house. *Keep breathing.* The wallet felt cool in her hand. She'd have to tell Noble it turned up. Open that bag of snakes.

Mr. Takeshimi appeared and proceeded to sweep the porch of his pristine cottage, his broom swishing a gentle rhythm. "Hey, Mr. T.," she called to him. He was a fighter, still holding onto his real estate despite million-dollar offers. Hank's plan had been to buy the house when it went for sale and open an art gallery. But now she was in debt and that plan was long forgotten. Someone would come along eventually and make it a tacky T-shirt shop. Or a competing dive shop.

When the elderly man straightened, Tina increased her volume. "Big storm coming in, Mr. T."

He nodded. "Doesn't scare me."

No, it wouldn't. He'd endured World War II as a Japanese American in Hawaii. Sixty-one years after the Pearl Harbor attack, he was sweeping his porch. He stared at her, his face a question in waiting.

"Me neither." She tried to believe in her own words.

Mr. Takeshimi nodded, as if this explained something. "Fall seven times and stand up eight, Tina." Japanese proverbs lived on the tip of his tongue. He'd once said, "Good things come to those who wait," and then Hank came into her life.

She stood. "I'm up. Thanks, Mr. T."

Back in the shop, Tina met the gaze of a fist-sized octopus in one of the aquariums. Staring directly into the cephalopod's eyes, she tried to convey an apology. Five days in an aquarium was too long for an intelligent creature. "I'll see you get released today."

It was eight a. m. Time to open the store. Flipping the wall switch, she illuminated all six fish tanks to create the underwater look to her Lahaina Towne shop. Hank had installed the wall of sixty-gallon aquariums to stylize the store and lure customers in. Even during the recent shutdown, the tanks had been maintained and viewed through the windows, still colorful, the fish vibrant, even though Hank was dead.

Walking around the room, she noticed the octopus watching her. Its scrutiny made her feel like she was not only being watched, but judged. A ridiculous thought. She tilted her head and contemplated what it must be thinking. "Being caged sucks," she said, not necessarily to the octopus.

Obi Wan bared his teeth in a smile, his usual reaction to any word ending in 'uck.' "It's okay. Mommy's having a good day." She scratched behind her dog's ears, and then moved to the back room and tucked the wallet in the top drawer of her messy desk. Her palm lingered on the metal front in silent apology to Hank for shutting him away.

Katie entered the back room. "Here, Boss." She set the double espresso with extra sugar on the desk. Ever since Ned, Katie's boyfriend, confessed that her constant talking drove him crazy, she'd been trying to use fewer words.

"Thanks, Katie."

Katie hovered over Tina, her smile hinting at all the unspoken sentences rattling around inside her mouth.

Tina arched her brows in question. "Is there something else?"

"Uncle Jamey's coming today." The words shot from Katie's lips like dice thrown on a table.

Tina attempted a genuine smile. "Your uncle from Seattle. My offer still stands. He can dive free on slow days." A soldier on leave from Afghanistan could dive on her nickel any day there was space. "He might have to wait until this Kona storm blows through." Predictably, bad diving conditions would put a halt on a lot of activities for the next few days.

She took a sip of the steaming coffee and wondered which problem to tackle first. The desk was littered with bills and phone messages from creditors but before she could open another letter from the bank, Katie's scream made her fly out of her chair and run into the shop.

A man grabbed Katie roughly and lifted her off her feet. The scream turned to a squeal that ended in a giggle. This was not the surfer boyfriend Ned, who was lean and scruffy and always looked like he just woke up. This was an adult, tall, with sandy-colored hair on the long side of a crew cut and muscular arms. His crisp white T-shirt reading *Maui Parasail* stretched across a broad back.

"I can't believe you're here." Katie pulled away from the hug. "I miss everyone, you know? How is everybody? I mean really. How's Dad and Grandpops?" She stopped to take a breath as her resolve to use fewer words went flying out the window.

"Everyone's good."

Katie did a little happy dance. "I can't believe you're here." She beamed. "I hoped you'd call this morning. I was just telling my boss that you'd come today, but you might have seen that the diving isn't looking good. Tina said it's not likely we'll dive tomorrow because a storm is coming in, but the weather here can change in a few hours, just like Seattle."

Tina stepped forward, knowing an interruption would be necessary. "You're Katie's uncle, I presume." She extended her hand.

As the man turned, Tina froze. It had been a while, but she knew this person well enough to know that when he slept on his back, he snored. And that he had a small birthmark shaped like South America below his belly button. Far below. She'd once pointed to Tierra del Fuego, and then inched southward...with her tongue.

His slightly lopsided smile was achingly familiar and once so dear to her, her breath now caught in her throat and produced a tiny warble that she hoped was inaudible. He must recognize her too. As their palms made contact, Tina felt a powerful surge pass between them, almost like an electric shock. Her eyes widened as a curtain of darkness moved in front of her vision and blackness invaded.

"Kristina?" The familiar timbre of James' voice sounded far away, muffled, as she fought for consciousness. Sinking to the floor, his arm moved behind her back.

∽∾

Check out Kim's novellas on Amazon, modeled after TV's reality show The Bachelor
THE HUSBAND HUNT – Kat's Season
http://amzn.com/B00CMY6Q14

ABOUT THE AUTHOR

KIM HORNSBY once earned her rent money as a singer on Maui, performing at convention shows and opening for acts like Jay Leno and Jamie Foxx. Those were the days she rubbed shoulders with George Harrison and Alice Cooper at Maui parties, days when she drove a sports car and got asked for her autograph in the DMV lineup.

She now lives in the Seattle area where she's only known as her children's mother. Writing stories in the rainy months, Kim edits in the sunshiny months. A wife, mother, dog owner and adventurer, she loves to hike, waterski, camp, and avoid housework. Living vicariously through her character's exciting lives, she creates stories to fulfill her reader's need for adventure and the thrill of romance.

She's over the moon excited to be an AMAZON BESTSELLING AUTHOR and to have her first self-published novel up for Best Indie First Book by Indie Rom/Con this year. She lives for good reviews of her books and loves to hear from readers. When she gets a nice email, she prints it off and puts it in a file marked "Favorite Readers".

Kim Hornsby
Commercial Women's Fiction
You only journey if you dare to leave home
The Dream Jumper's Promise
Necessary Detour
http://www.kimhornsby.net
www.kimhornsby.blogspot.com
http://twitter.com/kimhornsby
http://www.goodreads.com/author/show/676385
Kim Hornsby
www.facebook.com/kimhornsbyauthor

DEDICATION

This story is dedicated to Eliza, my number one fan and girlfriend extraordinaire. We are Libby and Jewell, add a few years and take away the quilts.

STILL LOVING CAT
By LORI LEGER

Chapter One

"You're killing me."

Zach's groan reverberated throughout the truck as Cathryn gave him one long, last, lingering kiss before slipping out of his embrace.

"Goodnight, Zachary."

"Oh God, don't go yet. Please Cat, let me hold you for five more minutes."

"Noooo…" She pushed gently at the strong hands trying to hold her. "We've already fogged up the windshield, and the mosquitoes are beginning to swarm."

She slapped at one that landed on her neck. "Besides, this is your request, not mine. No sex before the wedding, traditional ceremony in the church in front of all of our friends and family, remember? If it were up to me, we'd be married already, and I'd be all over that." She pointed at what surely must be a painful sign of sexual frustration in Zach's lap. "I could be enjoying that the way God intended."

He placed his hat over his lap to hide the acutely visible bulge. "I know, and as usual, you're right."

She beamed up at him. "You know, I *never* get tired of hearing that."

"Uh huh." He caught her for another soft nuzzle to her neck. "I know what turns my girl on."

Cat fought to keep her eyes from rolling back in her head as her already heated insides turned liquid. "Come in the house with me, Zach. Just this once?" She pushed his 'lap-hat' aside and reached for him.

"No!" He pushed her hand aside and straightened, setting her away from him. "It's only two weeks. We can wait some more when we've waited this long."

Cat pushed out her lower lip in what he called her sex-kitten pout, knowing damned well he couldn't resist kissing her when she used it on him.

Zachary played right into her hand as he leaned forward to pull her lower lip into his mouth. The warmth of his large but gentle hand settled at the back of her head, pulling her closer. This time, it was Cat's guttural groan to break the thick silence inside the truck.

"Why are we torturing each other this way?" She slipped her hands under his shirt, molding them to his hard chiseled abs. "Let's go find a J.P. and get married.

We already have the license. We'll go through with the wedding in the church when it's time and nobody else will know. We'll have our own, private ceremony, just for us."

He pulled his mouth from her neck, hissing under his breath. "Damn, girl, that's a tempting offer. I almost wish you were serious."

She pushed him back against the door of his truck and straddled his lap, grasping his face to make her point. "I am serious, dammit! Marry me, Zach. Marry me…tonight…now."

"Cathryn…"

"Zachary…"

"Where's the nearest J.P.?"

"Seriously? Can we?"

He kissed her hard and laughed. "Okay, beautiful. Let's do it."

She squealed gleefully, grabbing at her phone to access her search browser. Within minutes, she'd found the number to a Justice of the Peace, thirty minutes away.

"Thirty minutes? Wait, isn't Josh Cormier's grandpa a Justice of the Peace here in Lake Erin? And I know there is one somewhere in Jennings."

"Yes, he is, and yes, there is one in Jennings. But if we go to either one of them, someone in our family will know about it. How badly do you want to keep this a secret?"

He deliberated for two seconds before agreeing with her. "You ready to go now?"

She glanced down at the jeans and tank top she wore. "Can I run in and change into a sundress?"

"Sure you can. I should go home and change. I really don't want to marry you in old jeans and a T-shirt."

She cast a heated glance down his muscular body, thrilled that she'd be getting her fill of it two weeks sooner than expected. "I'd marry you in that, but your black jeans are here, along with that button down striped shirt. You know, from last week, when you changed a flat tire for that poor old lady?"

He nodded. "Just before the storm moved in. I forgot those were here." Zach followed her inside her home, nearly tripped over something solid but soft. He leaned over to pick up the blue-gray cat he'd given her as a homecoming gift months earlier. "Hey Chableu, how you doing, boy? Did you miss me?" The half-grown kitten purred loudly as Zach scratched under his chin.

"Here you go, babe. You can go ahead and change in the bathroom…" Cat's voice faltered as he dropped Chableu gently on the floor and pulled off his shirt in one swift movement, baring his tanned, toned, work-hardened torso to her hungry eyes. "Or not," she finished.

∽

He reached for the shirt, grinning at her. "Close your mouth." Zach chuckled as Cat snapped it shut and walked into her bedroom. He didn't dare follow, but instead kicked off his boots and dropped his faded jeans to the floor. He slipped into the new black ones, washed and pressed for him, as was the shirt.

A couple of minutes later, all buttoned, zipped, buckled, and tucked into place, he'd just slipped back into his boots when Cat appeared in the doorway. He sucked in his breath at the vision of her in a short, sleeveless white dress, overlaid with shimmery silver lace. Her hair, for the most part, clipped in a loose collection of dark curls, with a few escapees of long, natural ringlets.

"God Almighty, I am one lucky son of a bitch," he groaned, reaching for the girl he'd loved since sixth grade, the woman he'd waited for—for over eighteen *long* years of his life. Throughout every single one of those years, they'd been the best of friends. He'd waited patiently for her to see what he'd always known. They were good as friends, but they would be better as a couple. He could hardly wait to marry the only woman he'd ever loved enough to consider making his wife.

"Will this do?" she asked, smoothing the lace down over her slim, but shapely hips. "I bought it for our honeymoon cruise, but I thought maybe…" Her voice trailed off.

"You thought right, babe. It's perfect. From your hair, to the dress…" he glanced down at some shade of pink-something polished toenails peeking out from a pair of silver too tall to walk in heels, "…To those sexy as hell shoes you're wearing." He whistled. "Are you trying to give me a heart attack?"

She smiled, lifted her hand to his cheek. "I'm hoping to make a nice memory for us. Maybe someone will be around to take a couple of pictures during the ceremony?" She straightened his collar before stroking his chest. "Our secret ceremony."

"Bring your camera babe. I'll make sure there are pictures. Now where's that number so I can call the JP and get us married?"

～

An hour later, they'd climbed back into Zach's truck as the Justice of the Peace and his wife waved at them from their front door. Zach sat next to Cathryn and pulled their fresh marriage certificate from the envelope so he could stare at it.

"Babe? What'cha doing?" Cat glanced at the certificate, then up at her new husband.

"Just want to make sure I didn't dream it, that's all." He grinned, knowing that he was about to spend the best damned night of his life. "How does it feel to be Mrs. Cathryn Ferguson?"

She leaned in for a kiss. "Feels wonderful, for now, but take me home and ask me again after we've made love for the first time," she purred, rubbing her hand along his thigh.

Zach shivered, anticipating the night ahead. He lifted her left hand, kissed the ring he'd so recently slipped on her finger, and then pulled her tight against him for another kiss. "I still can't believe it. We're married."

"Yes we are. For better or worse."

"For richer or poorer," he added, kissing the tip of her nose.

"Forsaking all others as long as we both shall live, or *else*," she said, making a fist.

"Do you really think I'll screw up everything after waiting so long to get you to marry me?"

Her fist opened, turned into a gentle caress over his beard-stubbled jawline. "No. I always knew that whenever you married, it would be for life, and with total dedication. I always believed that your wife would be the luckiest damned woman ever, but I never thought it would be me."

Zach leaned in to give his wife a long, tender kiss then rested his forehead against hers.

"Take me home, Zachary," she whispered. "Our home."

"You got it." He started the truck and slipped one arm around her, pulling her close for a few seconds before swinging his arm back over. "You need to put your seat belt on."

"You first." Cat reached around to pull it across his body and buckle it up. She snuggled up against him, her arm wrapped around his waist, her head tucked securely against his broad chest.

"Cat...you *need* to buckle up."

"I will, just as soon as I get my fill of this."

"Cathryn Jade McDaniel Ferguson!" His voice filled the cab. "I'm not putting this truck in gear until you scoot over there and buckle up."

"Please don't make me move. It's so comfy right here." Her hand inched its way down his chest. "Just think how much fun I could have on the way home."

He pulled her hand up where he could see it. "Hell no! I'd drive off the road. Come on, you know the rules. Jeremy would still be alive if he'd been wearing his seatbelt." He shook his head, still unable to believe his friend wouldn't be around to stand up as 'best-man' in his wedding. The thought of the wife and two kids his friend had left behind gave him renewed determination as he slid her gently across the seat. "Seriously, I'm not leaving until you do."

"Oo-kaaay," she said, finally relenting. "You're right."

He leaned over to give her a kiss. "Yes I am. And *I* never get tired of hearing that, either."

Fifteen minutes later, he approached the bustling, brightly lit intersection in Jennings and stopped for the red light. "Damn, I should have stopped at the Super Center since we were passing through. I need to pick up a cartridge for my office printer."

"Oh, I forgot to tell you! I picked one up yesterday. I think I got the right one."

The traffic light turned green and he eased his foot off the brake, pleased that she'd remembered something he'd mentioned in passing. Damn, but she was thoughtful that way.

"I picked up the multi-pack of black and tri-colored. Is this it?"

He turned to inspect the box she'd pulled from her purse and held up for his perusal. He glanced at it, then shifted his gaze to something behind her—the yellow and black Hummer barreling toward his truck. Just for an instant, his focus shifted to his wife's beaming face before she turned to see what had caught his attention.

One split second later and life, as he had previously known it, came to a painfully abrupt, screeching halt.

Chapter Two

Cat blinked several times to clear her eyes. When she could keep them open without her vision clouding, she tried to focus on whatever was in front of her. Ceiling tiles? White institutional-type ceiling tiles, framed with white metal strips. She shifted her eyes from left to right, trying to see something other than the span of white. She caught sight of clear bags and tubing hanging from metal brackets. A steady beeping and soft motorized purr coincided with a tightening on her arm. A blood pressure cuff and pulse monitor? She closed her eyes, trying to remember what had happened. She caught a whiff of betadine, another dead giveaway of her location. Why the hell was she in a hospital?

Gripped by a sudden panic, she tried to lift her head. Her exertion rewarded her with an immediate explosion of pain. Cat cried out as it sliced through her head and neck. In an instant, someone was there with her.

"Cat? Oh, God, Cat…you're awake! Thank God! Thank you, God! Thank you!"

"Zach?" The word, spoken in a hoarse unrecognizable croak she didn't recognize as her own.

"What are you doing here? Why am I in a hospital?"

"We were in a wreck, Cat. Somebody ran a light and rammed the passenger side, where you were sitting."

"Was…was Chris hurt?" As Zach's face turned the color of chalk, her panic grew to monumental proportions. "Chris? Where's Chris, my fiancé? Is he all right?"

Zach finally nodded, and answered. "Chris wasn't with us, so he's fine, Cat." He sounded controlled, outwardly calm. But it seemed like a forced calm—the kind you see in one of those police drama hostage situations. Like when a thug holds a gun to someone's head, so they won't give him up to the cop at the door.

"How long have I been out, Zach?"

He walked toward the door and turned, his eyes dark with circles, his face lined with worry. "Two days. Only two days, Cat. We were lucky because the doctors didn't know when…or if…"

"I want to see Chris, Zach. Is he here?"

"You're not…He's not…Cat…you're with…" he stammered, until his voice cracked.

She nearly lost it then. In all the years she'd known Zach, she'd never seen him this close to breaking down. "What! Was someone else hurt?"

He shook his head and cleared his throat. "No. I'll get the doctor." He turned and rushed out of the room.

∞

"Zachary?" Ellen McDaniel, Cathryn's mother, rushed to meet him, carrying two cups of coffee. "What's wrong? Is it Cat?"

"She's awake, Ms. Ellen. She's awake, but…" He paused, not sure exactly how to finish.

"But what?" She placed the cups on a nearby table

and headed for the room before he caught her arm.

"The doctor's examining her right now. She seems to be fine, physically, but…"

Ellen's voice rose to fevered pitch. "What, Zach?"

"I don't think she remembers…the wedding…or even us being together."

Ms. Ellen's eyes grew wide as full understanding took hold. "Oh God! Zach…oh…I'm so sorry, surely it's temporary. Surely, it'll come to her. She'll get it all back."

He shook his head slowly. "I don't know. She's asking for her ex-fiancé. I think she still believes she's engaged to him." He slapped a hand tightly over his mouth to keep from screaming at the irony of the situation. He waited for her all this time…and now this?

"Oh. Zachary, I can't even imagine how you must feel." Ellen placed a comforting hand on his shoulder. "The doctor warned us about a possible memory loss, but he said it would most likely be temporary, too. You remember him saying that, don't you?"

He managed to give her a nod.

"Now you pull yourself together. Cat has loved you as long as you've loved her. She'll remember that, eventually."

"What if the injury destroyed that part of her brain, Ms. Ellen? That one part of her memory bank containing everything about me…about us?"

Ellen smiled and placed her hand on his chest. "Honey, you've been in her brain a long time, but you've been in her heart just as long. There is nothing wrong with her heart, sweetie. She'll remember, don't you worry."

They waited together, speaking in quiet whispers until the doctor came out of the room. He pulled them away from the door to discuss his diagnosis.

"There is still swelling in the brain that's causing mild retrograde memory loss. That would be memories from before the accident. She seems to have lost approximately the last year or so of her life. Now, I'm reasonably certain this loss is temporary. As the swelling recedes, bits and pieces of her memory will come back like pieces of a jigsaw puzzle. Don't push her because that can be just as traumatic for the patient as the actual memory loss. She'll need time to fit the pieces back into their correct order."

"How long?" Zach barely recognized the voice coming from his own mouth.

The doctor raised both hands and dropped them, shaking his head. "Could be a day or two, it could drag out for a month or longer. In extremely rare cases, the memory never returns. Let me reiterate that those cases are extremely rare. I'd say we should know something in a week or so."

"A week. See, that's not so bad, when you've waited this long for her." Ms. Ellen patted his shoulder.

"Here's the deal, Doc. She still believes she's with her ex-fiancé and they are planning a wedding. But, she broke it off with him earlier this year, and we've been together for three. We have a big church wedding planned for a week from Saturday. But…" He held up a hand to keep the doctor from cutting in. "I married that girl no more than fifteen minutes before the accident. She's already my wife."

Ellen's voice broke through. "You did what?"

Zach turned to his new mother-in-law. "We couldn't wait…she didn't want to wait, Ms. Ellen. We weren't going to say anything, just go through with the church wedding in a couple of weeks and no one would be the wiser." He looked down, shook his head. "I lost the marriage license in the accident; I don't know what happened to it. There were pictures on her phone but I don't know what happened to that either."

"How about her camera?" Elaine asked. "She never goes anywhere without her camera."

"She forgot to pick it up in all the excitement. I guess it's a good thing, or she'd have lost that too and everything on it." He ran his fingers through his hair. "God, what if she never…remembers? Maybe she won't want to be married to me. We should have waited. I should have been stronger. If we hadn't gone to Elton to get married, this wouldn't have happened!" He stared into Ellen's dark eyes. "What if it's God's punishment for not waiting for the church wedding?"

Ellen put her hands on his shoulders and gave him a good shake. "Stop that, Zachary! God doesn't punish people for trying to do the right thing."

"But, Ms. Ellen…"

"No! I don't want to hear that. I must admit I'm a little disappointed that the two of you planned this. On the other hand, I'm ecstatic that you were so adamant about showing her the respect she deserved that you went to this length. It's every mother's dream that the man her daughter falls in love with treasures her the way you do Cathryn." She placed her hands on Zach's face, made him look at her. "This is no one's fault. Sometimes things happen to test our resilience, our strength, our love for each other. You have to have faith. *Believe* it will all work out for the best. Now, I want to see my daughter."

He nodded, watching her disappear behind the door to Cathryn's room, with one thought ringing through his mind.

What if God's idea of what was best for Cat was a life without him in it?

∽

Cat turned toward the opening door, risking the pain in her head to see her visitor. "Mom!" She held her arms out to embrace her mother.

"Oh, my God!" Ellen burst into tears. "It's so good to see you awake and hear you talking. We've been so terrified."

"Who else is here, Mom? I'm so confused. Why am I in the Jennings hospital? Was I down for a visit? Was Chris with me?"

Ellen wiped her tears and sat back, staring at her. The poor woman looked every bit as confused, as Cathryn felt.

"Oh Lord, this is going to be tricky. What exactly did the doctor tell you, Cathryn?"

"Something about retrograde amnesia and partial memory loss. He said I lost some time, Mom. What did he mean? How much time?"

"What's the last thing you remember?"

Cathryn pushed past the pain in her head to concentrate, trying to bring up something that would give her a sense of time. "Chris and I just got back from our ski trip to Colorado the second week in January. I came home to a letter saying I was a finalist in a photography contest. They liked my stills portfolio. They were picking a winner the first week of June. I'm waiting on the edits to come back for book four of the latest series. Oh, and Chris and I finally set a date…we decided on a spring wedding, May of next year, the 4th, before it gets too hot. He wanted to make it this May, but I wanted at least a year to plan my perfect wedding. Where is he, Mom? Is Christian here, or is he in Dallas? Did anybody call him?"

"Oh, dear Lord." Ellen stood up to pace the room, wringing her hands. "I don't have the slightest idea how to go about this. I thought I did, but I don't."

At a complete loss as to how her normally calm, cool mother could be so distressed, she pointed to the door. "Go get Zach for me. He'll let me know what's going on."

"Sweetie, you don't understand. Zach is terribly...*terribly*...upset right now. I don't know if he's the one to talk to about this. Not just yet." She took a deep breath and sat on the bed, next to her daughter. "You were supposed to be getting married in twelve days."

"Twelve days! Is it April already? You mean I lost fifteen months of my life?" Her breath escaped in a rush as her mom's face grew even paler.

"It's not April, it's July... The wedding is set for July 6th."

Cat pressed both hands to her eyes, trying to fight back the tears. "July 6th? What happened to the May wedding? Why did we switch to July?"

"Sweetie, look at me."

Cat dropped her hands to gaze into her mother's eyes; somehow sensing her entire world was about to be set back on its ass.

"You called off the wedding to Chris in February of 2013 and moved back home to Lake Erin, in March."

Cat blinked, and blinked again. "That's impossible! I love Chris. Why would I call it off?" She took several deep breaths to calm herself, to keep her thudding heart from beating right out of her chest. Completely befuddled, she turned to her mother. "Mom, do *you* know...Can *you* tell me why I called off the wedding?"

"You tried to love him, Cat. You truly did. Or at least that's what you told me." Ellen fidgeted with her nails, a sure sign she was a bundle of nerves. "Christian is a nice man, but you never loved him the way you should have loved the man you were going to marry. He didn't...measure up."

Cat pictured Chris: generous, kind, tall, good-looking, hardworking, great in bed, trustworthy, one of the brightest, most successful architects in Dallas, and a man who treated her like a queen. "Measure up? To what?"

"Mm...Not to *what*, sweetie, but rather, to *whom*."

"Okay, he didn't measure up to who or *whom*...the flipping Prince of Persia?" She put up her hand, as something came to her. "And if I broke off the engagement to Christian, who the hell am I supposed to marry in a week and a half?"

Ellen inhaled and released it slowly. "Chris never measured up to Zach, sweetie." She raised her hands. "Your words, not mine. Well, they were my words too, but I only said them after you called off the wedding, because I've always known how you really felt about Zachary. Everyone knew, except for you...or so...it...seemed."

Thick, heavy silence followed Ellen's agitated outburst, permeating the air, until a deep, rich, baritone broke through from the doorway.

"Ms. Ellen, you mind if I take a stab at this?"

Cat didn't have to see the face. She'd known Zach for too long not to recognize his voice. She dropped her head heavily against the pillow and closed her eyes, trying to shut it all out. "I feel like I'm losing my mind."

"You're not," he said, his voice soft and low. "Just part of your memory, but it will all come back to you."

She opened her eyes as he stepped inside the room.

Ellen's gaze went from Zach, to Cathryn, then to Zach again. "You have the biggest stake in this, so it's only fair." She stood, relinquishing her seat on the bed, and patted his arm as she brushed by him. "Good luck, Zachary."

His gaze followed her out the door, and then landed on Cat as he pointed to the bed. "Mind if I sit there?"

She moved her leg to make room for him. "Not at all."

He sat, folding, unfolding, and refolding a long white envelope, as though to keep his hands busy. Eventually, he put it aside and took her hand in his, and gently rubbed his fingers along her bruised knuckles. "Do these hurt?"

She looked at the scrapes and scratches on her hands. "They're a little sore, but it doesn't hurt…you doing that, I mean." She flexed the opposite hand and found it didn't hurt at all. "What did I hit?"

"My truck's side air bag deployed. It bruised you up some."

"Your truck? What was I doing in your truck?"

"You were with me, and we were running an errand. Your injuries are pretty minor compared to what you would have sustained without that airbag and the seatbelts."

"Oh God, it was that bad?"

He nodded, unable to stop the shudder that came over him. "I could have lost you, Cat. I nearly did. That damn Hummer didn't even slow down. The driver was a sixteen-year old girl in her daddy's vehicle on her way to a party. No trace of alcohol, but she'd picked up four of her friends, on the way, so you know there were serious distractions."

"Dear God! Were any of the girls injured?"

"I think one of 'em scratched her eye pretty bad with some kind of make-up brush. Other than that, no. It's a Hummer, and the damn thing is decked-out with a heavy-duty grille and brush guard. Son of a bitch had minor damage."

"Typical teenage girl stuff…got to touch up the mascara on the way to wherever you're going. I nearly ran a light a couple of times, myself, with a car full of girls. I'm sure they'll all be more careful after this."

"Yeah, they were pretty shook up about it. The driver came by with her dad a couple of times to apologize and check on you. I called him earlier to let her know you're awake, so don't be surprised if she comes by later." He picked up the envelope again.

"Okay…what's that you have there?" She pointed to the envelope, now bent and creased.

"It's something the nurse just gave me that may help you to remember. Check it out."

She squinted, seeing her name on the envelope, along with the hospital logo. She reached inside, pulled out a small yellow envelope. After emptying the contents in her hand, she picked up the platinum and solitaire bridal set. "Somebody messed up somewhere. This set is gorgeous, just what I would have chosen for myself, but it isn't mine."

Zach almost looked sick, hesitating several seconds before taking the rings from her. Slowly, he placed them back in the envelope, she assumed to get them back to their proper owner.

"Okay, then. Do you need anything—water, some broth, something more for pain? Are you hurting or hungry?"

She shook her head, hearing the same kind of nervous rambling in his voice that her mom had exhibited. He was putting off telling her *something*.

"Zach?"

"Yeah?"

"What aren't you telling me?" She waited patiently as he struggled to speak.

"It was me, Cat. You were marrying *me* in less than two weeks."

She blinked, tried to swallow, but her mouth was suddenly bone dry. "Really?" She coughed, reached for the plastic cup containing ice water and took a big swallow.

He let his gaze fall on hers, and gave her a sad smile. "Does it offend you that much?"

"I wouldn't say offend, but it sure as hell surprises me."

"Why?"

"Because we're friends. You're my *best* friend, and we decided eons ago not to mess that up."

"Yeah, yeah…the friendship pact…I know. What a load of bullshit."

"Zach—"

"I love you, Cat. I've always loved you, and it turns

out you feel the same way. You were certain enough about it to call off your wedding and agree to marry me. So please, whatever you do, if you have the slightest bit of compassion, you won't talk about Chris to me."

The image of his face…pale, sad, sick with worry, flashed through her mind. One of the first things she'd done was to ask about Chris, ask if he was all right. If this was true, it must have been devastating for poor Zach to hear those words from her mouth.

"All right. I won't discuss him with you."

He swallowed, his Adam's apple bobbing, as though trying to control some heavy emotions. "Fair enough." He moved from the bed to the chair, looking every inch as disheveled and exhausted as he must feel.

"How long did you say I've been in here?"

"It's Monday, I think, and you've been here since just before midnight on Friday night. So, two and a half days, or something like that," he murmured.

"You haven't been here the whole time, have you?"

What was she saying? Of course, he had. Even as friends in high school, he'd stayed through her reconstructive knee surgery the summer after her junior year. He'd worked with her diligently, encouraged her through painful physical therapy until she was 100% ready for her senior year of varsity softball. He'd also been there to watch her catch at every game.

As *more* than friends, of course he'd have been that much more attentive.

"I don't have any other place I'd rather be, Cat."

"Look, Zach. The doctor said I'll be in here another couple of days at least. Go home, take a shower, eat a decent meal and get some rest. Who knows? Maybe by the time you get back, I'll remember what the hell is going on in my own life." She nearly laughed aloud as he assumed the position of stubborn mule—arms crossed, jaw locked, and chin jammed down into his chest. She sure as hell remembered that about him.

"I don't want to go."

"Don't be a stubborn jackass."

"I'm not going, and don't call me a jackass."

"Yes, you are and I'll stop when you prove me wrong, *Jackass*."

"Cathryn…"

"Zachary…"

He lifted his gaze, revealing the tiniest flare of hope, a soft sparkle of humor in his eyes.

"What?" she asked, more than curious to know what put it there.

"It's nothing. I'm just remembering the last time you talked me into something."

"Did it work?" Though he didn't smile outwardly, she did see another hint of it in his eyes.

"Yeah, it did."

"What did I talk you into?"

He studied her for several seconds, leaned forward to rest his elbows on his knees, hands clasped tightly.

"Zach?"

"Nah." He shook his head slowly. "You don't want to hear about that right now. This isn't the time or the place."

"Okay, but answer one question for me, please."

"It depends on what it is."

She pursed her lips in surrender. "Fair enough."

"What's the question?"

"Have we...did we? You know..." She faltered, suddenly shy around her old friend.

He raised one brow in a humorous display. "Have we gone to the movies recently, and did we enjoy ourselves? Yes, and yes."

She sent him as much of a glare as she could muster, considering how drained she suddenly felt. "*Must* you be such a smartass?"

He nodded. "Someone told me once it would be genetically impossible for me not to be."

Cat covered her eyes with one hand to block out the brightness of the overhead light. "Humph. I've told you that dozens—no *hundreds* of times since high school. You probably sprouted from your mother's loins cracking wise-ass comments."

"Oh great...*that* she remembers!"

"Come on, Zach. Have we slept together?" She held her breath, motionless as well as clueless as to the answer.

"No, we haven't."

"Oh, thank God!"

Zach popped to his feet, heading straight for the door.

"Where are you going?"

"Home. That shower and nap are looking pretty damn good right now."

"Wait!" she called out to him, realizing how callous she must have sounded. "I'm sorry, Zach. I didn't mean it that way."

He turned to face her, one hand grasping the metal handle of the heavy, oak door. "Are you sure? Because if you did, there's a fifth of Gentleman Jack at my place, and it's calling my name. I've been saving it for a special occasion, but what the hell! I figure this kind of dejection rates."

"I only meant that after all this time, it would be a shame if it happened and I didn't even remember it, that's all. Kind of like, having sex by proxy, you know?"

He turned slowly, leaned heavily against the door, one booted foot crossed over the other. "Yeah, I see your point, although, if it had happened and we did it again, you'd get to have two first times with me. That might be pretty cool."

"Unless it wasn't that great the first time, and I'd be disappointed twice."

"Uh unh...It'll be damn good."

"Hm...maybe for you."

He straightened, walked slowly toward the bed to lean over her, his hands burrowing into the mattress on either side of her hips for support. His face a scant few inches from hers, he spoke in a low growl. "You won't be disappointed. That, I *can* promise you."

Cat licked her suddenly parched lips, and swallowed, wishing she had some water to quench her thirst. "Really..." she whispered, wondering if he was going to kiss her, stuck somewhere between 'bring-it-on' and 'back-the-hell-off'.

Maybe he saw the uncertainty in her face, or maybe he had his own agenda. He settled for a tender kiss to her forehead, a friendly enough act he'd performed on previous occasions, though never before enacted in a manner as laden with barely concealed sensuality.

She jumped at the sharp rapping on her door. Cat looked up as her sister and brother-in-law entered, Kellie's significant belly breaching the doorway long before any other part of her.

"You're okay!" Kellie squealed, waddling her way over to Cat.

Cat gasped at the hugeness of her sister. "You're pregnant!"

Kellie placed both hands on her own belly. "Ya think?"

"My God, when are you due?"

"Yesterday, and I've been having Braxton Hicks contractions since I heard about you being in the accident."

Cat sucked in her breath. "Sorry." She placed her hands on the alien shape of Kellie's baby bump. "Do you have more than one in there? You're huge!"

Kellie's smile faded. "Just one, and yes, I'm aware of that, Miss Skinny Minnie. Think we could move past the fact that I may never get into my size 5's again?"

Zach scratched at his chin's three-day growth of stubble, and leaned over to his would-be sister in law. "Welcome to my world, Kel. Some fun, huh?"

Kellie's gaze flew from Cathryn to Zach. "Mom said something...you mean, she doesn't remember that you...that she...that you and her..."

Bradley stepped up to hiss at his wife. "Babe, your mom told us that she still thought she was engaged to Chris."

"What? I heard her say she remembered setting a date for the wedding, and then I had to go pee. I thought she was talking about *this* wedding." She pointed both fingers at Zach.

Cat grabbed at her aching head, and let it fall back against the pillow. "Look, I'm sorry if I hurt anyone's feelings, but how about the three of you stop talking about me as though I'm not right here in front of you?"

Kellie began herding the two men out of the room. "Out! You two...out, now. Zachary, go home! Mom's right, you do look like shit on a shingle. You need to shower, shave, eat, and sleep." She waved a hand over Cathryn. "She's obviously not going to die on us, though I may want to wring her skinny little neck before this is all over with. So, get the hell out of here and take care of *you* for a bit. Lord knows you've earned it."

Kellie waited until the men were out of the room before turning on her sister. "Look, here's the deal, big sister. You are *definitely* not yourself yet, so you are just going to have to trust that whatever I tell you is God's honest truth. You are head over heels in love with that man out there." She pointed at the door to indicate Zach.

"But what I remember is being in love with Chris. He's a good man...a wonderful man."

Kellie eased herself into the chair next to Cat's bed. "I can't argue with you on that count. You've always had fabulous tastes in men and I was very upset when you broke it off with Chris. The poor guy was heartbroken."

"Then why give me such a hard time about this?"

"Because you broke it off for the right reason. You and Zach...I don't know, it's like the planets aligned perfectly once you realized he was the one for you. The two of you are fantastic together. You belong together, Sis."

"Maybe we will one day, but not today, Kel. Why can't any of you understand that I cannot help the way I feel?" She wiped at her eyes, hating herself for hurting Zach, but wanting nothing more than to hear the sound of Christian's voice, to see his handsome face. "I think I'd like to call Chris."

"Cat, no! You can't do that."

"Just to talk to him. I need to hear from him exactly what I said when I ended our relationship."

"Oh my God. Do you have any idea what you'd be risking by doing that?"

"I don't think I'd be risking anything just by talking to him."

"You'd risk everything! Your eighteen year relationship with the man you were supposed to marry in several days."

"But—"

"What do you want to do? Give Chris false hope, then turn around and break his heart all over again when you remember how crazy you are about Zachary? Come on, Cat…even with amnesia, you can't be that cruel!"

"But, what if I never remember?"

Kellie's gaze turned to a hard glare. "You listen to me! You told me that when you and Chris first got together, you absolutely could not keep your hands off of each other. You told me later that you'd fallen in lust with him easily enough, but never in love with him. It wasn't there, Cat. I swear to God! You tried to love him. You did. You agreed to marry him because you thought it would happen eventually, but it never did. There was a reason for that. He wasn't Zach!"

Cat heard the words, but her mind would not let her comprehend to the point of belief. "So I just led Chris on for, what, a year? Had crazy good sex with him every chance I got, then just dumped him a month or so before our wedding? All because he wasn't Zach?"

"Because he wasn't *something*. You didn't know at

the time what the problem was, or if you did, you didn't tell me. It didn't penetrate that thick skull of yours until you came back home and met up with Zach at the club. The two of you started dancing, and that was the beginning of it. All the pieces fell into place." She leaned in closer, placing her finger in Cat's face. "I will not allow you to throw away what you have with that poor guy out there, by putting another poor guy through hell again, just so you can eventually dump him…again." Her chin lifted in grim determination. "If I have to stay with you every minute of every day until your memory returns, I will make damn sure you won't call Chris. It's for your own good, as well as Chris and Zach's."

Cathryn's low groan rang out across the room. "How do I deal with the fact that when I look at Zach, hear his words, as sweet as they are, I feel as though I'm cheating on Chris? I can't help it." She grabbed her temples. "Oh God, my head is throbbing from all of this. Please Kel, just come sit here by me." She wiped uselessly at the tears running down her cheeks and sniffed. "I can't take any more of this today."

Somewhat awkwardly, Kellie arranged her cumbersome body next to her big sister, and then hit the nurse's button to ask if they could bring something for Cat's headache.

Within a few minutes, a nurse brought pain medication, and ten minutes after that, Cat fell into a deep, blissful sleep, praying to wake free from her nightmare.

∽

Cat woke gradually to soft light and quiet movements in the room. She raised her head slowly, thankful for the absence of pain. Peering through the narrow slit of one eyelid, she scanned the room. Kellie moved awkwardly from the table holding her purse, to her room's single sink.

"What time is it?" she croaked, still groggy from her medication.

"It's four a.m. You slept for nearly ten hours straight," Kellie whispered. "Do you feel any better?"

Cat passed her hand over her forehead. "Much better. But *you* must be miserable."

Kellie met her at the bed and reached for her hand. "Of course I am, but that's the thing about being in the last stages of pregnancy. I can be miserable just the same in any location. There is no comfortable position in which to sit, stand, or sleep. So don't go feeling guilty on my account."

Cat couldn't help but smile at her sister's sharp wit and outlook. She patted the firmness of Kellie's baby belly. "Do we know what you're having?"

"Yes we do. A little girl, and her name is Diana Therese, after our two great-grandmothers."

"Nice choice. I like that."

"You should, it was your idea."

Cat frowned. "Was it?"

"Yep, but don't sweat that you can't remember. The doctor said it could take up to a month for your memory to return."

"Dear God...a whole month."

"Or as little as a day or two so don't look so depressed."

Maybe it was the result of a restful, painless sleep, but Cat nodded, deciding it would do her no good to panic. "You stayed with me all night in this bed?"

Kellie snorted. "Honey, at this stage I can't stay anywhere that long. I've been up and down to the bathroom all night, walking to ease the pains, out in the hall talking to the nurses and any doctor on call."

"I feel bad, sis. You should be home, in the comfort of your own bed."

"Have you not been listening? I'm not comfortable anywhere, and I won't be until I deliver this little bundle of joy. I'm delivering here, by the way, so it's actually a plus being here. The nurses have been monitoring the contractions."

"Still Braxton-Hicks, right?"

"As far as they can tell." A comfortable silence engulfed them for several seconds.

Cat tried to adjust her pillow. "You think they'd let me get up and walk around a little? My back and neck are killing me in this bed."

"Hm, I'm not sure about the walking, but maybe they'd let me take you for a spin in a wheelchair. I'll go ask."

"I'm not going to have my pregnant, contracting sister push me. You could hurt yourself."

"Then I'll find someone else to push you."

At the time, Cat didn't think much of the offer. Later, she'd remember the gleam in Kellie's eyes when she left the room, and realized she should have suspected something. As it was, the pain meds had her a little off her game.

She turned at the knock, expecting to see a nurse, but instead, Zach stood behind a wheelchair.

"Your chariot awaits, M'lady." He waved a hand

over the chair with a flourish. "I'd have confiscated the King Ranch edition, accessorized with saddle leather and chrome, but it was taken. The oil baron three rooms down called dibs, and he paid for the entire east wing…sooo." He finished with a shrug.

She smiled, despite trying to stay serious. "That'll do, and why aren't you home sleeping? You got your orders from Kellie. I heard her."

"There's only one woman I'd be willing to take orders from, and it ain't Kellie, sweetheart." He parked the chair next to the bed and stood next to her. "We have to wait for the nurse to come and transfer all these tubes and things before we can take off. Until then, I can rid you of some of that neck and shoulder pain you're having." He placed his hands on her neck and began a firm, kneading motion.

"That's not ne-cess-sar-rryyy. Oh God, that feels good." She knew her eyes had to be rolling back in her head but she couldn't stop herself. "Jeeze, Zac-attack. You should put a patent on those moves."

The room filled with his low chuckle. "Yeah, I've been advised of that before."

"Oh yeah? Anyone I know?"

"You tell me that every time I give you my special neck and shoulder massage."

"I do?"

"Yep, and I always say the same thing. Do you remember what that is?"

She tried to open her eyes but couldn't quite manage it. "Mmm…don't think so."

He leaned over and kissed her on the neck. "It only gets used on you, babe."

Zach continued to massage her neck in silence as she fought an onslaught of chill bumps from the intimate, though unexpectedly pleasant, kiss to her neck. That was definitely something a man would be comfortable doing to his fiancé. Soon, all she could think about was the last man she remembered who had kissed her that intimately. It wasn't Zach.

"I'm good, thanks." She pulled forward, trying to get away from Zach's touch, once again feeling as though she was cheating on her fiancée.

The nurse entered, extended the IV pole on the chair and transferred the bags over, before helping Cat into the chair. "There you go, you're mobile."

Zach grabbed hold of the handles. "All right, ready to burn some rubber, Cat?"

"Slowly please," the nurse said, holding the door open.

"Spoil sport," he grumbled, pushing his patient through the door. "Where do you want to go? I know there's an atrium in this hospital but I'm not sure if it's lit up at night."

"I think it is. It seems like I remember coming here with mom to visit a friend of hers. Let's check it out."

"Yes ma'am." Zach headed toward the double doors leading out of the wing. "Speaking of remembering things, anything new pop into that beautiful head of yours?"

Cat found herself feeling uncomfortable at his flattery, especially when it included some not so subtle interrogation.

"Nope, nothing new."

He pushed on in silence.

She thought of a detail that had been nagging at her just as she'd fallen asleep earlier. "Where had we gone, Zach?"

"Excuse me?"

"Saturday night. Were we on our way to or coming back from something?"

"Um…We were on our way home."

"From what?"

He pushed through the atrium doors and parked her chair near the fountain. "How's this?"

"It's fine, thanks." The gentle trickle of water falling in layers soothed her ragged nerves, nearly making her forget her line of questioning. "You said we were we on our way home. Where had we been?"

He took his sweet time answering, in itself a bad sign. Anytime Zach Ferguson had to think about what to say, there was a good chance he was about to feed her a line of bull.

"You needed—"

She raised one hand to silence him. "Don't bother. I don't want to feel responsible for making you lie."

"Hey! I don't lie…ever."

"Excuse me, I don't want to force you into telling one of your infamous "Zach-splanations". You know, one of those half-truths, where you omit the most important part of the story."

Zach had the nerve to act insulted at first, until his eyes lit up.

"That's a new memory, Cat. It's coming back, whether you realize it or not."

She narrowed her eyes at him. "What's a new memory?"

"You didn't come up with that "Zach-splanation" term until a couple of months ago."

She sent him a half-smile. "Sorry sweetie, but I've been saying that since high-school, just never to your face." She couldn't help but laugh at his expression of complete indignation.

"That's low. What else have you been saying behind my back all these years?"

Cat frowned at him. "Don't even think of acting all outraged, especially when it wouldn't have been necessary if you'd simply told the truth—the *entire* truth. By the way, this little sleight of hand diversion won't work on me. I know all your tricks, Zachary, and this is just a ploy to distract me. If you'd rather not answer, just say so."

"Okay." He sighed, sounding resigned. "You needed something, and we got it."

"What did I need?"

"I'd rather not answer."

"Dammit!" She slapped both hands on the chair's armrests.

He leaned over to place his hands atop hers and grinned at her. "When I think you're ready to know, I'll tell you. Right now, it would only complicate matters. I don't want you to feel pressured in any way."

"You're no help. Now I really want to know!"

He straightened to his full height. "Has anyone spoken to you about going home?"

"No, but I may have been sleeping when the doctor made his rounds."

"You were. He said you can go home this afternoon, if no complications arise."

"Home? Home where?" Her gut tightened with a sudden sense of not belonging anywhere.

"Well, if you don't want to go to your own home, you could go to your mom's, or Kellie's." He sat on the stone bench beside her wheelchair and stretched out one long, booted leg. "Or, you could come to my place, being that three-quarters of your stuff is there already."

"It is?" She must have looked at him as though he were a stranger.

"Sure. We've been gradually culling and combining household items for weeks to refurnish the house. I mean you were going to move in soon."

She took a deep breath to process even more information. "I hadn't thought of that, but it makes sense." Cat risked a look in his direction. "It sounds like something I'd do. I mean I was thinking about doing that with Chr…" She stopped cold, remembering Zach's plea from earlier. "I'm sorry, Zack. I just…I still…" The vision of him blurred as tears filled her eyes.

"It's fine, Cat."

"No! No, it's not fine! It may be fine a week from now, or a month from now, but today, I feel like I'm betraying my fiancé, and I'm sorry, but it's not you! Why can't any of you understand how out of place I feel here? I had a life in Dallas. It was a good life. I remember being happy. This…" She threw her hands up in the air. "This is the part that seems alien to me."

"Cat—"

"No, Zach! Every time I open my mouth, I hurt your feelings. I know I do. I don't know what to say or do, to keep that from happening. God, I *hate* this!" Her outburst annihilated the only barrier holding back her tears. A series of hiccupped sobs turned into uncontrollable blubbering.

∼⌒∽

Zach wanted to crawl in a hole, hide until things were back to normal. It didn't take long to realize that if he felt that way, surely she must feel the same…times about a hundred.

"Come here, Cat-tastrophe." He lifted her gently from the chair and wrapped her in a hug, his chin resting on the top of her head. "It'll be all right, and I do understand. I swear I do. We're all as clueless as you about how to handle this." He attempted to brush his hands through the mass of tangles and knots in her hair, and had to settle for rubbing her back, instead. "I can tell you one thing that will definitely help."

"What?" She sniffed, using the sleeve of her robe to wipe her eyes.

"You need a nice hot shower, someone to wash your hair, and maybe even a long soak in a tub afterward. I know *I* felt a hell of a lot better once I got to go home and shower."

"That does sound good." She spoke through watered down sniffles. "Do you think they'd let me?"

"It won't hurt to ask. You want to go now?" When she nodded, he helped her back into her chair and steered her to the double doors. Back inside the hospital corridor, he pulled up short at the intersection, nearly colliding with a nurse pushing an empty bed. "Whoa there! We don't need any more accidents."

Cat gave him a low chuckle. "Nope, and if you see anything resembling a giant bumble bee heading for us, run like hell."

"Don't worry, I will." He delivered her safely to her room, stopping once along the way to ask a nurse about a shower. Once Cat declined Zach's offer of assistance with the shower, he stepped out of the room to give her some privacy.

He sat in the lounge sipping on black coffee when something she'd said came back to him. He jumped to his feet, narrowly avoiding a lapful of piping hot coffee.

"Hell yeah," he whispered, the grin on his face widening. "That's what I'm talking about!"

~

"I live *here?*" Cat perused the neat yellow and white wood-frame house, its front porch bordered with flowerbeds filled with red and orange mums.

Zach opened the truck door for her and helped her step down. "Yep, for the last four months of your life."

"I've always liked this place. Who'd you say I was renting from?"

"Doctor Barton, a.k.a. your future step-dad, I'm thinking."

Her gaze flew to him to see if he was serious. "My mom is seeing Doc Barton? Are you sure?"

"Well, I'm sure they're a couple. I can only speculate on the future step-dad part, but they go everywhere together."

"That's…good…good for her. She's too young to spend the rest of her life alone."

"I think so too, and they both seem happy when they're together."

Cat took the front steps gingerly, wincing at the pain from bruised and battered ribs, and clinging to Zach's arm for support. She waited, catching her breath, as he unlocked the front door for her. As it swung open, she caught her first glimpse of the place she'd inhabited, barely recognizing some of her things in such a strange surrounding.

He helped her to one of four chairs scattered around the small living room.

She sat carefully, looking around. "Where's my couch?"

"You sold it." He sounded apologetic. "We agreed to start fresh. No pieces of furniture we'd…ah…had any *experiences* on…with other people. Or rather, you insisted, and I agreed."

Remembering the last time she and Chris had… She let her thought trail off as her face heated with embarrassment. "What'd you do with yours?"

"I took it to the dump. It…was…in pretty rough shape."

"No doubt!" she snorted, stopping short when something soft rubbed up against her bare legs. "Whose kitty?"

Zach leaned down to pick up Chableu and scratched his head. "It's okay, Chableu. She doesn't mean to hurt your feelings."

"He's mine?"

"Yep. I gave him to you as a homecoming gift your first week back. You adore him, by the way."

"Of course I do. Look at that handsome face!" she cooed as Zach settled the kitty in her lap. Within seconds, he'd pushed his head under her chin and began purring loudly.

"He missed you. You've never been away from him overnight before this."

"Poor Chableu. I love him, Zach. He's beautiful. Is he litter box trained?"

Zach nodded. "Neutered, litter-box trained, and what's even better, you've got him house trained as well. He scratches on the door to go out and you keep his litter box on the porch."

"That's quite brilliant of me, if I say so, myself."

"I thought so, too." He turned in a slow circle, both arms spread out. "You recognize any of this?"

She looked around. "My own stuff, but not the surroundings." She struggled to stand, finally accepting his arm to help her. She walked slowly around, surveying the small but extremely neat rooms, arranged exactly as she would have arranged them, decorated and accessorized to suit her tastes.

"It looks a little bare, though."

"Well, you've been moving stuff to our house. You'd planned on packing up some of this stuff and taking it to Goodwill this week."

She stopped in front of several framed shots around a bayou, gasping at the exact moment a heron emerged from the water with a fish in its beak. Another of a gator, up close and personal, had her sending Zach a curious gaze. "I'm not getting rid of this, am I?"

"No, you were looking for some special frames for them, and looks like you found them."

She studied the setting in the photos. "Where is this place?"

"I took you out to my secret spot and called old Wally gator in for you. He's inhabited that place for as long as I can remember." He pointed at the group and beamed down at her. "These garnered you a few first place prizes in contests, and a spot in a national magazine."

"It did? Where's the magazine?"

"It won't be out until this fall."

She nodded. "Secret spot, huh? Was I blindfolded during the drive?"

"Of course not."

"Well, I guess it's lucky for you I can't remember."

He snorted and shook his head. "That is so wrong."

She laughed and leaned in closer to study the photos, finally giving him a nod. "I'm not surprised about the awards and magazine. They're that good."

She entered the kitchen next, opened the fridge to examine its contents. It contained all the same items she kept in her *other* fridge, such as carrots, celery, sweet peppers, tomatoes, bagged salads, yogurt, thin sliced deli meats, assorted dips and dressings, and a container of left over pasta.

"Do I drink this kind of beer now?" She examined a six-pack of domestic beer, taking up space beside her favorite wine.

Zach came to stand beside her. "No, but I do."

She shut the fridge without a word, and then checked out her cabinets of dishware, drawers of silverware, and the well-stocked pantry. She meandered into the bedroom and bath; saw her possessions neatly arranged in the spacious rental, rather than her cramped Dallas apartment that cost triple of what he said her rent was on this place.

"Yep, I must live here, all right."

"Either that or we've arranged for a massive cover-up," Zach volunteered.

She coughed and couldn't keep from rolling her eyes.

Zach laughed and pulled down her largest suitcase from the closet. "Fill it up with whatever you think you'll need."

She hesitated before going to her dresser. "I still don't think I should be staying with you."

"You can't stay by yourself, Cat, at least not for a few days. You're the one who gave the thumbs-down on staying with your mom and Kellie. That leaves me."

"I could have gone to Marissa's. She offered, too."

"She also said since she has to be at the hospital twelve hours a day, you'd be better off with me."

Cat couldn't argue with that. Of everyone who'd filled her in on her current life with Zach, Marissa had been the most informed and adamant about her relationship with him. The two of them had been friends since pre-k and they knew each other inside out.

"You're crazy about him, Cat," her friend had substantiated. "And believe me when I say he feels the same way about you. If there is any place in this world you belong right now, it's with Zach."

Cat filled her large suitcase with everything she thought she might need for a week or two then headed for the bathroom. She stood in front of the medicine cabinet rifling through various bottles of vitamins and OTC headache and allergy relievers. She picked up her package of birth control pills, saw it was not only empty, but also two months past the last refill date.

"Um…do you happen to know anything about these?" She held up the package to Zach's reflected image in the mirror.

"You stopped taking them two months ago."

"No flippin' way!" Her immediate, somewhat violent response seemed to shock him as much as it did her. She turned on him. "Why the hell would I do that?"

His brow furrowed as blue eyes focused on her. "*You* insisted, Cathryn, not me. You said you wanted to start trying to have a baby immediately."

"I have a career!" she said through clenched teeth. "Two of them, actually, and I don't have time for babies." She leveled her best accusatory glare at him. "My writing and my photography are important to me."

Zach never even flinched. "That's how you felt with that *other* guy, Cat. Apparently you feel differently with *me* in the picture." He leaned in close to whisper. "That alone, should tell you something."

He straightened again and shrugged carelessly. "Regardless, I didn't talk you into anything. Like I said, that was your decision, and it still is. In fact, I would suggest getting back on them for a while, considering your injuries. You've got some fractured ribs I think ought to be good and healed before you put any kind of pregnancy stress on them."

She nodded half-heartedly, at a loss for words now that he had busted her balloon of righteous indignation. "I'll call..." she paused to read the label, releasing her breath in a rush of relief upon seeing the name of her old gynecologist. "Oh, thank God, it's still Dr. Richard."

Zach's laughter echoed in the tiled bathroom.

"It's not funny. You have no idea how traumatizing it is for a woman to switch gynecologists."

"If I did, I think I'd have some serious explaining to do."

Cat grinned. "I guess you're right." She threw several more items into her smaller case and zipped it closed. "I guess that'll do. If I think of anything else, I can always come back."

"Absolutely." Zach took the bag from her, along with her suitcase and put it in his truck. When he got back to help her, she stood there with her cat in her arms. "Mm…I have a dog, Cathryn. A big dog. I'm not real sure how Chableu will go over with him."

"Yeah? Well Zeus is just going to have to get over it. You gave me Chableu as a gift and I'm not leaving him here alone."

Zach gave her a sheepish nod. "Okay. We were going to do this eventually, so a few days early won't hurt. At least I hope it won't. Did I mention how big my dog is?"

Cathryn examined Chableu's paws and nodded, satisfied that his claws were sharp enough to defend himself. "He can handle your big, dumb dog."

Zach headed to her utility room, and came back wearing a huge grin, while hauling a pet carrier and some cat food.

"What are you grinning about?" Cat wished she felt as good as he obviously did about going to a place where she wouldn't feel as though she belonged.

"I'll tell you later."

"That list is getting longer, you know. I wish you'd start filling me in on some of that, now."

"All in good time, Cat-tastrophe." He placed Chableu in the pet carrier and got a good grip on the handle. "You ready?"

She scanned her surroundings, grabbed two bottles of wine from the fridge at the last second and met Zach at the door. "Now I am."

∼∽

"This is your house?" She gaped at the neat, mid-sized Acadian style home raised high off the ground, the pier-support section bricked-in nicely.

"Yep. Do you like it?"

"I *love* this house—the wrap-around porch and railing, even the staircase on the porch going up into the attic. Is it functional or just for show?"

"It's functional, but there's another one inside." He smiled as he helped her out of the truck, and then grabbed her two bags. "You know, nearly word for word, you said the same thing the first time I brought you here. I mean that *other* first time."

She studied the plot of land, just far enough from town to be considered country, but barely a mile from the nearest grocery store. "How long have you been here?"

"It'll be five years in October. Come on in and look around…again. I think you'll recognize quite a few items."

Cat walked inside and covered a gasp by slapping one hand over her mouth. "Oh my God, this place is fabulous!" She turned to Zach. "Is *that* what I said the first time I stepped inside?"

He guffawed. "Hardly. You see a lot of your stuff in here, don't you? Your personal touches?"

She nodded, looking around. "I do see some of my pieces in here."

"Now picture it with raggedy ass furniture, scuffed floors littered with junk mail, beer bottles, and dog hair all over the place. That's what you walked into the first time."

"Huh." She gazed at the gleaming floors, polished to a satiny gloss and the high quality leather furniture gracing the living area. This place was the perfect combination of rustic masculinity and sophistication. Built-in bookcases lined with classics, framed photography…her own work, some she recognized and some she didn't…and various relics pertaining to the Cajun culture. Upon closer inspection, she discovered an entire shelf dedicated to her own books, in regular print, large print, and several in other languages. She pulled several and read the inscriptions, even blushed at a few.

"Your words, not mine," he said, close enough that she felt his breath on her neck.

She fought to keep herself from flinching at his nearness, knowing it would hurt his feelings. "Yes, it's my handwriting. I can't deny that." She held up the last two books in the series. "The last I remember, I was waiting on edits for this one, and had just finished plotting this one. Do you have any idea how weird this is for me? First, I see photographs I have no memory of taking, and now I'm holding a book I have no recollection of writing."

"I know."

She gave her head an adamant shake while releasing a slightly hysterical laugh. "Um, no, I don't think you do."

"Look at the bright side, now's the perfect opportunity to analyze your own work. I guess if you don't like it, you have no one to blame but yourself."

"I can't argue with you, there."

"The same thing goes for the house, since I told you to run with it." He lifted his hands and spun slowly around. "This is all your handiwork. I don't know about you, but I love it."

"I do too, Zach. I've got to admit it's the perfect mixture of brawn and beauty." She placed a hand on her head, her breath hitching as a sudden shaft of pain filtered through. "Damn, the headache is back."

"You need to rest. You've been on your feet too long. Sit down and I'll get your medication."

He tucked her into a spot on the sofa and found the prescription he'd picked up from the pharmacy.

Within moments, she swallowed the pill with a sip of water from the full glass he provided, and held it out to him.

"Finish it. The doctor said to keep you hydrated, and resistance is futile."

She swallowed the water, knowing from experience, it would be useless to fight him when he wore that look of stubborn determination.

"Lay back for a minute until the meds take effect, Cat."

She resisted then. "But, I want to see this place. I want to see what you've done with it."

He paused a moment, gave her a nod. "All right, I'll take you on a tour to show you what *you've* done with the place. Keep in mind it was a typical messy bachelor's pad until you put your magic into it." He scooped her easily into his arms, ignoring her claims of being too heavy for him. "I haul two to three 50 pound sacks of feed at one time all day long. This is a pleasure for me."

She looped her arms around his neck, forgetting her self-consciousness once she got lost in their surroundings. She adored the living and dining areas with their authentic touches of Cajun culture, but the bedrooms astounded her. He took her upstairs first, to the two smaller bedrooms, both slope-ceilinged and decorated in a style she could only describe as country chic. Both were the perfect blend of style and utility, as was the shared bathroom located between the two.

Her stomach churned nervously as he headed down the first floor hall to what she suspected was the master bedroom. He pushed the door open and her gasp immediately filled the room.

"Oh my God..."

"Nice, huh?"

"Where...did you find this furniture?"

He took several steps inside the room and turned slowly, giving her the full three-sixty-degree view. "You mean where did *you* find it? You told me you found it online. The first time you stepped inside this room, you said it required something special. You did some research on furnishing French-Acadian style homes, and found a company that specializes in furniture from that era. You narrowed down some styles and we chose one we could both agree with. So, how'd we do?"

Cat felt the heat rising from the base of her neck to the tips of her ears, knew her face was flushed with a mixture of excitement and emotional distress. "The entire house is beautiful, but this room...this space..." The four-poster bed, the perfect cross of feminine beauty and sturdy construction, began to float in her vision as tears clouded her eyes.

"I *must* have done everything you said, because it's so absolutely perfect and pleasing to my tastes, my eyes, but..." Cat bit her lip to suppress a sob. "I can't remember doing it, Zach...none of it." She buried her face in his neck and sobbed quietly.

He settled them both in the chaise in front of the window and held her until she could control her sobbing.

She finally looked up, sniffling and wiping at her tears. "Dammit all, I feel so stupid, breaking down like a big ole baby. I don't know what's wrong with me."

"Seriously?" His blue eyes pinned hers. "It's called a head injury. You think you could give yourself the tiniest of breaks?"

She wiped her eyes with the back of her free hand and sniffed again. "It's difficult seeing all of this...stuff...I accomplished. I *see* my handiwork all over the place; books I've written, accessories I've acquired, pieces of furniture I know I must have agonized over, but I...just...I don't remember doing *any* of it. This is all so crazy—*scary* crazy!"

She dared to meet his gaze at that point, noticed the smile tugging at the corner of his mouth. The one he always got when he was holding back a comeback, ready to jump into the conversation to add something vital. "Spit it out, Zach."

The tug turned into a full-blown, single-dimpled grin. "I know something that may make you feel better. Want to hear it?"

"Absolutely."

"You *are* starting to remember some things, but you don't realize it."

She frowned at him. "What makes you say that?"

He thought for a moment. "Do you remember asking me what happened in the accident? I told you we were hit by a Hummer."

"Yes, I remember asking you that."

He nodded, continuing with his explanation. "This morning when we nearly collided with that bed you said something about looking out for anything resembling a giant bumble bee. I never mentioned the color of the Hummer to you, Cat, but it was bright yellow with lots of black trim. The damn thing did look like a giant bumble bee."

"You must have mentioned that at some point."

"I swear I didn't. Inside the truck, just before it hit us, I was looking past you and saw the Hummer coming. You were showing me the printer cartridges you'd purchased for me. You turned your head to see what I was looking at a fraction of a second before that thing plowed into us."

She stared at him, shaking her head, refusing to give in to the slim chance of hope. "I don't remember that."

"It doesn't matter. Your subconscious does, and that's a good sign." He twirled a lock of her hair around one finger and grinned. "There's something else, too."

"What?"

"Zeus."

"Your dog?" She looked around. "Speaking of which, where is he? And you need to bring in Chableu."

"Zeus is outside, and I'll get the cat soon, but how'd you know my dog's name? I've only had him about nine months."

She opened and closed her mouth several times before finally staring at him. "I have no idea. All you said was that you had a dog, a big dog. But I know he's a big, dumb dog and his name is Zeus."

"Hey, Zeus is not dumb. He's goofy as all hell, because he's still a puppy. He hasn't grown into his 'manself' yet." He grinned at her. "You know what I mean."

"Yeah, I do, Zach, and I guess you're right about the subconscious, but damn, it feels even stranger to know something, but not to know *how* I know." She gazed up at him. "You know?" As strange as the situation was, she couldn't keep the smile from her face.

∽

Zach couldn't suppress his snort of laughter as the woman he loved gave him the most bewildered, befuddled, but adorable smile he'd ever seen on her beautiful face. The fact that it happened without him having to force it out of her gave him even greater joy.

If he'd only been satisfied with that joy and left it at that, chances are the night would have been fine. Dumbass that he was, he couldn't leave it alone. Before his mind could warn him, his mouth was on hers in a crushing kiss.

At first she didn't move. Shock caused temporary immobility, he'd realize later—much later, after she'd pulled away from him and gave him a slap that put the "P" in Pain.

The ringing in his ear, almost as annoying as the sting from her slap, kept him from hearing her demand. It wasn't until she'd repeated herself that he fully understood.

"I want to go home." She took a step back and stood there, weaving slightly on her feet, one hand on her stomach.

"This *is* your home."

She shook her head, chewing nervously on her thumbnail. "No, it isn't. Not yet."

"Cathryn—" He stopped short when she began to ring her hands.

"Oh God…" One hand flew to her head as the other went to her stomach. "I'm…I'm gonna be sick!"

He jumped up, helped her to the bathroom they would eventually share—he hoped. "Can I help?"

"Close the door!" she moaned before crouching over the toilet.

He pulled it closed, sat on the bed until he heard the tap in the sink turn on. He went to the door and knocked. "You okay, Cat?" He waited until she opened it and looked up at him sheepishly.

"I'm sorry for slapping you. It just…you surprised me…I wasn't…don't do that again."

He gave her one nod. "It won't happen again. I'm sorry."

"I still want to go home."

"And I still say *this* is your home." Her glare had him defending his words. "You've known me for nearly two decades, Cat. You've got to know by now that I would never do anything to hurt you."

"I know that." She pressed her fingertips to her temples. "I need to rest, Zach. My head is killing me."

"Lay down, babe…here." He pulled the thick comforter back and fluffed the pillow for her. "Sit," he said, before kneeling to take her shoes off and then helping her into the bed. "I want you to know, you're the first to sleep in this thing. I've been sleeping on the couch until I can share it with you."

He placed a hand on her shoulder when she tried to rise. "No you don't, stay right where you are."

"But I could sleep on the couch."

"It'd be too crowded. Now go to sleep."

"Damn you're bossy."

He grinned down at her before giving her a shake of his head. "Well, hell. If that ain't the little ole pot, calling the kettle black, I don't know what is." He chuckled as he headed for the door. "You're killing me, Cat. You're killing me." He left the room, pulling the door closed quietly behind him.

Chapter Three

You're killing me.

Cat's eyes flew open at the three words floating around in her head.

You're killing me.

Had someone spoken them to her in a dream? If so, in what context had they spoken them? Her eyelids drifted closed again as she stretched in the comfortable bed. When her hand brushed the pillow next to her, she pulled it close. She cradled her arms around it, crushing it until it released its delicious scent in the air. Zach…it smelled like Zach. He must sleep with this pillow on the sofa. She buried her face deeper into the pillow trying to breathe it in.

Tom Ford. Extreme.

She jerked her face away from the pillow. How did she know that? Christian wore Ralph Lauren. Always. No matter what anyone gave him as a gift, he'd return it and come home with Ralph Lauren. Good cologne. Just not on him.

So, how the hell did she know this was Tom Ford? Had she bought it as a gift for someone? She tried to relax. Let the memory come to her. Mall of Acadiana, in Lafayette. She gasped, as the memory developed. She and

Zach were together and he had tried the tester. He'd bought it because of her reaction to it.

What reaction?

She closed her eyes, trying to replay the scene in her head until it came to her in complete detail. She slapped her hand over her mouth to cover the groan. She'd wanted to tear his clothes off right in the store and she'd begged him not to wear it until the wedding. Her eyes flew open. He wore it for her, hoping to jog her memory.

She sat up slowly, studying the massive four-poster bed and the rest of the room's furniture. Nothing. She still didn't remember picking it out. No memories of planning any wedding other than to Chris.

Somewhere in the house, she heard the chirp of a cell phone. A quick glance at the nightstand told her it was 8:15. Another glance at the windows told her it was p.m. not a.m. She'd slept at least four hours.

Damn drugs.

Where was her phone, anyway? She remembered pictures, asking someone to take pictures, but of who, of what? Frustrated and annoyed, she was relieved when Zach finally answered his chirping phone. She heard him talking, soon after he knocked at the bedroom door and opened it.

"Cat, we need to get to the hospital. Kellie's baby is coming!"

∽

Cat pushed through the door into the waiting room, followed by Zach. She saw her mother sitting next to Dr. Barton, holding his hand. "Mom!"

They locked gazes the exact instant the strongest feeling of déjà vu came over her, so stout it weakened her knees.

Zach caught her before she hit the floor. "Hold on babe! Are you alright?"

"Cathryn!" Ellen rushed to her daughter.

Cat held up a hand as a distinct memory came to her. She'd done this before…with a pregnant Kellie, and Zach by her side. "I'm okay." She couldn't say why she didn't want to admit it right away, maybe to keep the pressure off.

"I'm okay! I just need to sit down. How's Kellie?"

She knew from the pinched, worried look on her mother's face that the news wasn't good. She also knew her mom was trying to keep it from her, to protect her somehow.

Zach helped her to the couch across from her mother. "What happened?"

Doctor Barton finally spoke when her mom couldn't seem to form the words. "She started hemorrhaging and they took her into surgery."

Cat stared at her mother, but only saw herself through her eyes for an instant, knowing she must look like she was about to lose it. She was. As a matter of fact, Cat was so damn close to losing it she wanted to scream out. Her head felt so funny and fuzzy. In contrast, memories began to take shape, sharpen, becoming crystal-clear. Earlier memories of the exact moment she knew Chris wasn't the man for her…and more recently…realizing that Zach was—had always been. Everything came flooding back to her in a rush—nearly as quickly as the pain.

"Ahhh...Jesus!" Cat cried out, clamping both hands to her head. She felt herself falling forward, heard Zach's voice as he caught her in his strong arms. Just for a second, she saw his face appear before her. Her Zach...so handsome, even in his obvious state of terror.

He'd always been her Zach. She wanted to tell him that she knew it now. She remembered. Wanted to do or say something to remove the worry and panic from his striking eyes, his handsome, tanned face framed by coal black hair. She wanted to, but she couldn't find those words, or any words, for that matter. She couldn't speak. As her eyelids fluttered and closed, the very last thing she heard was Zach calling her name, and her mother screaming.

∽

The medical terminology merged in his brain, like cranky customers at an overcrowded Wal-Mart on Black Friday. Cerebral aneurysm, localized dilation, endovascular coil embolization, and catheters...to phrases and words he could understand, but hoped wouldn't be relevant, such as leakage, rupture, stroke, and death...to those he hoped *would* be relevant, such as repaired and miracle.

A miracle she's alive.

Zach crouched over Cat's hand, holding it, stroking it, while listening to a conversation spoken in hushed tones. The three speakers, Ms. Ellen, Doctor Barton, and Doctor Collins, the neurosurgeon, who had successfully repaired Cat's aneurysm, stood on the opposite side of her bed.

This was her second miracle, her second chance at cheating death in less than a week. If every cat truly had nine lives, *his* Cat had used up two of hers already. He'd do his damnedest to make sure she kept the other seven safe and sound.

"Zachary, do you have any questions for the doctor?"

He glanced up at Ms. Ellen, then Dr. Collins. "How long before she wakes up enough to stay awake?" She'd been in and out since coming back into the room, murmuring some things no one could understand, and then falling asleep again.

"She should be starting to come out of it pretty good in another hour or so. She'll be groggy for the next several hours. Some patients are extremely sensitive to the anesthesia." He placed a hand on Zach's shoulder. "Don't worry, she'll be fine. When I asked her some questions in recovery, she answered them all correctly."

"What'd you ask her?"

"The usual—her name, birthday and year, her mom's name, how many siblings she had, how many fingers was I holding up—that sort of thing. She has good muscle control, good reflexes. All signs she'll make a full recovery. We caught the aneurysm before it ruptured, which I find absolutely amazing, since she's been walking around with it steadily ballooning for God knows how long."

Zach's gaze zeroed in on the doctor. "You mean since the accident, don't you?"

Dr. Collins shook his head. "Considering the location, I have serious doubts as to whether or not the accident caused the aneurysm. Of course, we can never be sure exactly why or when they occur, but it's still amazing that we caught it before it had a chance to do any real damage."

"It's amazing, all right." Zach crouched over Cat's hand again to place soft kisses upon the delicate fingertips as one thought repeated itself like a marquee in his mind.

Does she remember us?

Too bad he couldn't have asked the questions. If she'd been on the verge of remembering, would this set her back? He wouldn't know a damn thing until she woke up.

A soft touch to his shoulder had him looking into his mother-in-law's face—an exhausted face, judging from the shadows and circles under her eyes. She had reason to be. In twelve hours, she'd made the round-trip between the Jennings hospital, where Kellie delivered her baby, and here in Lake Coburn to see Cathryn, at least three times.

"I keep forgetting to give this to you, Zach." She handed him a large, white-handled, plastic bag bearing the Jennings hospital logo in bright blue lettering. "It's some of the things recovered from the wreck. I'm not sure how, but somehow, in all the commotion, it ended up with me."

Zach pulled out the yellow envelope with her name on it. He peered inside, reached for the smaller envelope containing the rings he'd bought for her, along with his own matching wedding band. He'd slipped his inside the envelope with hers when she wasn't looking. If she couldn't remember them being engaged, no way in hell would he tell her they'd already tied the knot. He slipped the envelope in his pocket, just in case he'd need it later, and then examined the rest of the items in the plastic bag. He opened the business type envelope, holding his breath as he pulled out the folded marriage license, signed, sealed, and now delivered safely back into his possession. At the back of his mind, he had always known he could get a copy of it at any time, but a copy wasn't the original. He breathed a sigh of relief as he refolded, and tucked it safely back in the bag.

He dug around and found her small shoulder bag that she called an organizer. It always amazed him that she could manage to fit so freaking much into one tiny purse. He pulled out her wireless phone; saw the single, long crack along the faceplate. Considering what it had gone through, it could have been so much worse. He hit the power button, satisfied to see the wireless company's logo appear for several seconds before it beeped twice and disappeared. Other than the battery being dead, he suspected it was perfectly fine. He placed it in her purse, pulled out a tri-folded piece of paper that caught on his roughened knuckles. Zach unfolded the paper carefully, gazing at the handwritten words through eyes suddenly wet with tears. The contract…the agreement he'd written, in the hope she'd say yes to marrying him. He had recited it to her on Easter Sunday just before giving her the engagement ring.

He wiped his eyes and smoothed out the paper on her bed sheet, and began to read in a low voice, cracking with emotion.

"I, Zachary Cade Ferguson, agree to allow Cathryn Jade McDaniel, upon her marriage to me, all the time she needs to pursue her dual career of writing and photography for as many years as she wants or needs to. I also agree to pull my share of daddy duty should she agree to bless us with children as beautiful as she is. In the event that occurs, I will gladly, and without complaint, share in changing dirty diapers, both number one and number two, participate in midnight feedings, rock colicky babies, treat boo boos, wipe snotty noses, clean spit-up and vomit, both regular and projectile, as well as clean and sanitize after cases of diarrhea, both regular and explosive. I do, however, reserve the right to an occasional gag or barf during above-mentioned situations. In the occasion that any child of ours survives our incessant doting and spoiling, I do, also agree to share in both dropping off and picking up of said child or children to and from any, and all lessons and practices. This includes dance, gymnastics, tee-ball, baseball, softball, soccer, volleyball, football, basketball, chess, wrestling, swimming, water-polo, golf, synchronized swimming, track, singing, cheerleading, dance squad, piano, guitar, band, etcetera, etcetera, etcetera."

"I also reserve the right to love you unconditionally until the end of our time together on this earth, and beyond that, if God is willing. I will be your lover, your best friend, your ear to listen to your problems, your shoulder to cry on, and your cheering section."

He chuckled lowly. "This is where I stopped reading and pulled out the ring." He wiped his eyes again, touched the side of her face with one hand. "You need to wake up, babe, and when you do, you need to remember the rest of that speech. How I promised to do all that stuff if you'd agree to be my wife."

He clasped her fingers tightly. "You remember, don't you? I told you how I'd loved you since sixth grade, when you racked me during dodge ball?" He laughed then, having to stop to wipe his eyes, yet again. "But you *did* apologize in the most adorable way."

At that point, he cleared his throat and proceeded to tell her in her own words.

"You said, and I'm quoting the best I can remember, *'I sincerely hope I didn't damage any of those man parts, Zachary, but it's not my fault you weren't paying attention.'*" He laughed again. "And you were right. I wasn't paying attention. I was too damned busy watching you, and falling in love with you."

He drew in a long breath and released it slowly. "You know, I told you all of this once, at Easter, Cathryn Jade, but I need you to wake up and remember so I can tell you again. Please wake up remembering, baby. I want to ask you again what I asked you that day, to please, *please* marry me."

He smoothed the sheet and white cotton blanket over her stomach, and then laid his head gently on top. He held her left hand tightly to his lips as he asked God to give her strength.

That's when he felt it—the touch, the lightest, most delicate touch on his hair. He held his breath, praying he hadn't imagined it. He felt it again, stronger this time, and followed by the five most wonderful words in the world.

"We're *already* married...aren't we?"

He lifted his head slowly to stare into eyes the color of rich chocolate, framed by lashes so long he'd always told her using mascara was a waste of time and money.

"Or did I dream that part?" she asked, looking a little confused. "I didn't remember, but then we went to the hospital for Kellie, and it all came back to me. There was pain. I remember a lot of pain, too." She reached up to touch her bandaged head.

"You had surgery, but you're fine now."

Zach kissed her and smiled, pulled the tiny yellow envelope out of his shirt pocket. He emptied all three rings into the palm of his hand and picked up hers.

"You didn't dream a damn thing that had to do with marrying me, and it so happens I've got the proof."

He slipped the rings onto her left ring finger before giving it a gentle kiss, and then slid his own band back into place. He reached for the plastic bag, pulling the second envelope into view.

"I couldn't find this for a while, but it was in your mom's car this entire time." He unfolded their marriage license and held it up in front of her.

"How long?" she murmured. "How long has it been…this time around?"

Zach shook his head at the look of sheer terror on her face. "Not even twenty-four hours."

"Is that all?" she slurred.

"Yep, that's all. Close your eyes now and sleep a little longer. Looks like you're having some trouble keeping those gorgeous peepers of yours open."

"No!" she forced her eyes open. "What happened, Zach? I want to know if I'm remembering it correctly."

"We went in to Jennings last night to see Kellie, and you collapsed as soon as we got there. Is that what you remember?"

She gave him the slightest of nods, as though she was afraid to make any sudden movements. "Uh huh. What about Kellie? Do I have a niece, yet?"

"Yep, healthy and beautiful. They had to do a C-section but mommy and daughter are both wonderful, and Daddy Brad is over the moon."

"Good." She smiled, half asleep. "Keep going."

"Doc Barton made them rush you by ambulance to Lake Coburn because they had the best neurosurgeon around. They got CT scans, and X-rays, MRI's, and some other tests I can't recall, and first thing this morning, Dr. Tanner Collins did the surgery. He inserted this tiny little coil into the aneurysm to keep it from rupturing and bleeding out. You were in surgery for about four hours, I think, but you did fine and there's no danger."

By the time Zach had finished the story, the sound of soft snoring filled the room. He stood slowly and watched her for several minutes, thanking God for bringing her back to him. When he thought he could bear to leave her side, he leaned over to kiss her gently on the lips and went to find her mom.

Chapter Four

August 10th

Zach held his breath, waiting to catch the first glimpse of his bride as the double doors opened at the opposite end of the church. His gaze zeroed in on Cat...his Cat. Her bare, lightly bronzed shoulders contrasted nicely against the white sleeveless halter dress she'd chosen. Its skirt shimmered, catching glints of reflected light from whatever covered the front in some kind of delicate pattern. The dressed hugged her curves before flaring in gentle folds to the floor...God he'd like to be that dress right now.

He couldn't see many details from this distance, didn't even notice her escorts until she was halfway down the aisle. Cat had both arms looped through Kellie's elbow on one side, and Ms. Ellen's on the other. Neither of the women, dressed in non-matching, black and white gowns, elegant and beautiful, were a match for the woman with whom he planned to spend the rest of his life.

Cat's hairstyle, her locks of chocolate brown, highlighted with natural auburn, was a testament to their ability to compromise. The style...somewhere between his love for it down and flowing around her shoulders, and the 'up-do' she longed for. Half of it pinned in a loose cluster of curls, while the rest cascaded in graceful loops and spirals down her luscious neck. His mouth watered, thinking about getting his mouth on that neck tonight.

As Cathryn neared, her exquisite beauty took center stage. Those huge, sexy, brown eyes he loved gazing into sparkled with sheer joy, and a hint of excitement. Her smile…God he loved seeing Cat smile…Loved the sexy as hell curve of that bottom lip.

How the hell did he get so lucky?

Cat stopped before him, her long lashes lowered, resting on lightly flushed cheeks as she took a deep breath and released it. She hugged her sister before turning to her mother. After a brief exchange in emotional whispers, Cat clung to her mom for a moment, before she stepped back.

Zach hugged each woman and waited as Cat turned slowly to face him, her glorious eyes focused and serious, all hint of laughter gone. Her classic 'let's get down to business' look.

So, it's that way, is it? He lifted one brow curiously, wondering what had happened to her desire for a fun, relaxing wedding. That's when he saw it…The barely noticeable lift of one corner of her lip. That one movement, the slightest reveal…told him to expect the unexpected.

She leaned in, her voice a tantalizingly low, seductive whisper. "Zach-attack…You are looking mighty fine today in your GQ tux."

He smoothed down his lapel, adjusted his tie. "You think so, Cat-tastrophe?"

"Mmm…I'm thinking if all these people weren't here, I could show you just how good I think you look."

He grinned at the woman he adored. "Bring it on, beautiful," he whispered. "People in this town would find something else to talk about soon enough." A sudden loud clearing of a throat forced him to pull his gaze from his gorgeous bride, to face their local priest.

"If, ahh…you two are finished admiring each other, I have a wedding to perform." Father Hebert spoke quietly, his deep baritone reserved, though his eyes sparkled with barely concealed humor.

"Sorry, Father." Zach took Cat's right hand in his own.

Her face beaming, she placed her left hand gently upon his jaw. "I adore you, Zachary."

He brought her left hand up to his mouth for a gentle kiss before lowering it and covering it with his right hand. "I know."

Lucky…lucky man.

∞

Cat snuggled closer into Zach's arms, tried to catch her breath as she relished the feel of his corded muscles holding her.

"You know that saying," Zach panted, "about good things coming…to those…who wait?"

She grinned, already suspecting where he was heading with this. "Uh huh."

"It *should* be…*great* things." He panted heavily. "Oh my God. This is the best night of my life, already, and…" He stopped to pant again.

"And it's only started," she finished for him, thankful that her heartbeat was finally returning to normal.

"Yeah…I was gonna say that…as soon as…I could," he gasped.

"Let me know when you can," she said, nibbling on his chin. "So we can go another round."

He pulled her close for a kiss. "As soon as I'm able...I'm willing."

She laughed and sat up, pulling a light robe around her before crawling out of their massive bed. "You hungry?"

"Mm...for you...always." He grinned at her, pulled on the belt of her robe until it hung open.

She chuckled and pulled her belt from his grasp. "I don't know about you, but I'm starving! I was too excited to eat before the wedding and too busy to eat during the reception." She leaned over to lift the lid of the cooler her mom and Doc Barton had packed and placed in their get-a-way vehicle.

"Just a little something to tide you two lovebirds over until your flight leaves tomorrow evening." Her deliriously happy mother had patted their cheeks and grinned. *"You'll thank us later."*

"Mm...What do we have here?" she said, lifting a storage bag full of crust-free sandwiches to the bed.

Zach sat up, obviously lured by the aroma of chicken salad, ham and Swiss, and sliced turkey. "Sus-te-nance! I don't care what kind it is. I'll eat it!"

She popped one in his mouth, pulling back her fingers with a screech, as he wolfed it down. "I wonder what other goodies she packed for us." She shoved the bag at her husband, giggling when he hissed at the cold plastic hitting his bare belly.

She dug into the chest, squealing in victory as she pulled out a container of shrimp dip, crackers, a relish tray, and assortment of sliced and cubed cheeses. They feasted on smoked gouda, black olives and crackers covered with the delicious dip.

Zach nodded and smacked his lips. "That's all good, but I need meat for optimum performance...lots of protein."

Cat dug into the cooler again, pulled out a container of sliced ham, turkey and roast beef. "Will this do?"

Zach took the container from her and grinned. "I believe it will."

She opened another container and gave a delighted laugh. "Don't eat too much of that, babe. I found dessert!" she said, showing him strawberries dipped in chocolate.

"Wow, Doc and your mom thought of everything, didn't they?"

Cat pulled out a chilled bottle of excellent champagne, along with a corkscrew and two flutes. "They sure did."

An hour later, with *all* appetites finally and fully sated for a while, they lay together, talking in quiet whispers.

"I wonder how many other married couples wait until their second wedding to have sex?"

He snorted. "In this day and age? Not too many, I'd wager."

Cat traced her finger lightly over the profile of his nose. "Are you sorry we waited?"

He caught her finger between his teeth, sucked on it softly before releasing it. "Absolutely not. It made it even more special, in my opinion. Besides, I made you wait, first."

"Yeah, you did. And for a while there, you were really strong."

He shook his head, remembering the fateful night they'd talked each other into getting married early. "You know, I was angry at myself, thinking I could have saved you a lot of pain if I had only been stronger."

She shrugged. "Until Dr. Collins told us that the aneurysm was most likely there prior to the accident. Things *do* happen for a reason. That accident could very well have saved my life."

Zach pulled her closer, as though afraid to let her go. "God definitely works in mysterious ways."

She ran her nails lightly through the hair on his chest. "Speaking of Dr. Collins, I saw him yesterday morning, and he gave me a clean bill of health."

"Oh yeah? So you're released and everything?"

"Yeah, and you know what that means, don't you?"

"You're probably going to say that I can quit worrying about you so much, but I doubt *that'll* happen anytime soon."

"Well, that, and we can start trying for a baby anytime we want."

He lifted his head off the pillow to lock his gaze onto hers. "Sooo…just what is it you're trying to say?"

She smiled seductively at her husband as she slowly straddled him.

"I'm saying…I want."

If you enjoyed this story, please leave a review on the Amazon page or Goodreads, if you are a member.

STILL LOVING CAT
By Lori Leger
PG 13
15,690 words
Contemporary romance

Other Works by Lori Leger

La Fleur de Love Series: Book One
SOME DAY SOMEBODY
(Full First Chapter Excerpt)

Chapter One

Late July, 2000
Damn the bad luck.

Carrie Jeansonne groaned at the sight of her soon to be ex-husband.

There he stood, in all his conceited glory, the dark-eyed Cajun boy she'd been idiot enough to fall for. He leaned casually against her car door, smirking and smug, like he didn't have one thing better to do than bug the hell out of her. His tight jeans hugged lean hips while his tee shirt...tight, white and two sizes too small...outlined the perfect torso he was, oh-so-damned-proud-of.

"I don't have time for your crap today, Dave," she growled through clenched teeth. She shifted her armload of groceries, clutched her keys in one hand like she'd learned in self-defense class, in case she'd need to knock some sense into him.

He didn't move a muscle.

She struggled not to smash the bread, while trying to keep the contents of her purse from spilling onto concrete hot enough to blister bare feet. "What do you want?" She tapped her foot, falling into rhythm with an old Zeppelin tune blasting from the sound system of a passing car while Dave said nothing.

Silence from her husband.

Carrie hefted one bag in an awkward attempt to check her watch. "Look, I hate to interrupt your dramatic pause-for-effect, but I have to pick up our daughters before I can go home to cook." Keys jingled from one finger as she shifted her bags from one aching arm to another.

God's-gift-to-women-kind finally graced her with words. "We need to talk, Babe."

Carrie's stomach soured at the sound of the endearment aimed at her. "I don't have time, and I'm *not* your babe," she said, wiping the sweat from her forehead. In less than a minute, she'd migrated from air-conditioned comfortable, to hot as hell. It didn't take long for her fair skin to betray her by turning sun-kissed pink. "I need to go."

"You *need* to rethink this divorce." He glared up at her from lowered lids, his black eyes daring her to talk back. "You know you can't do this on your own."

She sent up a silent prayer for a sensible way out as an older couple approached. The old man, who had served during WWII alongside her father, stopped to stare. She watched him nod, as his wife quietly reminded him of Carrie's parentage.

"Is there a problem here, young lady?" the old man said.

Dave spoke, his voice tight and contained. "I'm speaking to my *wife*."

The man glared at Dave. "Are you a young lady?"

"No, sir."

"Then I wasn't talking to you, was I?"

Dave leaned in close to Carrie, his breath hot on her face, and spoke in a steely whisper. "Don't you do it."

Carrie anchored her gaze on Dave as she spoke, too apprehensive of the consequences to lose sight of him. "Mr. Bubby, could you ask someone to call the police for me?"

The man grunted while leaning on his walking cane. "If I were twenty years younger I'd take care of him for you myself, hon." He grabbed hold of the door and turned to shake his cane at Dave. "You're lucky her dad isn't still around. In his younger days, he would have whipped your ass good, boy."

Carrie grinned, watching the old man disappear into the store, before Dave's comment jarred her back to the present.

"You bitch."

She gave her soon-to-be-ex-husband a smug look, part satisfaction, part justified anger, bordering on devilish amusement. "That's what happens when you go public with private business." Carrie heard the *pop* of his jaw as it tightened, then saw him relax in reluctant acceptance.

Dave took a step back and gave her appearance a prolonged perusal. "Why didn't you look this good when we were married?"

"Why are you still an idiot?" she shot back in a tone as dry as a piece of unbuttered toast.

"You're looking hot these days, Carrie."

"There's an easy explanation. I'm the shiny toy dangling out of your reach." Carrie leaned forward to invade his space. "You're the dog who always wants what he *can't have*."

His dark eyes narrowed. "Are you screwing around already?"

Her eyes sparkled with amusement. "You're kidding, right?"

"You're looking good for somebody, and it sure as hell ain't me. Besides, you must want it by now," he goaded, casting a lustful gaze over her ample curves.

"It?"

He nodded.

"Trust me, David—whatever *it* is that you think I want— you don't have it."

"Who does?"

"None of your damn business."

He closed in on her, hot breath in her face once more, his tone low and dangerous. "You'll never know another man if I can help it."

She jerked away, overpowered by a repulsive mixture of cologne, stale tobacco, and beer. "Is that supposed to be a threat?"

He cupped her chin roughly. "That's a promise."

Carrie pulled away from his touch, ignoring the chill his words caused. She clucked her tongue as one of the town's black and white units made a U-turn on the boulevard and hit the lights. "They're hee-erre," she said, standing her ground until the cruiser carrying two of Gardiner P.D.'s finest pulled up to the store.

The Chief of Police hitched his jeans and *harrumphed*, sounding somewhat like an outboard boat motor. Rob LeDoux stood an impressive six feet two inches, and even in his mid-forties, came across as solid as a wall of brick and mortar. In his prime, he had been a hell of a linebacker for Gardiner High. Carrie watched him approach and make one final adjustment to his navy blue cap.

"Carrie," he said, with a slight nod.

"Hey, Rob. I see you survived the slumber party. I'm on my way to pick up Lauren and Gretchen from your place." She smiled up at the Chief, whose daughter had been friends with her girls since first grade.

Rob glanced at his watch. "Yep, they might be awake by now. When I called at noon, Mona said Abbie and your twins were still asleep." He focused a scowl on Dave. "So what's the problem?"

Carrie jerked her head toward Dave. "He won't let me by."

"We need to talk," Dave growled.

"We're done talking."

Before Dave could respond, the big man in uniform clasped his shoulder in an iron grip, giving him a back-the-hell-off glare only a fool would ignore.

The younger officer, a T. Hardin, according to his pin, stayed behind to question her. He relieved her of the grocery bags. "Ma'am, are you hurt?"

Carrie unlocked her car and popped the trunk open. "Nope, inconvenienced is all."

The officer placed the bags into the trunk and slammed it shut. "What's his excuse for bothering you?"

"Our divorce is finalizing soon, and he's not happy about it." She peered around his bulging biceps to keep an eye on Dave.

"Maybe he thinks marriage is too important to walk away so easily."

Carrie whipped her head around to face the officer, a good-looking man in his late twenties to early thirties, well groomed and muscular. His hunky looks did nothing to quell her irritation at his judgmental comment. "You're not from around here, are you?"

"No, ma'am."

"If you were, you'd know how many times he's walked away in the last eighteen years."

Carrie watched the man's hooded gaze turn to scrutinize Dave. She could tell the moment the officer's opinion morphed from 'desperate husband' to 'perpetrator'.

"I'm sorry, ma'am," he said. "Maybe you are better off without him."

"And maybe you'd be better off not jumping to conclusions before you get the whole story." When he turned his gaze back to her, Carrie didn't falter, still too full of heart-pumping adrenaline to back down from anyone.

"You may be right."

She jumped at the slam of a truck door, and pulled her gaze from the young officer's mesmerizing green eyes. She turned in time to see Dave tear out of the parking lot as if he was late for a fire sale at a whorehouse.

Chief Rob walked over to meet her. "He won't give you any more trouble."

She raised her hand to block the sun's glare from her eyes and squinted up at her old friend. "You don't believe that, do you?"

The chief pulled a plastic wrapped toothpick from his shirt pocket. "If he does inside city limits, I'll find his ass." He popped the pick in his mouth then pulled a business card out of his wallet to write something on the back before handing it to her. "As soon as I get back to the office, I'll call the Sheriff's office and fill them in. You call this guy if you have any trouble outside of town."

Carrie glanced at the card then put it in her wallet. "Thanks Rob, and—" She turned toward the other man. "Mr. Hardin."

The younger officer touched the tip of his cap and gave a little nod, like he knew her,

"That'd be Tim, ma'am."

She cringed in mock horror at the label. "I wish you'd quit calling me that. I'm not a ma'am. My *mother* is a ma'am."

His gaze grew somber. "It's not an age thing, but a gender thing for me, I assure you."

"It still makes me feel old." She thanked them both and left to pick up her girls from the slumber party.

She parked her sedan in front of a wood-frame home and tapped on her horn.

Mona LeDoux came to the door and waved. "I'll send them out," she called from the front door.

Carrie nodded then settled back to wait for her girls. She stared out at Mona Ledoux's collection of garden gnomes. What in hell would she have to look forward to for the rest of her life? For one thing, no husband to bring her down. She'd have sole responsibility for herself, and her kids when they were with her, with nobody to blame but herself if things didn't work out.

She dropped her head on the back of the seat and closed her eyes for a moment to consider the 'Dave situation'. Over the past six months of their separation, he'd made some half-hearted attempts to get her back, but she knew the truth behind his empty promises. He'd still be the unfaithful, controlling, unsatisfied man he'd always been. Would he continue to cause trouble for her once the divorce was final, and she moved into her rent house in January?

She wasn't afraid of him...for all his bluster, Dave was harmless, but she was tired of trying to avoid him. She wanted to skip the next six months...fast forward to a time when he'd already have someone else so he'd leave her the hell alone.

That thought made her wonder what she would be doing six months from now. She adjusted the rearview so she could see herself. "I won't be with a man, that's for damn sure," she murmured, wiping a smudge of mascara from the corner of one eye. "Dave cured me of that for good."

What baffled her was the way her almost-ex had fought this divorce every step of the way. Lately, his attempts to win her back had grown to the level of desperation.

Carrie rubbed her eyes, exhausted from the hour commute after a long workday. She yawned, wishing there were good job opportunities for computer drafters closer to home. As long as she lived in Gardiner, it was a given that she'd be stuck on the road two hours a day, five days a week, for God knew how many years. It exhausted her just thinking about it. Her mother had suggested that she move closer to her work, but how could she uproot her kids in the midst of a divorce? Her mom's words from their last discussion came back to her. "*Carrie, kids are resilient. We relocated twice when you kids were young and you all survived.*"

"But our parent's weren't going through a divorce," she said, readjusting her mirror.

Carrie tightened her grip on the steering wheel, recalling her husband's hateful words. *"You know you can't do this on your own..."* The comment ate at her, made long-dormant feelings of inadequacy rise to the surface like dead fish in a stagnant pond. Feelings she thought she'd buried with the college degree she received. No...Earned...Fought for, by defying Dave's demands she stay home and be *just* a wife and mother. He'd always said it like there was no effort involved. As though the years she spent raising children and tending to the household was a minor thing, but still, all she could handle.

Bitterness and resentment rose from the pit of her stomach to sour in her mouth. She sought the image of the middle-aged stranger staring back at her in the rearview mirror. She raised a finger to the worry lines creasing her forehead. "What made you think you could do this, you stupid, stupid woman?"

Carrie inhaled a deep, cleansing breath before side stepping the self-doubt. "What you should be asking is what made you think you couldn't? Or who?" She shook her head forcefully, disgusted she'd let him get to her. "Damn you, Dave."

Long after Gretchen and Lauren joined her in the car, she continued to launch low curses targeted at her ex.

"Mom?" Gretchen asked, interrupting Carrie's personal rant.

"Hmmm?"

"Are you okay?"

"Yeah, you look kind of mad," Lauren chimed in.

Carrie gazed back at the looks of concern on her twins' faces, and knew she couldn't give in to her fears. Years from now, she wanted her kids to remember she was strong when she needed to be.

"I was, but I'm over it," she said, pinning her gaze back on the roadway.

"At Dad?" Lauren asked.

"I was scared more than angry, but it's my fault for letting him get to me."

Gretchen turned in the front seat to face her. "Are you still scared?"

Carrie reached out and brushed Gretchen's golden brown curls back from her face, then smiled at Lauren in the rearview mirror. "Not anymore."

∞

She wasn't afraid...Not until the two a.m. phone call the next morning. The caller spoke no words, made no sounds, but she could somehow feel the threat, more dangerous because of its ominous silence. What was worse, she couldn't be certain it was Dave.

You'll never know another man if I can help it.

The memory of Dave's threat haunted her, kept her awake, tossing and turning, until the five a.m. alarm sounded for work.

∞

One week later
Lafayette, Louisiana

The young woman's sightless eyes fixed on the ceiling, her face, void of expression—vacant—as though she'd taken herself far from the tiny apartment.

He stared down at her, pleased with the effects of their latest session. Vivid, red whelps combined with the pattern of purple, black, and blue, mimicking the patchwork quilt draped across the back of her couch.

He leaned closer and whispered, watching for any reaction from her. "You're tough, I'll give you that."

He fastened the sturdy, square buckle and threaded his belt through its last loop. Recalling the sharp *whack* of smooth leather meeting her skin, made him long to hear it again. No time for another round with her. Several weeks of careful planning had culminated in three glorious days of self-indulgent pleasure.

His motivation to maintain the carefully structured schedule had been the same for nearly a decade. Freedom. To play...Without having to pay.

He pulled on his boots and straightened, studying her one last time. "Maybe that mulish pride will keep you fighting long enough to survive." He paused to brush the back of his hand down the length of her face and neck. "If you do, maybe I'll pay you another visit one day soon," he murmured, mildly disappointed his threat hadn't produced fear in eyes that were otherwise useless. Some would consider her unlucky for being blind since birth, but he knew the truth of it, and so did she. No sight—no way to identify him—a chance to live.

∽

Early August

Damn, my life sucks.

Sam Langley gazed up at the August evening sky from the front porch of his home. Today marked the unwelcome anniversary of his first year as a single man—middle aged, single, and not enjoying it in the least. Funny the divorce should finalize on the exact same day.

God it was hot. The dog days of summer were upon them, with no relief in sight for at least another month, maybe even two. July had broken records for heat and humidity levels, causing temperatures to rise into triple digits. He braced both hands on the porch rails, and breathed in air that was hot and dense with moisture. Nothing compared to summertime in south Louisiana.

As fast as it got here, it'd be gone. Before long, he'd be surrounded by the sights, sounds and smells of Fall...Parents calling kids in to do homework, music and cadences drifting over from the stadium as the high school marching band practiced routines for Friday night's game, the smell of leaves burning, or the occasional lit fireplace as someone took advantage of the first cool snap. Fall meant lower temps and drier air as humidity levels dropped, causing the entire population to breathe a collective sigh of relief.

Normally, he'd welcome the sights and sounds of the fall months. It meant the reddish gold of leaves as they turned, and the calls of Speckle Bellied and Blue geese flying in from the north, precise in their V-formations. Unfortunately, along with football season and shorter days, the fall season would also bring the long, lonely nights he dreaded.

He walked inside to answer his ringing phone, thankful for the interruption of his personal pity party. A smile crossed his face as he recognized his married daughter's number on the caller ID, no doubt calling to check up on her old man again.

"Hey Pop, how you doing tonight?"

"I'm okay, Amanda. You and Joe just making it back from your mom's?"

"Uh huh, I know how you worry so I called to let you know."

"I'm glad you did. Is your brother walking home?"

"One of Nick's buddies picked him up. He asked me to let you know he'll be riding around for an hour or so."

"Okay, hon." He paused. "How are your mom and everyone on that end?"

"Everyone's okay."

Sam heard a catch in her voice and waited through the awkward moment of silence. "What?"

"It's just that, I was a little surprised when she told me the divorce went through."

Sam heard the hesitation in her voice.

"Why didn't you tell us, Pop?"

He clenched his jaw and took the phone out to the porch with him. "I didn't want to involve you in our mess."

Amanda spoke quietly. "I would rather have heard the news while I was home, so I could mope in private."

"I'm sorry." He released his breath in a long, slow hiss. "One year ago, I never would have believed I'd be facing another summer—another fall, and all of those damn holidays—alone again." Being single for the holidays was number one on his list of least favorite things.

"You have us."

"I know. I appreciate having you kids around, too. But..." *That won't put a damper on those long, lonely winter nights.*

Sam stood still and listened to the sounds of small town life. The young mother from next-door, pleading with her husband to help get their two rowdy boys settled—a barking dog down the street—the slow steady rhythm of the train's freight cars clattering along the rail six blocks to the west. "When your mother left me a year ago, I really believed she'd be back by the end of the month." *Like all the other times she left in our twenty-one year marriage.*

"We all thought the same thing, but I guess Mom had other plans."

Sam grunted in agreement, as he heard Amanda cover the phone and speak to someone else in a muffled voice.

"I need to go now, Daddy. Are you going to be okay?"

Sam smiled at the label that called to mind images from years past. His little girl, with banged up knees, big brown eyes, a constant pixie grin, and long, black pigtails...now twenty years old with a husband of her own. "You go on and get back to Joe. Don't worry about me."

"Love you."

"Love you too, baby girl."

Sam ended the call and stood there, remembering the day Linda left. How the first month's confidence in her return had slowly disintegrated when two months stretched into three, then four. The loneliness had eaten at him, eventually forcing him to accept the death of his marriage. It ended the only life he'd known for over two decades, with the only woman he'd ever known, in the biblical sense, anyway.

He found himself twisting the plain, gold wedding band he'd continued to wear, even though Linda had discarded hers immediately.

He pulled it off and raised it skyward to view the partial moon telescopically through the circle of gold. Sam palmed the ring before walking to the end of the sidewalk then out to the middle of the street. Without giving it another glance, he wound up and pitched it as far as he could into the night. He never heard it land but knew it was gone, long gone, like his wife and marriage.

Heat enveloped him as he made his way back to the porch. Sam dropped heavily onto the top step, feeling the residual warmth from the cement. As miserable as it was out here, he dreaded going back inside.

Sam gazed up at the star-studded sky, amazed at how much he sucked at going solo. He'd have at least thought he'd enjoy being able to watch what he wanted on television, but he didn't. He hated being alone, hated shopping for groceries alone, and hated not having a reason to shave. Scratching at his three-day growth of beard, he thought of his king size bed, and how much he hated sleeping alone. It wasn't even the sex, although he missed that, too. It was being in that big old bed, with nobody to talk to at night.

Sam wiped a hand roughly over his eyes. *I'm lonely, damn it all.* He stood up slowly and shoved his hands deep into the pockets of his denim shorts. He looked up at the sky as though he were talking to God. "So what the hell do I do now, huh? What do you have in store for this old man?"

Old man? He shifted uneasily at the thought of his birthday around the corner. Being thirty-nine and single hadn't done much for his mood at work. He doubted moving into the fourth decade of his life would be any better. He'd gone from the office clown to *'Oscar the Grouch'* in no time at all. At first the nickname his survey crew gave him had been an inside joke, but his ever present surliness had made it too easy for the rest of his co-workers to adopt it. He prayed something changed before it became a permanent condition. Sam emitted a low growl at the thought. The last thing he needed was to be forever associated with one of Jim Henson's Muppets.

God must have one hell of a sense of humor.

*****

La Fleur de Love series: Book One
SOME DAY SOMEBODY: http://amzn.com/B005JNAJ3Q

Also from Lori Leger
Halos & Horns Series: Book Three
MEAGAN'S MARINE
(Full First Chapter Excerpt)

Chapter One

"Well, I'll be damned!"

Master Sergeant Mitchell Hebert threw his cell phone on the cot and dropped beside it with a pensive sigh.

Sergeant Matthew "Tex" Broussard swaggered over to Mitch. "You're already in Afghanistan, the arm pit of the middle east. How much more damned could you be?" The east Texas drawl that prompted his nickname in boot camp twenty years earlier, was still present and accounted for. "What's up, Cajun Heat?"

"Looks like I'll have time for that barbeque at your place after all, Tex. My only sibling is getting married in a week and my soon to be brother-in-law called to see if I could walk her down the aisle in my dress blues next Saturday. He and I were in cahoots about me coming home, anyway. I wanted it to be a surprise so I asked him not to tell her. It seems he finally talked her into a wedding and wants me to show up just in time to escort her." He grinned at his friend, his Marine brother he considered as close as blood. "That means I'll be able to make that homecoming celebration of yours in Beaumont Friday afternoon."

Tex beamed at him, revealing his pearly whites. "That's great, man. She still doesn't know you're going home for good?"

"Nope. I want to surprise her. She's been wanting this for so long."

"She'll be surprised all right," Tex snorted. "You're gonna give that poor girl a heart attack on her wedding day. So, what gives with the guy she's hitching? You think he'll be good to her?"

"I think this one's worthy of her, Tex."

"Well, if he ain't, I'm sure you'll be there to whip him into shape."

Mitch stretched out on the cot. "You got that right. I dropped the ball for years with that first son of a bitch she married. That ain't happening again."

"Man, you couldn't stop what you didn't know about. She kept all that from you."

"I know. She took beatings so I wouldn't be distracted over here." He muttered a mild curse. "I owe her, man. She had to deal with my mom's cancer, then dad dying, and she did it all on her own. She was just a kid when I joined up, and she's had it rough."

Tex grunted in agreement before tossing a dirty sock at Mitch. "Well, if that dude's really a brain surgeon like you said he is, she won't have it rough anymore. Big brother will be around this time to make sure nobody is mistreating his little sis. I can understand how you feel, though. God help the poor bastard who *ever* lays a hand on my little sister, Haley."

"Damn straight." Mitch shuddered at the stinky sock and threw it at Tex's back as he left the room. He settled back on his cot and thought about his sister and her impending nuptials to Dr. Tanner Collins.

For nearly a year, he'd beaten himself up about nearly losing his sister to an abusive husband. She'd tried hard to escape, had moved into a woman's shelter and began divorce proceedings. The selfish bastard had tracked her down, kidnapped her and her twin babies. After beating the hell out of Sarah, he'd left her and the girls locked up with no food for nearly a week while he went to work on a land rig. Her breast-feeding had sustained the infants, but had nearly killed their mother. Finally, someone heard the babies crying when their mom couldn't feed them anymore. It had resulted in their rescues.

Mitch clenched his fist, regretting his no good brother-in-law had met an untimely demise in the treacherous storm waters of the Gulf of Mexico. What a waste. He'd longed to give the bastard a painful reminder of what a jarhead could and would do to protect his family.

He settled in for an unaccustomed nap, on what would be his last afternoon in Afghanistan. He owed it to his sister and nieces to be *there* for them. Maybe after twenty years as a Marine, he owed it to himself as well.

His eyes drifted shut, and his thoughts shifted from his sister, to a pair of cobalt blue eyes surrounded by long, black lashes. A face materialized suddenly, one with a perky nose, slightly cleft chin, and high cheekbones, framed with hair as black as coal. He pictured the engaging smile of a certain bar maid in Lake Coburn, Louisiana—her straight, white teeth and pouty red lips—lips made for kissing, though he hadn't had the opportunity on their one and only date his last visit home. Not one that counted, anyway.

The initial image faded, turning instead to one of her, this time holding a little boy…the spitting image of his mama. His gut wrenched painfully. No way in hell was he ready for the commitment of a woman with a child.

He winced as Tex's drawl floated to him from outside the tent. *Why*, he asked himself, for the thousandth time, did Meagan have to speak with the same East Texas twang as a guy he saw and heard nearly every day since he'd been back here? Each time he heard that accent, he couldn't help but think of her.

Mitch folded his pillow over his head, issuing a silent plea for Tex just once to shut the hell up. It didn't work, of course, as the twang filtered through the barely there pillow.

Meagan.

Not good. Not good at all.

Meagan Hutton released her breath in a rush as she entered the room where the bride waited impatiently. "Oh, honey! Tanner is going to flip when he sees you."

Sarah faced the full-length mirror and ran both hands down her sides. "I can't believe it's me in this gorgeous dress." She looked up, catching the reflected gazes of her friends. "It still feels like a dream. No way could I ever be this happy." She smoothed down the delicate layers of champagne colored silk and lace clinging to her slim body. "I just wish my brother could have been here to give me away."

Meagan stepped forward, taking her by the shoulders. "Today's not the day for regrets, Sarah. You know Mitch would be here if he could, and he sure as heck wouldn't want you to be sad about it."

Sarah dabbed at the corner of her eye with a tissue. "I know, and you're right, Meg. No regrets, not today." She spun around, letting the dress flare out around her. "I'm so ready to marry Tanner. Is it almost time?"

A swift rapping on the door had them all pivoting in that direction.

"Is it safe to come in?" Daniel LeBlanc's voice sounded muffled through the thickness of the wooden door.

Tiffany McAllister headed to the door and opened it a crack for her father. "As long as you don't have Tanner with you. I don't want him seeing his bride until she's walking down that aisle."

Daniel chuckled, tugging on his elegant black tux. "No, but I have someone nearly as important to her. It seems I'm being robbed of my bride escorting duties for the day."

Tiffany released a shocked gasp a second before opening the door wide enough for the U.S. Marine to enter the room.

Sarah flew to Mitchell and threw her arms around him. "What are you *doing* here, big brother?"

Mitch wrapped his sister in a bear hug. "You didn't think I'd miss your wedding, did you?"

Sarah laughed, straightening her dress as he finally released her. "I didn't think they'd give you leave again this soon. How did you manage this?"

He shrugged a sharply jacketed shoulder. "Turns out your timing was impeccable. I'm out, Sis. For good, this time."

Sarah waved her hands in front of her eyes, trying not to cry. "Seriously? I don't want to ruin my make up, but this would be so worth it."

Even through Sarah's tears and squeals of excitement, all Meagan could do was stare at the vision before her. Mitch Hebert in plain old jeans and a T-shirt had been a pleasure to behold nearly a year ago during their first meeting. The sight of Master Sergeant Mitchell Hebert in full dress blues, complete with his cover, and white gloves, was enough to turn her insides to liquid heat.

Out for good. Permanently. No more praying for his safe-keeping while he was in Afghanistan; without his knowledge, of course. *Maybe now she could manage to relax a little?*

A second later, his gaze found hers, pinning her to the spot.

Meagan's breath hitched in her throat at the perceptible widening of his eyes. *Or maybe not.*

Red cleared his throat and spoke, breaking her out of her trance.

"Time to get this thing rolling, people. Father Carlos has another wedding in two hours."

Meg managed to slip out of the room without a word to anyone, and made her way to the pew reserved for wedding participants. Although Sarah only had one bridesmaid, Melanie Finley, she'd thoughtfully included her other friends for readings, gift-bearers during the communion for mass, or as witnesses. She'd chosen Meg as a reader for her favorite reading from Corinthians.

Meagan stood with everyone else in the church as Melanie Finley and Red McAllister appeared, each carrying one of Sarah's twin daughters. Audible waves of admiration rippled through the guests at the sight of the toddlers. Sarah's adorable girls, dressed in matching pink gowns, pristine white shoes, with their glossy curls framed in delicate flower braids, worked the crowd like the little hams they were. Appreciative gasps turned to laughter, as Sammi and Danni shrieked with delight upon catching sight of

Leah and Daniel LeBlanc, seated in the first pew. Essentially, the couple filled in as welcome replacements for Sarah's deceased parents, and the twins adored them.

The bridal march began and all eyes turned to where Sarah and her escort began their leisurely walk up the aisle.

Meagan tried...she honestly did, to concentrate on Sarah, the beautiful and glowing bride. She must have failed at some point, because she found herself gazing at Mitchell instead. He carried himself straight and tall beside his sister. Already agonizingly handsome, his uniform gave him an air of masculine elegance that called forth heroes from decades gone by.

She hadn't even realized her mouth had fallen open until his soft brown eyes found hers, rooting her to the spot. She blinked, and closed her mouth in order to swallow a groan of appreciation at the sight of him.

Meagan watched his approach—close—closer still. Close enough to notice a scar at his left temple, just missing his eye. Had that been there before? No. She would have noticed it. What horrors had he seen since he'd been away? What horrors had he survived in his twenty years in the Marines?

Survived. A cold sweat overcame her at the thought. She'd spent weeks tracking down her dead fiancée's Marine brothers, hoping to find someone who could fill her in on the last days of his life. No one else had understood her need to know, but at the time, it had been important to her. In the end, she'd heard more than she should have heard, seen more than she should have seen. Everyone else injured in the same incident had survived, in one form or another. Some without limbs, but with enough strength of character to bear their losses well. Others hadn't coped so well. One man, who'd lost both legs, had called *her* dead Marine, the lucky one.

During the months that followed her fiancé's death, pregnant with his child, heartbroken and alone, she'd even found herself agreeing with him occasionally. Until the night she'd given birth to her son.

She pictured her handsome little boy, dark haired, with eyes as blue as her own. But that's where the genetic similarity ended to his mother. Once she'd set eyes on him, she knew Chris hadn't left her completely. He was there, in the shape of his son's head, to his ears, chin, and nose. Other traits manifested themselves later, such as his dad's walk and the tilt of his head to study something. Buck was his daddy made over, and her reason for battling her way out of the darkness.

All too soon, it was time for Meagan's reading. On shaky legs, she crossed the aisle to approach the reader's lectern, suddenly terrified at having to read in front of the packed church. She took a deep breath, trying to relax her shoulders. What was *she*, an unwed mother, doing up here in a church about to read from the holy bible? Where was that archangel—the one on the lightning bolt committee? Any second now, he'd be throwing a bolt in her direction, just for being present in God's house.

Heat infused her face to accompany her feeling of complete unworthiness. She managed to look up, intent on finding an escape route, but instead found Mitchell. He sent her a nod of encouragement from his seat directly in front of her. For some reason, it helped. She took a second deep breath and found her passage.

"Love is patient. Love is kind. It does not envy, it does not boast, it is not proud..." She continued, making a conscious effort to read slowly, steadily, with full range, finally reaching the end. *"And now these three remain: Faith, Hope, and Love; and the greatest of these, is love."*

∽

She stood with everyone else, applauding the newly married couple, and grinning from ear to ear as Sarah and Tanner clasped hands and headed down the aisle, practically at a run. Red, the best man, took Melanie's arm to lead her out, leaving Mitchell standing alone. He smiled and offered his arm. She slipped her hand through and let him lead her back down the aisle.

"Well done on the reading, Meagan. You did good."

"You think so? Lord, I have never been so terrified in my life. I seriously thought I was going to lose it up there until I saw you."

Laughter rumbled in his chest. "I channeled courage in your direction. Did you feel it?"

"I believe I did," she said, with a nervous laugh. "Thanks for that, Master Sergeant."

"Glad I could help, Ma'am. Where do we go from here?"

She craned her neck, barely able to see Sarah and Tanner standing off to the side, surrounded by well-wishers. "I'm sure you'll need to stick around here for pictures, but the reception is at Red and Tiffany's ranch. They have a pavilion out back by the pond."

He gave her a curious lift of one brow. "Will you be there?"

"For a while. I have to go pick up my son first. My roommate watched him during the ceremony, but she has other plans tonight."

"Oh…yeah. Your little boy."

She shouldered her purse strap, trying not to feel hurt at the immediate change in his demeanor—the tightness in his face, a tension in his shoulders she couldn't ignore. "That's right—my son, Buck. I'm glad you could make it in for this, Master Sergeant. I know it meant the world to Sarah to have you here." She headed off in the opposite direction, without another word.

∽∾

Jesus, she can't get away fast enough. Mitch stared after Meagan, knowing he'd upset her, though he sure as hell hadn't meant to. He'd barely laid eyes on her, and just for a few moments, he'd forgotten about the kid. The son, *her* son, Buck. Seriously disgusted with himself, he wondered how in hell he could have forgotten the existence of a child.

"Because you're a jackass, jarhead—" he mumbled, with a sharp shake of his head. Only one of many reasons he wouldn't be good for her.

After enduring twenty minutes of a photographer barking orders like a sharp-tongued drill instructor, the group headed over to the reception venue.

Against all good reason, Mitch began searching for Meagan as soon as he arrived on site. Her soft drawl reached him first. He made an immediate one eighty and spotted her with two others. Mitch took that time to study her without her knowledge. Her formerly coal black hair was a shade or two lighter, as though she'd spent lots of time in the sun. Now it was a rich, brownish-black, an even more becoming shade on her. Rather than short and spikey as it had been nearly a year ago, it had grown out to past her shoulders. She looked good—too damned good—and still had the bluest eyes he'd ever seen. A few steps over, he settled at the bar to watch her, and accepted a beer from the guy tending to drinks.

Meagan's son, Buck, had grown a good few inches since the one and only time he'd seen him. His face had thinned out, giving him more the look of a little boy, rather than a toddler. Despite his mom's best efforts to rein him in, the boy wanted to cut loose. Meagan knelt in front of him, pointing to the pond in the distance before poking him gently in the belly, most assuredly warning him about going near the water. The child took off toward a group of other children, most of whom looked older, but a few a little younger than himself, including Mitchell's own nieces, Sarah's twins.

He sat through his sister and new brother-in-law's first dance as a married couple, and then danced with the bride. After handing her back to her new husband, he found himself touring the floor with the maid of honor.

Melanie Finley's eyes creased with secretive laughter. "Hello Marine. How've you been?"

"You mean since you left me alone in a Lake Coburn hotel last year? That was my first post-it note good-bye…ever!"

She gave her head a quick shake. "It wasn't a post-it note, it was a deposit slip from my checkbook, and it had my info on it. Which you did *not* use to contact me, I might add."

"Oh. I didn't realize that."

Her face blanched. "What did you do with it?"

"With what? The note?" He shrugged. "I think I just left it where it was."

She paused their dancing to stare up at him. "Seriously? Well, that's just great. Whoever found it knows I had a one-night stand with a marine, not to mention my name and all my contact info."

He laughed softly at the look of horror on her face. "I wouldn't worry too much about it. I saw the cleaning woman at the hotel. She was seventy if she was a day and barely spoke English. I doubt seriously she could read it." He nudged her into continuing their dance. "Besides, that was almost a year ago. If she'd wanted to steal your identity, I'm fairly certain it would have happened by now." He stopped suddenly and stared down at her. "You don't have any other news for me, do you?"

"Like what?"

"Like 'Guess what? The condom broke and you're the father of a bouncing baby… whatever…"

She looked serious for a moment. "Come to think of it, I did receive a blessed little addition to my household as of one month ago."

Mitch felt the blood drain from his face as he stood there contemplating the weight of her words. "You're serious, aren't you?"

She nodded. "Absolutely."

"Is it…he or she…mine?" He felt as though he'd be sick at any moment.

"He, and I named him Shots, you know, like 'shots' of tequila."

He pictured her as she was that night at the bar, downing shots of Patron with salt and lime. "You named my kid after booze?" he seethed, suddenly furious at the indignation of it all.

"Hold on, now, Marine. I haven't said he's yours. Although, now that I think of it, I guess he could be. I mean….we did do it doggy style…"

"What? What the hell does that have to do with…" He stopped as she burst into laughter.

"Oh God, your face! I got a new puppy, Mitch!"

"Ohhh…oh damn, Mel. I think I'm gonna puke." He rubbed at his belly, shaking his head at the woman doubled over in laughter. "Man, that ain't cool, Detective. Not cool at all."

"Maybe not," she finally managed to spit out between delicate snorts. "But it was funny as hell."

He took her in his arms again, determined to finish the dance with some nuance of dignity. "Says you…shithead." He managed to smile as her joviality finally faded to soft chuckles. "You realize, of course, this means I owe you one."

Melanie made a fist and punched him playfully in the chest. "Well, you go on and give it your best shot, Marine. You've already taken out the element of surprise. I'll be waiting for it, now."

"You'll never see it coming, Detective. *That*, I can promise you."

∽

Meagan laughed as Tanner regaled them with how his mom used guilt to persuade him and Sarah into having a larger wedding than planned.

"I told Sarah she'd do it, gave her plenty of opportunity to get her anti-mother-in-law mojo brewing, so she could resist her. Did it do any good? Noooo! We could have been married a week ago, if she had."

Sarah slipped an arm around Tanner's waist. "Oh, it wasn't that bad. You barely had to lift a finger. Besides, she insisted on a society wedding in Houston that would have taken a year to plan. I held her to one week and convinced her how beautiful it would be here at Red and Tiffany's ranch. I'd already seen the pictures of Giselle and Jackson's wedding here, with the pond all lit up at night. It was gorgeous! I wanted a church wedding but I knew I had to have the reception here."

Tanner gave his new bride a resounding kiss on the mouth. "Ours is beautiful too. I've got to hand it to you, babe, my mom isn't easy to sway once she sinks her chops into an idea. Society weddings are important in her inner circle."

"Not nearly as important as keeping my new daughter-in-law happy." Heads turned as Celine Collins joined their circle, carrying one of the twins. "As much joy as she's brought into our lives with these two angels, it's the least I can do."

Tiffany stepped forward with Sarah's other twin. "Besides, after this, all of Ms. Celine's Houston friends will probably decide that outside fall receptions are the thing to do. It really is lovely."

"Oh thank you, Tiffany. Leah LeBlanc and I had such fun planning this. Maybe I ought to do it for a living. It'll keep me from sitting around and growing old in between visits with my new granddaughters." She leaned in, speaking in a loud whisper. "Along with any future grandchildren they decide to bless us with one day."

Meagan listened half-heartedly, while keeping one eye peeled on her child. All this talk of grandchildren and their doting grandparents made her a little sad for her own son. Sarah's parents had died, but no doubt, they would have loved to be around their granddaughters. Poor little Buck had four living grandparents, none of whom wanted a thing to do with him.

Sometimes life sucked.

Who would he have to teach him the things her own grandparents had taught her? Things like when to plant your vegetable garden so the plants don't get frost-bitten, how to cook popcorn the old fashioned way…in a kettle, not a microwave, and how to season a black iron pot.

Misty eyed with old memories and a sudden feeling of homesickness, she saw Buck pull to a sudden stop in the middle of chasing a balloon. She smiled, recognizing that look on his face—Christopher's look—the look he got when he saw something he couldn't resist. He started a slow walk toward whatever had garnered his attention. Meagan's vision tracked ahead to see what it was and froze at the sight of the lure.

Warning bells went off in her brain, but she couldn't seem to move. Had she traded her heels for lead boots since the ceremony?

"Oh God, no," she whispered, finally taking a step, then several more, but not before her son made it to his destination.

∽

Mitch felt a slight tug on his jacket and looked down. Meagan's little boy stood there, his face cloaked in childlike innocence and wearing a look of awe. "Hey there, buddy. How ya doing?" No training, military or otherwise, could have prepared him for the single question uttered by the boy.

"Are you my daddy?"

Mitch contemplated the strange question while studying the face so much like his mother's, but then again, not. He obviously bore a heavy resemblance to his father. His father…Meagan's Marine. He'd just made the connection by the time Meagan reached the two of them.

"Buck! Hey! There you are. I've been looking for you. Are you having some fun playing with all these kids?"

Her breathless overly enthusiastic act fooled neither Mitch, nor her son, obviously. After casting a glance toward his mother, Buck looked up and repeated the question.

"*Are* you my daddy?"

"No! Buck…No! He's *not* your daddy. He's just a friend of mine." She knelt beside her son, obviously struggling to stay calm in a situation she'd never found herself in before. "His name is Mitchell, and he's a Marine, like your daddy was."

"Is." The word left Mitchell's mouth before he could stop it.

Two sets of identical, blue-eyed gazes landed on him.

"What?" Meagan said, her eyes wide with worry as Mitchell knelt before her child.

Mitch looked from the mother to the son while keeping his tone steady and calm. "No, I'm not your dad, but I want you to know something. Even though your dad isn't where you can see him every day, he still *is* a Marine, Buck. One you and your mom can be very proud of." He took his cover off and played with the brim. "I bet you have a picture of him at your house, and he's dressed like I am, huh?"

Buck gave him a shy smile and a vigorous nod. "It's in my woom."

Mitch chuckled. "In your room, huh? I figured as much."

Buck gave him one more nod. "He looks like you," he said, reaching out a chubby finger to touch a shiny brass button. "You look like him."

Mitch swallowed hard, suddenly aware of the presence, the man that the ugly side of war had taken from this child's life, permanently. He offered his hand slowly. "I'm Mitchell, Buck—Master Sergeant Mitchell Hebert. It's real nice to meet you. And it's an honor to meet the son of a fellow Marine."

Buck looked up at his mother to get her approval before offering his own pudgy hand to return the handshake. "I'm Buck. I gotta go." In an instant, he was gone, off chasing another balloon, leaving the two adults staring after him.

Mitch rose slowly to his feet, even as Meagan began muttering apologies.

"I'm so sorry, Mitch. I didn't mean for that to happen."

"No apology necessary, Meg. It wasn't difficult to figure it out. The dress blues are designed to make an impression, but to a little kid, we must all look alike. How old is he, anyway?"

"He'll be four in one month."

Mitch nodded. "So, his dad never—"

"Chris died before he was born," she rushed, before he could finish.

He stared off after the boy. "That's too bad."

"Yep." She crossed her arms as though to ward off a sudden chill.

"Are you cold?" He started to take off his jacket to offer it to her.

She raised her hand to stop him. "No, I just get this feeling every now and then when I talk about him. My granny used to call it 'knocking on a coffin'. It's almost as though I can feel his presence." She ran her hands up both arms. "You'd think I'd feel comforted, but, for some reason, it freaks me out a little. I never was good with ghost stories and things like that."

"Yet you like to watch scary movies, like the one we watched at the theater last year."

"I don't have a problem with Hollywood spirits, Mitch. It's the real ones that give me the heebie-jeebies."

"You believe in that stuff?"

"Oh sure. My granny had too many stories and real life experiences of her own for me to be a non-believer."

"You don't think they were just that…stories?" He knew he sounded skeptical and there was good reason. He wasn't a believer of ghosts and spirits.

She lifted her chin. "You know, I'm not trying to persuade you to believe. It makes no difference to me one way or the other what you think."

A second later, she'd left him standing there, with the realization that he had, once again, shitified the entire situation.

"One of these days you'll learn to shut the hell up when you need to, you dumb son of a bitch," he grumbled while heading to the opposite end of the reception area. He finished off his beer, deciding it was probably for the best she'd high-tailed it when she did.

∾

MEAGAN'S MARINE
By Lori Leger
PG 13
CAJUNFLAIR PUBLISHING
Contemporary Romance W/Paranormal Elements
Look for it August 2013

LA FLEUR DE LOVE series

Book 1: SOME DAY SOMEBODY
Some Day Somebody: http://amzn.com/B005JNAJ3Q

Book 2: LAST FIRST KISS
Last First Kiss: http://amzn.com/B005RBZS6I

Book 2.5: HART'S DESIRE
Hart's Desire: http://amzn.com/B006JARUEE

Book 3: BROWN EYED GIRL
Brown Eyed Girl: http://amzn.com/B007B50JEE

Book 4: HEAVEN IN YOUR EYES
Heaven in Your Eyes: http://amzn.com/B0087NVG2I

HALOS & HORNS series
(Spinoff of La Fleur de Love)

Book 1: GREEN EYED TEMPTATION
(Previously named GREEN EYED LADY, and was originally planned as Book 5 of first series)
Green Eyed Temptation: http://amzn.com/B0094OVB1K

Book 2: SARAH SMILE
Sarah Smile: http://amzn.com/B00BAO177A

Book 3: MEAGAN'S MARINE
Coming Summer 2013

Book 4: RAINY SEASON (Title subject to change)
Coming Late Fall 2013

SEASONS OF LOVE series
Anthology Series of short stories

Book 1: HEARTS, HEARTHS & HOLIDAYS
Anthology of Christmas themed short stories
"Bells Will Be Ringing"
Hearts, Hearths & Holidays: http://amzn.com/B009ZP5R86

Book 2: SPRING PROMISE
Anthology of Spring themed short stories
"Loving Cat"
Spring Promise: http://amzn.com/B00C4O8KFM

Book 3: SWEET SUMMERTIME LOVE
Anthology of Summer themed short stories
"Still Loving Cat"

ABOUT THE AUTHOR

Lori Leger lives in south Louisiana with her husband of eighteen plus years. Between the two of them, they have five wonderful children and a passel of grandchildren, ranging in age from six months to seventeen years of age. In March of 2012, she resigned an 18+year career in road design to write full-time. Lori is the owner and editor of Cajunflair Publishing Company. She has six full-length novels, one novella, and three short stories published, with an article in a non-fiction book soon to be published.

Find Lori Here:

Website: http://www.lorilegerauthor.com
Facebook: http://www.facebook.com/llegerauthor
FBPage: http://www.facebook.com/lorilegerauthor
Twitter: http://twitter.com/lleger641
Blog: http://cajunflair.wordpress.com
Pinterest: http://pinterest.com/lleger641
Goodreads: http://www.goodreads.com/author/show/5171074.Lori_Leger

DEDICATION

I want to thank my beautiful granddaughter for letting me borrow her name for this story, although *that* is where the similarity ends. I love you, bunches, Cat.

Many thanks go to Karen, Kimberly, and Carmine for contributing to this anthology, and for allowing me to publish it through Cajunflair Publishing.

Much appreciation goes to my husband, Michael, for helping me to perfect my office 'space'. As always, love you, babe.

THE LAST BLIND DATE
By CARMINE VALENTINE

Chapter One

I was lucky to get a taxi on this Friday evening. A Broadway play had opened at the Fifth Avenue Theater and the Rolling Stones were somewhere rocking the house.

Tonight, I would rather have remained home on my sofa indulging in my passion for historical romances and eating a bowl of popcorn with my cat *Gov'nor*. I say it with an English accent and try to sound like Audrey Hepburn when she starred in My Fair Lady using that wonderfully horrid dialect.

To please my best friend, I've fancied myself up in one of my floor-length evening gowns that I own for the various charity and fundraising events I attend and here I was in a yellow taxi cab hurtling through city traffic because this driver seemed to think I was late.

The day had finally cooled as summer weather had come unusually early to Seattle in this first weekend of June. The joke in Seattle was that our summer weather really didn't start until the day after the Fourth of July. I guess you'd have to live here and sit through a rain-soaked firework display before you would start to appreciate the humor in that joke.

The lapis blue of the dusky sky held a tinge of pink and gold and the star Venus already twinkled overhead. I loved summer evenings like this, balmy breeze, the smell of freshly cut grass and the heady sweet scent from the honeysuckle climbing the trellis near my front door.

"What's the big hurry?" I said to the driver as we sailed down Queen Anne hill. There were no seatbelts in the back and my daffodil yellow, satiny-slick gown wasn't exactly letting my butt grip the seat.

"Behe nigh, behe nigh." The driver barely looked at me in the rearview mirror as he hunched over the wheel. With the many times I'd watched My Fair Lady, I considered myself an expert on broken English, even if that was just my opinion. So I easily interpreted this to mean, *busy night, busy night*. Yes, I was quite the linguist.

The driver just drove faster and so I gave up and held on. I was off to a black-and-white-tie dinner at the Columbia Tower. I wasn't too keen on the elevation. I've been there before and I swore to God I would never go back. Heights were not my thing, especially when wind gusts way up there had the building moving just a smidgen. Some people never feel the building moving. Unfortunately, I'm one of those people who needs a drink before the plane takes off and wouldn't say no to a drink before I stepped off the elevator at the top floor of the Tower.

So, here I was, wearing this elegant sleeveless, off the shoulder evening dress with a heart shaped neckline that dipped low in front and even lower in the back. The satin wrapped my torso in a warm hug then flared out below the knee to trail the ground. The type of dress that made a girl feel glad she was a girl, made her believe she was darned attractive and just a little sexy. Who would have thought she'd find a dress like this in a consignment shop?

I adjusted my chiffon shawl of the same color around my shoulders, trying to hide my half-bared breasts from the cabby's furtive glances in the rearview mirror. All I needed was for him to plow into the rear of a car while ogling my boobs. My friend thought I should show off my breasts more often. Sure, I'd replied mischievously, for two hundred dollars. She thought I was kidding.

My best friend does this every year, invites me to this fancy annual dinner hosted by her employer. She acts as though it's the highlight of my life. The agency where she's employed investigates possible arsons and other naughty things that people do. I keep teasing her that I'm going to pull the fire alarm one of these years, but she keeps inviting me anyway as she thinks it's a special treat. I, in turn, feel like I'm giving her a gift by going because these dinners are almost always exceedingly boring.

One year I raised my hand and asked if the three-piece orchestra could try a little AC/DC. I tell you, these people my best buddy works with really need to check the dictionary for the meaning of *fun*.

This is the fourth year I've gone. Every year, she has somehow convinced me to attend these functions under the sham that she didn't have a date. Every year, I show up and there are two men waiting for us: one for her, one for lucky me.

You'd think that because I'm the guest, she'd let me do the 'eeny meeny miny mo' thing. She never does. She pre-selects *her* date and brings me his buddy. Each year I threaten never to go again because I abhor blind dates. But I'm a sucker for a fancy dinner and a chance to dress up, especially wearing ridiculously tall, four-inch stilettos.

It's my curse, this unwanted assistance I repeatedly receive from my friend who thinks I need a man. She feels that I need to settle down…which reminds me. Why is she bugging me to settle down when she herself has a new beau every six months? I will have to ask her that.

My excuse is that I'm too busy to settle down. I'm an Executive Director for a non-profit and participate on a board for another non-profit. The indoor rock climbing class I never attend is to conquer my fear of heights, and the two-mile daily run is just basic therapy. Throw in my classic movie addiction and my aversion to sharing my checkbook balance with members of the opposite sex, and yes, I do believe I'm too busy to settle down.

Then there's that moonlighting job I've taken on to assist in my dream of having a mortgage of my own one day.

My name is Mimi Goodenough, and I swear this is absolutely the last blind date I go on, ever.

∼∽

We screech up to the entrance at the Columbia Tower. Before paying for my roller coaster ride, I wipe my pink lipstick off the back of the driver's seat and steal a look in his rearview mirror to see how well my shoulder-length layers of blond curls survived the whiplash.

The handsome valet helps me from the car, earning my smile and an unintentional flash of cleavage as reward.

A light wind coming up from Elliott Bay blows in the slightly fishy smell of the wharfs. That, along with the car exhaust and hot asphalt mix from the road project a block down, makes an interesting consolidation of odors. I longed for the smell of fresh air. Someday soon, when I move on out of here.

It takes a moment to situate myself in my tight dress. I smoothed it down at the hips and tried to remember the small steps I'd practiced in order to walk in this satin tube while still looking like a woman. Small steps, like I'm not in a big hurry, with hips swinging gently side to side. Must be working because the doorman is smiling big.

I do this quite often; go places in fancy dresses to help raise money for this and that. As a result, I'm accustomed to doormen and valets and screeching taxi rides. It's getting old. This city is getting old as well. The glam is gone, the lights are too bright, the sirens too loud, the pan-handlers too annoying, and then there's the shoving, crime, and hair in my take-out.

As I ride the elevator with a pack of others also dressed up in fine attire, I add crowded elevators to my list of reasons I'm ready to leave this metropolis. On second thought, I wouldn't want to move too far away from the glam. Where else would I wear my collection of evening gowns?

Just six more months and I will have enough money to purchase a house. Actually, I could start house hunting sooner than that, but I'm willing to work a few additional months at this moonlighting job for the extra cash. That is if I can continue to put up with the owner hitting on me. At least I think he's hitting on me. He's a well-dressed Italian whose behavior walks a fine line between creepy and acceptable. I could have sworn I saw him in a town car a few weeks ago following me home on the Interstate. After losing sight of the car in the heavy traffic, I decided I had imagined it. It had only been my over-active imagination at work again. But anyone who knows me knows I'm a careful girl. The next opportunity I had to moonlight, I asked the manager if the owner ever frequented the Seattle area. Along with receiving a cold look, I was told that if I wanted to continue to work there I should not ask so many questions. Fine, I'd thought. I suppose I could not be curious for the few remaining months while I built up my savings. As far as I was concerned, case closed, due to a rude club manager.

The elevator dinged, I let go of my death grip on the handrail and we all poured out and onto the luxuriously plush maroon and gold carpet of the restaurant. Out through the expanse of floor to ceiling windows, the sunset painted the horizon in shades of gold. Over the roofs of the smaller skyscrapers, the city's lights reflected like hundreds of dancing stars off the calm surface of Elliott Bay.

A saxophone played Frank Sinatra tunes and waiters stood at the ready with silver-colored trays of slender champagne goblets of gleaming golden bubbles. I began to relax. Sexy music and bubbly: the perfect distraction for my aversion to heights and to recover from the elevator whooshing us up to the top floor at the speed of light.

Betsy Maverick waited for me, looking fabulous in a white slinky gown with no back. We shopped at the same consignment place, a boutique where the wealthy women of Seattle dropped off their worn-once gowns they wouldn't dare be seen in again. At a smidgen of the price of which they paid, we were happy to be seen again in their gowns.

Betsy was taller than I, bustier than I, and with kinky red hair that curled every which way. My 5'2" frame had a tendency to be slender in some places and exhibit my love for donuts in others.

The way I figured it, I had a good balance going. I worked out, kept the rear firm, the legs and arms toned, and even without a rock-hard tummy, and only one donut per week, I still received admiring looks.

Personality-wise, I was tame compared to Betsy, and I actually enjoyed table dancing. Not really, well maybe, if you twist my arm and dare me to take a couple of shots of tequila.

Betsy, on the other hand, hung from the ceilings in comparison. Even now, in our early thirties, there was always fun to be had with Betsy. She liked to say we were old enough to know better but young enough to do it three-times again. I've seen that on a lot of T-shirts so I know she didn't originate the saying. She likes to think she did.

My friend was all smiles, too big of a smile if you ask me. She and her exotic perfume enveloped me in a big hug.

"What?" I looked warily up at her. Even in my skyscraper strappy stilettos, I had to look up at this woman, whose father and brothers all played college basketball.

"You are going to *love* him." Betsy all but jumped up and down. Her glossy red lips were spread into the biggest grin I'd seen on her face in a long time. Her eyes dropped down to my cleavage. "Good. You wore the booby dress."

I covered my pale flesh protectively with one hand, and couldn't help but roll my eyes. "Betsy, why do you do this to me? Have some compassion, girlfriend."

She took me by the arm and urged me through the crowd of rented tuxedos and fancy gowns. Ahead, two handsome gentlemen in evening black caught my eye. They stood to one side of a glass showcase of valuable North American Indian weavings. They looked our direction, most likely admiring Betsy's curves.

Not too far from them, stood two more gentlemen, both in tuxes as well. One with a pony- tail and an earring, and his finger on his way to his nose, the other was as short as I and looked pregnant.

Damn that Betsy, I told her no more men who looked like they still lived with their mothers.

"No." I tugged away from her. It was time to take a stand. "Betsy, could you at least, for once, produce a

George Clooney look-a-like? It's going to take four margaritas before I even begin to like that man's shoes."

I dug my stilettos into the patterned carpet and stubbornly refused to budge.

Betsy looked down at me in confusion. "What are you talking about? This guy is a hunk."

"Have you been mixing Midol with tequila shots again?" I scrutinized her carefully.

She laughed, her red curls quivering on bare shoulders. "You goose." She pushed me ahead of her. "Your date is straight ahead, two o'clock."

I took two steps forward and stopped. 'Lives With His Mother' was at eleven o'clock. I let my eyes swivel past the glass case and land at one o'clock. I purred.

Betsy was right behind me. "One o'clock is mine, keep going."

One o'clock was delicious. Did I really have to move on? He had dark curly hair, a sexy smile directed right at us, playful eyes waiting to see what we were up to, and the body of a linebacker. Of course, he would be Betsy's. I guess if she went to all this trouble, she should get first pick.

A nudge from Betsy and my eyes traveled to two o'clock. Holy moly! Here's the quarterback!

"Nice, huh?" Betsy murmured in my ear. "And you thought I didn't know your taste." She urged me forward.

"Mimi, I'd like you to meet my date, Travis Norton, and his brother, Derek Black." Betsy paused and did this thing she liked to do when introducing me to men. It was a poor drum roll. "*Da,da,ta,da*. This, gentlemen, is my best friend, Mimi Goodenough."

I wasn't even looking at her date, Travis, when he shook my hand. I'm embarrassed to say that I had gone completely ga-ga over his brother, Derek.

∽

The second Travis eased up on his grip I quickly pulled free and offered my hand to Derek. I could hardly *wait* to touch him. It wasn't that he was movie-star handsome. The attraction was deeper than that, and an immediate one to boot. I think they call it primal. Thank goodness a decade or two of romance novels had educated me enough to put a name to this sensation.

His height and broad shoulders drew me in, as well as his overall athletic appearance of a man in top physical condition. I wondered how soon before I let this handsome devil know that it's best to assume I'm always right.

Derek's strong hand closed around mine in a solid handshake. You can tell a lot about a man in a handshake. There's the limp-I-don't-want-to-be-here handshake and the feather-weight-will-you-be-my-mommy handshake. Both will scare a girl off anytime. Then there's the solid, strong handshake of the man who doesn't miss the opportunity to check out your backside yet in the next breath could spring into action and fearlessly rescue you from a burning building. My knees went weak as he smiled down at me.

"Pleasure to meet you, Mimi." He paused. "Goodenuff?" His eyebrows rose curiously.

He wasn't the first to have fun with my name. Yet something in his tone played with my hair trigger temper.

"Yes," I answered him with a lift to my chin and barely a threat in my eyes. "It's Mimi Goodenough and nothing else." And here I'd thought I had outgrown my fieriness.

What was this man doing to me? Within the first five seconds of our introduction, I was hot, bothered, *and* ready to step into the boxing ring with him. I didn't have a category for this sensation in my to-date-or-not-to-date reference manual. My heart palpitated in its brief moment of panic.

His smile told me he knew he'd gotten under my skin.

"Let's find our table, shall we?" Travis had an arm around Betsy's waist and they both set off across the dining room without waiting to see if we would follow. As always, Betsy assumed I was a big girl and could converse with whatever life-form she set me up with.

I felt his hand lightly at my back as he directed me to follow his brother.

"You don't look alike," I commented over my shoulder. And they didn't. Derek was taller. His hair cut rebelliously short and silvery-blond. I could almost picture an earring in his ear, just like Sting, the rocker.

He didn't answer immediately. With a warm hand at my back, he gently maneuvered me through the crowded room of guests, all yet to take their seats.

When we caught sight of Betsy and Travis seated at a window table for four, Derek's deep voice resonated over my left shoulder. "We're half-brothers. Same mother, different pops."

We threaded our way to the table. Betsy noticed Derek's hand at my back and didn't try to hide her pleased smile. As for the question in her bright eyes of whether I approved of Derek, I wouldn't give her the satisfaction just yet.

I could give her a thumbs-up for the goose bumps and racing pulse, but he'd yet to earn a perfect ten rating. His hand at my back, I thought a tad pushy, like he was used to taking charge. Nothing wrong with that, except that I was used to it as well. Ask my cat.

Derek pulled my chair out for me. Betsy smiled. Okay, score one for a gentleman.

The waiter stopped by our table.

"Would you care to order a bottle of wine?" he asked.

Travis turned to Betsy and inquired about her drink preference.

"We'll try the '09 Chateau St. Michelle Cabernet." Derek spoke as if he were used to ordering for his date.

Putting on my nicest boardroom smile, I countered, "I'm fine with a glass of your merlot."

Now how could anyone refuse my request? Heavy eyeliner, lots of mascara, and you were looking at blue eyes that could convince a man to give her what she wanted every time. I let these Cleopatra eyes of mine slide over to Derek to let him see that this modern woman could order her own wine, thank you very much.

Derek glanced down at the wine list. "The '09 Cab is far superior to their merlot."

"How nice," I said.

Betsy sucked in her breath.

Derek turned to the waiter. "We'll take the '09."

I opened my mouth but Betsy kicked me under the table. An antiquated mode of communication, but still immensely effective. Betsy knew how I felt about men ordering for me.

I smiled at Derek. For now, I would be pleasant. "I'm sure the '09 Cabernet will be fine."

Derek held my glance for a few moments. "I know my wines, trust me."

I'd let this one go based on the attraction ratio and because of Betsy's pointy-toed shoes.

I glanced across the table to the cozy couple. You couldn't slide a dollar between their heads. Between working my day job and my moonlighting job, I apparently had fallen behind on keeping up with my friend's social calendar.

The lights from the neighboring skyscrapers twinkled like a galaxy of stars, clearly visible from our viewpoint. The spotless windowpane reflected our table of creamy linens and gleaming silver, along with four adults in evening dress. It also revealed Betsy getting her back caressed by her new man.

It was all I could do not to sigh aloud. Betsy counseled me many times regarding my process of qualifying men, saying that I needed to relax and just enjoy the attention and stop worrying about how we would get along down the road. It's just a date, she would say, just a touch, just a kiss. Enjoy it like a glass of champagne. Perhaps she was on to something. She was certainly happy all the time with the wining and dining on her social calendar.

"You work for the agency?" said the man responsible for the erratic pulse at the soft place on my wrist.

Betsy's words repeated in my head: It's just a touch, it's just a kiss. Enjoy it!

I reached for my glass of ice water. "No." I took a sip of the water and promptly returned the glass to the table because my shaking hand had the ice cubes clanking together. "Which of you is older, you or Travis?" I clasped my hands together on my lap.

"I'm four years older."

He perused the room in a careful manner. I'd seen that look before. I've known and dated more than a few cops. They always cased a room as though they were investigating a crime scene.

"By chance, are you in law enforcement?"

He paused in playing with the butter knife. "What makes you ask?"

I liked his voice; *almost* enough to forgive him for the '09 Cabernet that had arrived at our table.

The wine steward uncorked and Derek waved away the cork sniffing ritual and told the steward just to pour. Travis and Betsy had ordered martinis so declined the wine.

Derek waited for my reaction to the vintage I held to my lips. Darn-it, but it was better than any merlot I'd ever had.

I shrugged, attempting an attitude of indifference. "It's not bad."

His glass to his lips didn't quite cover his smile.

∞

I took a second delicious sip. "So you're a cop and a wine expert too?"

"Who said I was a cop?" He leaned back in his chair.

We were sitting so close, I suppose it couldn't be helped that his hand rested on the back of my chair. All it would take was for me to lean back the last few inches and he could play with my hair if he desired.

His warm brown eyes raked over me, showing obvious interest. I hadn't allowed a man into my personal space like this in a long time. My senses tingled with nerves and excitement, and my breathing quickened. I felt like I'd been left alone with a hungry tiger. I needed rescuing but friendship rules kept me from interrupting the intimacy going on across the table. Betsy and Travis were like two teenagers sharing sips of their martinis.

I leaned forward, casually resting my arms on the table before addressing him. "I bet the twenty dollar bill in my shoe, that you are carrying a badge."

"Why is there a twenty dollar bill in your shoe?" His mouth lifted at the corner.

"For emergencies." I sipped at my wine.

"What kind of emergencies?"

"Good dates gone bad, and I need a taxi ride home." I sent him a smile that didn't start out being flirtatious but somehow ended up that way.

His eyes sparkled with amusement, but his answering smile hinted that I could have this man wrapped around my pinky by dessert.

At the announcement that the first course would be served once everyone took their seats, the room buzzed with activity as guests searched for their tables.

Out of the corner of my eye, I noticed that Derek unconsciously fingered the silky fabric of my shawl where it draped across the back of my chair. He looked lost in thought, staring down at the blank canvas of the linen tablecloth. What girl wouldn't take an opportunity to study the profile of a handsome man? Across the bridge of his straight nose lay a faint scattering of light freckles leading me to wonder if this man liked the outdoors year-round. His thick brown eyelashes fanned out in the shapes of crescent moons, looking silky enough to tempt a woman into blowing gently across his high cheekbones, just to see what would happen. The small white scar on his square jaw brought up the question of whether he'd earned it playing team sports or earned it in a fist fight.

He glanced up and caught me looking at him. I quickly averted my gaze.

Betsy and Travis momentarily stopped orbiting each other.

"How did you two meet?" I asked, eager to focus on something other than the man at my side.

"A case he'd been working was linked to a local string of arsons." Betsy sent Travis a sweet look. "I brought him the file he needed. He works on the Vice squad with the Seattle Police Department."

I wondered if Travis picked-up on the adoration in Betsy's voice.

"Interesting." I felt it safe enough to meet Derek's gaze again. "Is everyone in your family a cop?"

"Derek tell you that already?" Travis sent Derek a curious look. "He generally doesn't discuss what he does for a living."

"Actually, I guessed." I held my smug smile in check.

Derek kept his silence, eyeing me with a dry-deadpan look. I didn't let this put a damper on my fun.

"Cops are quite easy to spot," I added.

"Are you really an officer as well, Derek?" Betsy said. "What division?"

"He's sort of freelance," Travis contributed. "Use to work out of Las Vegas. He's up here for the month leading an investigation."

"What sort of crime kept you the busiest in Las Vegas?" Betsy asked. She loved her cop shows.

Travis volunteered for his brother, "Strip clubs that were a front for money laundering."

Derek finally spoke. "Thanks, Travis. Anything else you want to tell them?"

Undeterred, Travis said, "My brother follows the need-to-know rule."

Leaning back in his chair, Derek glowered at his brother.

"Alright, alright," Travis raised his hands good-naturedly. "Enough talk about Derek." And suddenly the attention was on me. "Tell us about you, Mimi. What do *you* do for a living, and how do you like my brother, so far?"

∽∽

I set down my wine glass before my jitters had me dumping the contents all over the crisp, too-close-to-white-for-comfort linens. Why was I so nervous? Was it the reference to something I didn't dare write in my diary? Or was it Travis's direct question as to whether I liked his brother? Struggling for an answer to either question had me asking the dating gods, how old would I be before I no longer blushed?

The only good in either of these questions fired at me was that we were no longer discussing what Derek did for a living. I wondered if I could utilize Derek's need-to-know rule.

I was about to give it a shot when Betsy came to my rescue.

"She's a director for a non-profit. Think Twice is an agency that informs and educates people on how their actions, on both a personal and political level, have lasting global affects."

I sent Betsy a smile, but not because she'd memorized my agency's mission statement. She'd left the other unanswered question alone knowing that how I felt about Derek could keep until we had some girl time.

The salads arrived at our table on chilled clear glass plates and we set to enjoying our first course. Derek seemed deep in thought beside me and I soon learned why.

"Is there something on the political agenda right now that you are hoping to change your fellow American's minds about?"

I turned to him in surprise. Never before had a date of mine asked that question nor even cared what I did for a living. Non-profit seemed to scare most people off. They assumed I either worked at a soup kitchen or chained myself to trees.

The saxophone player across the room began to play. Frank Sinatra's *Fly Me to The Moon* spilled tantalizingly through the air, drawing a few couples out of their chairs to dance to its hypnotic rhythm.

"Actually, there is." I set down my fork and took a sip of the wine.

Betsy sent me a cautious look.

My return look told her not to worry.

Derek waited, and as he looked attentive, I eagerly turned toward him. "Gun control. Most Americans forget that our ancestors wrote the constitution well over two hundred years ago when we did not have government agencies to protect us like police and military. Every man shall have the right to bear arms pertains to those times. Now that we can pick up the phone and dial 911, do we really need to keep ourselves armed? We could drastically reduce the number of deaths contributed to a loaded gun in the home if Americans were not so obsessed with maintaining this right. Furthermore—"

"I would never give up my right to own a gun."

I stopped with my mouth open. I blinked at Derek. Yes, this was a typical male response, but he seemed intelligent and practical. I was sure I could convince him. "Well, yes, you are a police officer. Of course, *you* wouldn't be asked to give up your gun. Your duty is to protect those of us without guns."

Derek set down his fork and shook his head. "No, I mean I would never give up my right to own a gun, personally."

Betsy's pointed shoe grazed my shin and I tucked my legs further out of her reach and continued. "What if a drug addict broke into your home, stole your loaded gun, and went off to rob someone and shot them to death? Don't you think you would be partially responsible?"

"No, I don't." Derek's voice was firm. Very firm.

"But you would be because you supplied the weapon."

He turned in his seat to face me. "No, I wouldn't be. My house would be locked, my gun in a locked cabinet, and the bullets kept separate. Anyone bent on committing a crime like that is not going to let any lock stop him."

I drummed my fingers on the table and met him look for look. "What about all those people out there who do not lock up their guns nor keep the bullets separate? And the crazies who are allowed to walk right into a gun show and purchase semi-automatic rifles without a proper background check?" I did my best to keep my tone at a moderate level but Derek would have had to be made of stone not to sense the intensity growing in my voice.

He seemed to ponder my question as the waiter removed our salad plates and set out the main course of prime rib, mashed potatoes, and pan seared asparagus. A quick glance across the table revealed Travis and Betsy's attentions both focused our conversation, although for different reasons. Travis's expression showed amusement…Betsy's, concern.

"I agree that careless gun owners should be held accountable as well as those licensed to sell. These are areas of concern and with careful review of the current laws and guidelines, some changes may be necessary—"

"After careful review? What do you think this is, a football game?" I sliced right into his moderate reply with a waspish tone.

We had a nice little candle flickering on our table and it did a fine job of illuminating the angry expression on Derek's face. He wasn't pleased I had interrupted what had sounded to me like a reply read from something a press secretary would write.

In a dangerously quiet voice he said, "You're not going to solve the problem of people dying by gun shot with the removal of our right to bear arms. Consider that the majority of Americans owning a gun today are responsible gun owners. A few whackos out there shouldn't be allowed to jeopardize our constitutional rights. Now if you were thinking more clearly, you would have more respect for the importance and value of those rights."

"Isn't this delicious, Travis?" Betsy said louder than necessary.

Travis agreed. He also sent his brother a look that implied this was not the time or place.

I didn't care to take the hint, but I was willing to change the subject, slightly. This wasn't my first time in battle. Generally, I was in a business suit with my reading glasses on the tip of my nose, and let me tell you, I have put my share of know-it-all people in their places in my time. Tonight, however, I had to be careful not to split a side seam in this satin cocoon. As it was, I'd been steadily grinding my teeth since his *thinking more clearly* comment.

"I suppose you're a member of the NRA?" I said.

Just a fraction of a pause before Derek set down his knife and fork just so and removed his wallet from the inside pocket of his tuxedo. He flipped it open and held it up to my face.

I had to lean back a bit to allow my eyes to focus on his identification, as well as his NRA membership card.

"Well," I said to Agent Black. "You certainly like to flaunt that don't you?"

"Mimi?" Betsy said in a very sweet voice. "Shut up and eat your dinner."

∽

Derek snapped his wallet shut and returned it to his breast pocket. His attention went to his prime rib and mashed potatoes.

I was furious. I poked at my asparagus and drank my wine too fast.

Without a word, Derek reached over and refilled my glass. He set down the bottle and went back to cutting his meat like there was nothing more important. Betsy's look implored me to let it go. Too late. I was seething.

"I suppose you're a Republican?" This was said softly enough for only Derek to hear and with no intention of having it sound like an invitation to war.

The corner of Derek's mouth moved just the slightest as if he might smile. He checked that smile and for a moment there, I thought he wouldn't take the bait.

"You're good at this aren't you? Guessing what people do for a living and how they vote. While you're at it, why don't you tell me how old the milk is in my refrigerator and whether or not I had sex last week."

The first thing that happens when I do lose my cool, is that I take in a deep breath and my eyes open up really wide, because I simply cannot believe someone had the nerve to say or do what they just said or did. My eyes bulged and I took a breath—a very deep breath. Before I could dish out a well-deserved comeback, Betsy started bouncing up and down in her chair, squealing and pointing at the MC.

"Look, look. They're going to announce the winner of tonight's door prize." She clapped her hands like a gleeful child. "I know what it is. I know what it is." She turned to Travis, bubbling over with excitement. "It's an evening for four to this wealthy man's hunting lodge in the Cascades. Tonight, the winners get whisked away in a limousine with all the champagne they can drink, to this mountain retreat for an evening of romantic leisure. It will be an all-night party. The lucky winners won't be brought home until tomorrow. There's even a hot tub and swimsuits provided."

I heard the words, without comprehending any of them. How could I? I was far too pissed at Derek, whose disapproving gaze had currently locked with mine. Regardless of how clever he thought his answer to be, and how cool his demeanor, I could tell I had riled him. Gone was the male approval I had seen in his eyes at our introductions.

So, my approval rating had dropped. Well his had too. A ten? Hah! Due to his backward views on constitutional rights and his error in whose political party he leaned towards and his nasty bit of humor, he was barely striking a one at this moment.

The saxophone player took a break and relinquished the microphone to the prize announcer.

"And the winner is . . ." the announcer said.

Everyone around us, including Travis and Betsy, waited in anticipation with their eyes on the card propped up in the center of their table. "Table sixteen," the announcer called out.

Betsy leaped to her feet. "We won! We won! We won!"

I snapped out of my glacial stare-down with Derek.

In perfect unison, we asked, "Won what?"

Applause broke out around us. Travis looked pleased, Betsy looked as if she had just been crowned Miss America. Derek and I exchanged a look of confusion that made us temporary allies.

There was so much clapping and cheering that I couldn't hear the words coming from Betsy's mouth.

Derek put his mouth next to my ear. "What's going on?"

I had no idea.

Then the host of the evening was at our table asking us to follow him.

Thinking along the same lines, I took one last bite of my asparagus and a gulp of my wine just as Derek took one last bite of his potatoes and drained his glass. At that point, Betsy literally jerked us out of our chairs and away from our unfinished dinners.

Derek re-buttoned his tuxedo jacket, and I barely noticed him settling my gauzy shawl around my shoulders.

I picked up my tiny evening purse that matched my dress, and followed Travis and Betsy, Derek's hand once more at the small of my back.

At the elevator, I stopped and turned around, not realizing he was so close behind me. So close, I found myself staring at his bow tie and the crisp pleats of the shirt beneath his tux. Instinctively, I raised my hand to his chest, to stop him from coming any closer. The healthy, masculine beat of his heart beneath my hand electrified me, making me forget our lack of political or personal common ground.

A heartbeat like that, coupled with a warm look from its owner, could go far toward weakening a woman's resolve. Over the top of my head, Derek attempted to catch his brother's attention while keeping one of his hands lightly at my waist as though acknowledging we were a couple . . . at least for one evening. Wherever they were whisking us off to, he clearly intended to look after me. In a zingo of a second, I knew I liked having his hand there, touching me, claiming me. I wanted it to stay there, permanently.

Wrong!

I wanted to shake myself. Twenty-four hours with him in a locked room and one of us would require an ambulance.

I lifted my gaze to his. "Where are we going?"

Derek's warm smile spread over his face, transforming him. "Your guess is as good as mine."

He obviously wasn't one to hold a grudge over dinner-table sparring. His look, full of warmth and concern, told me, without a doubt, that politics aside, this man was interested in me. My heart pounded rhythmically, as I struggled to keep my distance from this man.

Sexual attraction didn't solve world hunger, nor correct the poor distribution of wealth, or get a Republican out of office. It was best I remembered that.

∽∾

Betsy and Travis received instructions from our host and when the elevator door opened, he ushered us aboard.

My idea of keeping a safe distance from Mr. Tall, Dark and Wrong About Most Things So Far, failed when the elevator dipped and my knees buckled. Derek's strong bicep was the closest security blanket.

His arm snaked around my waist and held me steady as we plummeted. At least it felt like a death dive to me. I closed my eyes and tried to breathe evenly.

"You'll live through this, I promise you." As comforting as those words sounded, I also detected a trace of amusement in his voice.

I didn't care. I clung shamelessly to his biceps until the elevator settled and the doors slid open. I recovered in record time, stepped out into the foyer and put a hand to my hair, pretending I was not a marshmallow in the elevator.

"Do you know where we're going?" I said.

His hand again claimed the small of my back as we rushed keep up with Travis and Betsy.

Derek raised his voice so his brother could hear him over Betsy's excited chatter. "Travis? What's going on?"

The doorman swept open the glass door and we were on the sidewalk with the balmy evening air rustling the satin of my gown and caressing my bare shoulders. We assembled next to several large container plantings of palm trees and fragrant blossoms. I shivered.

"Cold?" Derek asked.

I sensed he was about to shrug out of his jacket. How chivalrous. I didn't want him to be that nice. I couldn't see how the two of us could possibly get along. Life was a lot longer and much more complicated than a five-minute elevator ride.

The sleek extended length of a jet-black limousine sat at the curb. Travis and Betsy climbed aboard and the small driver in suit and matching hat stood holding the door for us.

I will shamelessly admit, then, that I panicked. The only way I knew to keep this man from making me like him too much was to continue sparring with him.

"Just for the record," I said, "the NRA is just a group of men who feel they can't be men without guns."

Derek's attention was on a black sedan parked at the corner with its driver, a tall skinny man with blonde hair and an alabaster-white face, leaning against the car with his chauffer's hat pulled low over his eyes as if he were napping.

Betsy yelled at us from the depths of the limousine.

"Get in! It's time to party!"

"You know what you need?"

Derek took me by the elbow and I had no choice but to climb into an interior smelling of leather, whiskey and Betsy's perfume.

"You need a warning label."

Chapter Two

The driver shut the door behind us. A giggling Betsy sat deep inside the limousine happily sharing that darkened end with Travis, who struggled to pop the cork on an iced bottle of champagne.

Derek and I had the rear bench seat to ourselves. Our only light source being tiny white lights encased in clear tubing bordering the ceiling and floorboard. These lights reflected like tiny fireflies from the limo's mirror-lined bar behind the driver's seat.

Betsy's silver and rhinestone finery worn around her neck, wrists and at her ears glittered in the cab. Light sparkled off her date's gold cufflinks. Derek pressed a few controls in the door and both his and my window rolled down to let in cool air. The full moon out my window illuminated enough to reflect the white of his dress shirt and the shimmering sheen of my satin dress, bouncing off the clasp on my purse.

"You're very funny," I said to Derek. "Warning label, I'll have to remember that one."

The limo pulled away from the curb and Derek gave a look back through the rear window.

"Travis, Betsy, fill us in here. What the hell is going on?" Derek said.

The cork flew out and Betsy held out flutes to take the bubbly liquid. She answered for Travis.

"We're heading for the Cascade Mountains to Livingston Lodge. It's a private home owned by the CEO. His private chef and butler will take very good care of us tonight. It's going to be so much fun. This man has an in-home theater, an Olympic-sized pool, a private gym, indoor go-carts, and I hear there are secret rooms and tunnels everywhere. It's like an adult playground."

I was immediately on my guard. "What do you mean an adult playground?"

Betsy giggled as she scooted down the length of the seat that ran from front to back in order to hand off two flutes to us. "Not kinky adult, silly. Fun, let's-be-a-kid-again-playground. Relax, you two, and try to get along." She smiled at the both of us. "I think for tonight that you two should not be allowed to talk politics or go anywhere near a controversial subject. Agreed, Travis?"

"Agreed," he said. "You're restricted to only talking about your childhood or hobbies."

"Boring!" Betsy exclaimed after downing her entire glass of champagne. "They can talk about fun vacations or …sex."

Heat swept into my face and I could not have been more thankful for the dark interior of the car. Still, I couldn't bring myself to look at Derek.

Our limousine driver accelerated, merging onto the freeway. Derek rolled up the windows to shut out the wind and freeway noise. So much for the cool wind across my heated cheeks.

"Truce?" He smiled and held out his hand.

I wasn't sure about this. I found him too attractive. It wouldn't take much for this man to turn me into a marshmallow. My independent nature wanted to resist, while my romantic side desperately longed for a good long kiss and some heavy petting. Which would win? I know what Betsy would like to see, and I was beginning to sense what I would like to feel. Tell that to my stubborn inner me, the one that refused to budge an inch, or surrender under any circumstances.

However, I was a civilized, mature woman. For Betsy's sake, I could be nice to her date's brother.

I slid my hand into his for the second time that night. I discovered that truce handshakes with men you're attracted to have a certain effect on a woman. I couldn't seem to release his hand. In the dimly lit interior of the moving car, I sensed the heated emotions in his eyes. Emotions that even my nasty comments about his choice of memberships and affiliations hadn't dampened. I slowly pulled my hand away.

"It might be safer if we talked politics." I drank from the chilled champagne as if thirst were my main priority.

"Okay, how about the next election." Derek seemed just as eager to change the atmosphere.

Betsy shook her finger at the two of us. "You're breaking the rules."

I ignored her and rattled off my opinion of my politician's opposition.

Derek raised his eyebrows. Then he sighed heavily as if the world's burdens were his. "I think I'm going to need something stronger if I'm going to survive this night with you." His slight smile added teasing to the equation. He leaned forward and dumped his champagne in the bucket for this purpose.

"Anything else in this wagon besides champagne?" He spoke to Travis, who was occupied with a lapful of Betsy.

Travis pulled a bottle of whiskey from the bar and handed it to Derek. "Better?"

"Whiskey?" Derek offered me a shot on the rocks.

I shook my head. "I don't care for the hard stuff. And I don't need to liquor up to be able to handle you."

Derek really did smile this time as he tossed back his drink and poured a refill. "I can handle you, whiskey or no whiskey."

∽

Shivers, goose bumps, and heart beating overtime; I kept it all to myself as I sipped casually from my flute. I laughed the sophisticated laugh of a woman in control, or one that thought she was.

"I feel like we're being kidnapped." I gazed out the window as we sailed over the I-90 Bridge that spanned Lake Washington. Mercer Island loomed ahead, where lights sparkled in windows of mansions on the shoreline and tucked in amongst the lushness of this tree covered island.

Once over the island, we continued across another bridge that spanned across the water until we reached the opposite shore. From here on, it was a straight shot toward the Cascade Mountain range.

"This seems to be more of an evening for Betsy and Travis." Derek directed my gaze towards the far end where the two other occupants of the vehicle were occupied with nuzzling each other. "Too bad they can't drop us off somewhere."

I was curious. "What would you rather be doing tonight?"

He turned sideways in his seat, his arm along the back. He sent a casual look out the rear window before replying, "Well for starters, I'd be watching the game on television in my hotel room."

"You would prefer that to fencing with me over political issues?" I was kidding, really I was.

"I didn't say I would be there alone." He looked pointedly at me.

I sucked my breath in. "I don't like watching sports." There, that ought to change his mind about wanting my company.

"Who said we would be watching sports?"

I leaned back against the door. "Stop it." My shaking hand set the flute into the holder designed just for this purpose. "In case you hadn't noticed, we have nothing in common."

His eyes warmed. "It seems that way so far."

The driver of the limo suddenly swerved to one side as a black car raced passed us in the lane on the left and then cut abruptly into our lane to accelerate ahead.

The motion sent me sliding across the leather upholstery to slam into the side of Derek. He saw me coming and raised his arm up and out of the way.

"Oh!" Every single inch of my right side smashed against every single inch of his left side.

Betsy had tumbled off Travis's lap and he helped her back onto the seat.

"Crazy driver!" Betsy brushed at the spilled champagne on her dress.

"What's wrong, Derek?" Travis asked.

Derek looked concerned, but quipped, "Where's a cop when you need one?"

Reluctant laughter filled the limo and I moved to reclaim my half of the seat. Derek's arm dropped around my shoulders and held me there. The heat from his thigh and torso against mine warmed me quite nicely.

I needed words to fight this sudden threat. "The death penalty, do you not agree it's inhumane?"

"Do I think psychotic killers and those who rape and murder children should be allowed to exist on my tax dollars? No, I don't. I don't believe they can be rehabilitated and that we should just put them out of theirs and our misery."

I pursed my lips. I could go either way on that issue. It all depended on the crime.

His arm tightened about my shoulders and I stiffened. "I will always vote Democrat."

"It's your right." He sipped at the whiskey still in his hand.

"I hate sports, crass language, I would never have a gun in my home, I believe that wealth is poorly distributed and that a woman should be president if only to keep us from listing too far over to the act-before-we-think side—"

His finger on my lips stopped me. "Do you want to hear what my beefs are?" He didn't wait for my reply.

"I think that those who *don't* work to improve their lives *should* be left to live in the conditions that result from their choices. I think that democrats spend *too* much money on social services. We *do* need to increase the strength of our military and I wouldn't miss one damn season of the 49-er's."

"You two have certainly improved foreign relations." Betsy giggled.

I suppose she would think that, as there were very few air pockets between Derek and me.

"We're working on a few domestic issues," Derek replied without taking his gaze from me.

"Of which some will never be resolved." This was way out of my comfort level. I scooted away from Derek. He didn't try to stop me.

Betsy and Travis were back to improving their own relations.

"You're in town on a temporary basis?" I said this to make a point…basically, this was useless. He would be leaving town soon, so why bother with starting anything.

"I'm here until this investigation is over."

"What investigation is that?"

He swirled his drink around in his glass for a moment. "Can't talk about it."

But I wanted to talk about it, or anything other than his suggesting his hotel room again.

"Are you after someone?"

He smiled down into his drink. "You are persistent."

"I'm curious."

"Yes, we're after someone."

"What did he do?"

Derek checked the time on the glowing face of his wristwatch. "What's our ETA at this place?"

Avoiding my question or tired of my prying? I guess that changing the subject was better than him telling me to mind my own business.

We were speeding along I-90 having left behind the City of Issaquah. We began to climb slightly in elevation as we headed straight for the darkened silhouettes of the mountain range.

"It's been a long time since I've been to North Bend," Betsy said. "If I recollect, it's only about another twenty minutes."

She wiggled and giggled on Travis's lap. I wondered how much of this wild night I was going to be up for. I almost would rather have sat through an evening of watching a game on the television than have to watch Betsy and Travis in what was obviously good old fashioned foreplay. I was darned envious of her and damned miffed as to why Derek now found it more interesting to check his text messages.

∽

If Derek looked out the back window again, I was going to start believing that he really would rather be back in his hotel room watching a game.

"So, Agent Black," I began, "when you've caught this person, will you be returning to Las Vegas?"

"Agent?" Betsy said. "You're an FBI Agent?" She sounded impressed.

"Hey!" Travis said. "Where's *my* admiration? My job is tougher than his."

Betsy returned to fawning and adoring her date, much to his satisfaction.

"Where were we?" Derek said.

"I asked if you're returning to Las Vegas."

"No. I don't live there any longer."

The ice cubes in his glass clinked together as he took another sip.

"Where do you live?"

"Where do *you* live?" he countered with his own question.

"I live on Queen Anne Hill, here in Seattle." This was a fairly safe subject area from my fairly safe place on this seat in a dark car with my back against the door. I'd braced myself in such a way that the next time the driver tried some evasive moves I wouldn't slide into Derek.

"I live in Taos, New Mexico." Derek set his empty glass in the drink holder in the door.

"So when you're finished here, that's where you'll return?" I tried to ignore the sounds of smooching coming from the opposite end of the car. Derek's gaze turned slowly in that direction, then returned to me.

"Depends on how long this investigation takes. I may end up in Vancouver for a spell."

"Vancouver, Washington?"

"No. Vancouver, Canada."

"Is this all the same investigation?"

"It will be if I don't get what I want down here."

"What is it that you want?" I asked. He hesitated for a moment. "To catch this guy who owns strip clubs that front illegal activities. He's an elusive son-of-a-bitch."

"You mean exotic dancing establishments."

"Same thing," he said. "He owns them all over Canada. Aren't you Canadian?" he added.

My dress was suddenly so tight I could barely take in a breath. "I have dual citizenship. How did you know?"

He nodded toward Betsy.

"What else did she tell you about me?"

"That you're a hard worker, you like beer and you're thinking of buying a house. She said that you belonged to a dance troupe in a former life."

"College," I said. "So this exotic dance club owner, what happens to his businesses when you arrest him?"

"They'll be closed temporarily as part of the investigation. Depending on the illegal activity, they may be closed for good."

"But what about the dancers?" My pulse beat with anxiety. I found it hard to swallow. "Will you be interrogating them?"

"Depends." He smiled. "Going to tell me that I should vote yes on an initiative to help the less fortunate stripper?"

Offended, I squared my shoulders. "There is nothing illegal about a strip tease. These girls pay their taxes and most of them are honest women just trying to make ends meet. Some put themselves through college."

His brow wrinkled. "Sounds like you know them personally."

"I, I know someone who knows someone who has a sister that, that performs on stage. She doesn't necessarily strip down to her birthday suit. You know, lots of those girls wear a bodysuit that's the same color as their skin tone and is as sheer as pantyhose. It covers about 97% of their body."

"Really?" Derek drawled. "Only 97%? What's covering the other 3%?"

Okay, so I set myself up for that one. "Maybe you'll find out when you bust his club." Take it easy, girl, I counseled myself. You're getting dangerously close to what he doesn't need to know.

I turned to look out the window. The lights of the city were miles behind us as we climbed in elevation and the road wound its way toward the mountain pass.

"Tell your friend to tell her friend to be careful."

I whipped my head back around. "Why?"

"Just in case she works for this guy."

"How bad is he?"

"He's smart and, unfortunately, has good lawyers. He's also paranoid. He's been known to threaten and stalk employees he suspects might be FBI agents. Some of his employees have restraining orders against him."

I found myself looking instinctively over my shoulder.

"How much longer?" Derek asked our tour guide.

Betsy lifted her head from Travis's shoulder and rapped on the driver's window.

The driver slid open the window between his section and ours. "Good evening." His heavy accent couldn't be missed.

"How much longer?" Betsy asked.

"Good evening." The driver repeated his greeting with such careful pronunciation he sounded more like a recording. He smiled into the rearview mirror as he bobbed his head. His eyes returned to the dark road ahead.

Betsy sent an amusingly puzzled look back towards the rest of us. She turned to the driver and tried again.

"How—much—longer?"

"Too ee ble teh." He slid the window shut.

No one said anything for a moment.

"What did he say?" Derek looked to Travis who could only lift his shoulders and shake his head. Betsy only giggled behind her hand. "Anybody speak mumble jumble?"

I leaned forward, happy to be of assistance. "He said, soon we'll be there."

"You understood that?" Derek's eyes widened.

"It's easy once you get used to it. It's just broken English."

"You have no idea what he said." Betsy shook her head and laughed.

"Sure I did." I was mighty confident. "Ask him something else."

Betsy rapped on the window again. The driver slid it open.

"Where are you taking us?"

"Ooo eh un t'ouse."

Betsy turned back to us, a hand over her mouth and trying not to laugh. "Did you get that?"

I certainly had. "He said, to a haunted house."

Betsy burst into laughter, nearly drowning out a chuckle from Travis.

Derek wasn't so sure I was right. "That can't be correct." He turned to Betsy as if seeking the correct answer. "Where is this place we're heading to?"

"Livingston Lodge. It's a ski lodge, Mimi, not a haunted house. Surely you couldn't have translated that correctly."

"I'm certain that's what he said." Her teasing didn't bother me. I was extremely confident that I was correct. "Not that I want to go to a haunted house this evening, but, Betsy, maybe it's you who got the information wrong from the get-go. Who told you this was a ski lodge we are heading to?"

"The host, right before he announced the winner, he read the description of the prize. Weren't you listening?"

I stole a quick glance at Derek. He sent me the same guilty look. We had argued our way through dinner.

"Weren't you paying attention?" Derek teased.

"I believe I was educating you in what is best for our country."

He stretched out his long legs and settled back against the leather upholstery looking ready to take a nap. "I believe you were wasting your time."

"For once, I agree with you."

Derek straightened in his seat. "I meant that your point of view isn't going to change my mind."

"I think I liked your first answer." I tried not to show him how pleased I was to be having the upper hand of our second round.

"Will you two cut it out?" Betsy sounded like she was losing her patience with us. "Or you'll both do a time-out when we get there." She looked at me then Derek. "In the bedroom."

∾

My reply came out without much thought of the consequences. "We can't."

"Why not?"

"Well we would first have to wait until you were finished with Travis, again, and again, and again.

Derek burst out laughing. It was quite contagious, that laugh of his. I found myself joining him. Travis did as well only his was an uncomfortable laugh with an odd look thrown in Betsy's direction.

Betsy wasn't quite sure she liked being the center of the joke. To my surprise, she squirmed in her seat and wouldn't look at Travis. "Well at least I get some now and then."

That remark cut my laugh short quite abruptly. I narrowed my eyes at Betsy. Comments about my sexless sex life were cause for manning the battle stations. "Thank you for that, Betsy."

"You're welcome." She crossed her elegant arms and her elegant legs and her pointy-toed shoe was now bobbing angrily up and down.

Derek cleared his throat uncomfortably. "So how about those Mariners, Travis?"

"Doing okay, doing okay." Travis kept a watchful eye on Betsy. He was probably concerned she might blow while he was within striking range. "More champagne, ladies?" He held up the bottle.

"No, thank you." I said in between my slow count to one hundred.

"I'll have some. Thank you, Travis my darling. Pour Mimi some as well, she needs to loosen up."

"Champagne gives me a headache." Thus the reason I'd barely touched my glass. Betsy knew that.

"Lightweight," Betsy murmured from behind her glass.

"I can out drink you, Betsy Lou." I knew she hated her middle name.

"Watered down beer doesn't count, Mimi Babette."

"Mimi Babette Goodenough?" Derek ran this over his tongue making it sound like a name for a Madam. He sent a slow grin towards Travis.

My pulse beat angrily. "Hand me the whiskey, Derek." I said this without looking his way as I tried to turn Betsy to ice with my go-to-hell look.

"I thought you didn't like the hard stuff?"

"Whiskey," I snapped at Derek. The next thing I knew, there was a tumbler in my hand with amber liquid barely covering the ice. I looked down into the glass. "Are we rationing?"

"I think you should." His smile seemed friendly enough, but I didn't need him cautioning me to take it easy.

I tossed the whiskey down with one swallow and gasped for breath. Holy hell—that burned. I coughed. "*That* was horrible."

Derek patted me on the back as I leaned forward fanning my hand frantically in front of my face.

I could hear Betsy's tinkling laugh.

Derek leaned in and spoke in a low tone. "Ignore her." I noticed then that there was no longer room between us for two large people. At some point, he'd slid over to my side of the bench seat. His hand gently rubbed my lower back.

"I'm fine." I leaned back to purposely squish his arm. He tugged to pull his arm free and I pushed back harder against the seat. I felt the need to take my aggravation toward Betsy out on him.

"Easy," he said, "I'm not the one who commented on your sex life, or lack thereof."

I squished even harder. With another tug, he pulled his arm free, and draped it across my shoulders instead.

"Just relax," he said. But he wasn't even looking at me. Did he not think that I couldn't see his cell phone on the seat beside him? Was he checking his text messages again? Did I care? I couldn't figure out what I said that had upset Betsy.

With a dangerous look in my direction, she deliberately snuggled in closer to Travis as if to say "*I am loved and getting some*".

I snuggled in closer to Derek.

We drove this way in silence for several miles before the driver finally decreased in speed as he exited the Interstate.

The burn of the whiskey had turned to a mellow hum. That and Derek's nice aftershave were likely contributing to my relaxed state. Then there was the warmth of sitting so close to him. The man should come with red warning strobe lights, because I was dangerously close to crawling onto his lap.

The limousine came to a stop sign. To our left and under the overpass were the bright lights of the small sleepy town of North Bend. We turned right and headed up a steep hill, dense with pine trees and with very few homes lit with welcoming lights. In fact, the homes we passed had darkened windows with nary a lit porch light.

Derek dipped his head. "How good of friends are you two anyway?"

"We were roommates in college and have been friends ever since."

"I bet she'll forget why she's mad at you by the time we get there. Travis and I go at each other now and then as well." He seemed quite comfortable lounging beside me.

"I'm not worried." I liked the easy conversation we'd slipped into.

It was warm in the limousine. Derek loosened his bow tie and unbuttoned the top button of his white dress shirt. "Can we get the A/C on?"

Travis had removed his tuxedo jacket and rolled up his sleeves to his forearms. Betsy fiddled with some buttons on the ceiling and cold air blew from the vents.

Derek, even with a faint sheen of perspiration at his hairline, had elected to keep his jacket on. Tanned skin gleamed in the low lights and it was obvious that Derek worked out. Muscles strained against the fitted jacket and slacks. One tanned hand rested casually on his knee. He had nicely shaped hands with fingernails filed straight across. His other hand was along the seat behind my shoulders. Every now and then, I thought I felt him touching my hair but I wasn't sure. Only a few inches separated our hips.

The driver reduced his speed and turned slowly onto a dark side street. He drove a short distance before coming to a complete stop. Over the tops of the trees on our left, you could see the lighter dusk outlining the mountain-tops and the lights along the valley far below. On our right, the evergreen-covered mountain rose like a looming dark shadow.

The window suddenly slid open and the driver said, "Ee b'dare. Ee b'dare. Ich ouse? Ich ouse? I got no mo ime."

They all looked at me.

"He said, we be there." I bit down on my lip and knew this was going to be a tough one.

"And?" Travis looked at me inquiringly.

I drew my brows together. "Which house?" My eyes flew to Betsy. "He wants to know which house, Betsy."

We were suddenly chums again. Her claws were in and my thoughts of doing something evil to her were dissipating.

Betsy lowered her window to stare out at the darkened neighborhood. Only a few of the houses had porch lights lit. The rest stood in darkness.

"It's a big one, that's all I know." She got to her knees and hung her head out the window, leaving her date to admire the view she presented.

The sweet smell of sun-warmed pine trees poured into the car. A symphony of crickets chirped their evening song, clearly audible over the purr of the car engine.

"What else did he say?" Derek asked.

I had been trying hard to figure that out myself. I suddenly had it. I snapped my fingers. "He got no time. I mean, he said, he's got no time. He wants to know which house and to tell him quick because he has no time."

∽∾

I looked at Derek. "What does he mean he has no time? He's going to wait here for us isn't he? To take us home?"

Derek looked back through the rear window. "Hell if I know."

Curious, I looked over my shoulder as well but saw only the dark road.

"Just drive slowly around the cul de-sac so I can read the mailboxes." Betsy continued to keep her upper body out the window.

The driver did as she requested and slowly drove the complete circle.

Betsy pulled her head in to give us a report. "No luck."

"Ich ouse? Ich ouse?" The driver grew more anxious. He held up his wrist and tapped at the face of his watch. "I got no mo ime."

"Go around again," Betsy said.

"What name are you looking for?" Travis moved over to help Betsy read the mailboxes.

"Livingston." Her voice came in through the open window. "Look, there's a driveway with a gate at the end of the cul de-sac." She pulled her head in and instructed the driver to point the car towards the gate. He did so and his headlights lit up stone pillars and bars of wrought iron. There were two gates, side-by-side.

"Well," Betsy pulled her head in again. The wind had tossed her curls about quite a bit but it only made her more beautiful. "Looks like we have two choices: one sign says *Estate*, which could very well be the Livingston mansion. However, the other sign is so worn that only an L is legible. So, it could be either one." She looked at Travis. "Which one do you think it might be?"

I could hear Travis asking her if the party host had given her an address when I heard the distinct sound of someone texting.

"Girlfriend?" I asked Derek.

He quickly shoved his cell phone into his jacket pocket.

"Work. Sorry."

"Not a problem."

"Having fun yet?" he asked.

I didn't want to smile but I did. "Are you?"

"From the moment you asked me if I was NRA."

I jabbed him with my elbow.

"Look, there's a speaker phone on each pillar." Travis said. He rapped on the dividing window and asked the driver to ring up to each of the houses.

The driver climbed from the car to press the speaker button on the intercom to the right. We could not hear the conversation, but the short driver hurried back to the car. As he climbed in and shut the door, the wrought-iron gate slowly began to open.

I sent Derek a frown. "How does he know if this is the right house? Who the heck can understand him, other than me?"

Betsy rapped on his window. "Is this the Livingston Estate?"

The gates slowly opened and the limousine moved forward.

"I guess that's your answer," Travis said.

Chapter Three

The limo maneuvered up the long winding driveway. We climbed and turned, and climbed and turned again, until we came to a level area and there before us was what appeared to be a very old hotel. Lights flickered on lampposts, and from the many coach lanterns lining the stone exterior of the mansion. Dark shapes of trees bent in the wind and the shadows from the high turrets stretched out far and wide across the grounds.

"Oh my," Betsy said.

I swallowed my apprehension. "This is not a ski lodge."

As the car slowed to a stop in front of a grand pair of steps, Derek added his two bits. "It's the Munster's house."

"Not unless the address said 1313 Mockingbird Lane," Mimi snorted. She gazed at Derek, who had swiveled suddenly in his seat to gape at her in astonishment. "What?"

"I can't believe you know the Munster's address," he said, with the slightest hint of admiration.

She made a show of rolling her eyes to keep from beaming. "I guess I can say the same thing about you, Mr. FBI agent."

"Well, I don't give a damn what the address is, at least we've finally arrived," Travis sounded relieved.

The driver opened the door and we stepped out, each one of us obviously amazed at the sheer size of the mansion. Betsy pulled me by the arm towards the wide stone steps.

Once we were out of earshot, she whispered in my ear, "Sorry for what I said. It's just that…we haven't exactly done *it* yet." Betsy's cheeks were a bright pink beneath the porch lights.

This brought me to a halt. In all the time I'd known her, Betsy never delayed on the intimacy portion of any date. "Is something wrong?" I said.

"I'm not sure. He walks me to my door after a date and kisses me goodnight and then splits." She laughed in embarrassment.

I picked up the skirt of my dress and walked with her up the steep steps. "Maybe he wants to get to know you better. There's nothing wrong with that." I stopped as we passed a gargoyle head on a stone pillar. "I don't know about this, Betsy. This house is not what I expected."

"Don't worry." She tucked her arm through mine. "At least we'll get some fantastic food." She gave my arm a squeeze and lowered her voice. "What do you think of Derek so far? Ready for a summer romance?"

"He's very attractive and very annoying all at the same time."

Betsy smiled. "He's perfect then."

I looked at her, shivering in the cool mountain air. "How is that perfect?"

"You'll never grow tired of him. There's attraction to get the juices flowing and annoyance to keep you on your toes."

"Is that how you feel about Travis?" I'd been dying to ask. I'd also wanted to ask something else. "When did you meet him anyway? I thought you were dating that delivery guy."

Betsy shrugged that off. "History. I just met Travis last week. He came into the agency needing information. He's a fast mover, too. Came right up to me and asked if I would like coffee. We've been out several times, and each time, he asked if I had a friend for his brother who was in town. I know you don't like blind dates, but he sort of pushed for this." She smiled. "Turns out, it was a good idea."

I looked over my shoulder to see the limo pulling away

"Where is he going?"

Derek and Travis turned in surprise. "Hey!" Travis tried to wave down the driver.

Derek swore.

I stood there shaking my head. "I can't believe he left us."

"I'm sure he'll come back. After all, this is an all-night party. We can't expect him to wait out in his car. Come on you guys," Betsy urged our dates, both still standing there watching the vanishing lights of the limo. "I'm sure he'll be back in the morning."

I could hear the men murmur in low voices, obviously having a private discussion. They headed toward us, the ominous frowns on their faces causing my stomach to churn.

I turned to my friend. "Betsy?"

"What?" She took a few steps toward the door.

"Can you help me with my zipper, please?"

Betsy stopped in her tracks then pivoted to face me. Fixing the zipper on a dress or a hem or a lost earring were all code for must-have-girl-talk-right-now. Something was bugging me. I couldn't figure it out, but this was one burden I didn't want to handle alone.

She approached, her right brow raised in curiosity. "What's wrong?" She pulled me away from the men and pretended to examine my zipper.

"Something's off about this, Betsy. I don't know, but I get the feeling we're being kept in the dark. I mean, check out the guys. They both look so serious and uptight."

She fiddled with my zipper, casting a glance over to our dates. "Oh, yeah. They're in cop mode, all right. I'm still hoping to have some fun, but we'll definitely have to keep our eyes and ears open."

∽

We rejoined the men on the doorstep and Betsy rang the doorbell. Melodic chimes sounded beyond the grand door.

We waited a moment and looked at each other.

"Try again," Travis said.

Chimes rang out again. Still, the door remained closed.

"I say we go on in." Travis reached past Betsy and put his hand on the door just as it opened from within, startling us.

We all took a step back. I bumped into Derek and both his hands came up to steady me by the hips.

Beneath his breath, Derek swore softly.

The tall man was bone thin in his dark suit and tie. He was as pale as the moon overhead with lips so thin they were more like a dark bluish line on his pale face. He looked familiar, if indeed this *was* a man who stood on the threshold. The person's features were delicate, with finely arched eyebrows and a thin nose. Whether man or woman, blood donating was a definite no-no for this person. A receiver maybe, but not a donor.

"Bin 'spect'n you," he said.

"Good God, is this how it's going to be all night?" Travis muttered beneath his breath. "What I would give just to hear a complete sentence."

"What did he say?" Betsy asked.

"I think he said he's been expecting us."

"Well of course he has," Betsy said. She held out her hand. "Hello. We're the winners of the door prize."

Her outstretched hand was ignored and the man didn't blink an eye, giving no registration that this meant anything to him.

He stepped back and held the door open. Dimly lit sconces sent a yellowish hue into the foyer of dark paneled wood and old paintings.

"Come on, everyone." Betsy was all set to get the night rolling.

Travis hung back for just a moment before Betsy reached for his hand.

We stepped into the foyer and the door closed behind us with a solid thud.

"Come with me," said our pale-faced butler.

With a hand to my hip, Derek held us back. "Hold on a sec," he said in a low tone and one that sent ominous shivers down my spine. As soon as the others started down the length of the grand foyer, he pulled me over to a Grecian-style pillar with a fern perched on top. He startled me, by pulling me into an embrace as if to nuzzle my neck.

He spoke softly into my ear, "Whatever happens tonight, stay close to me, and if I say get down, just do it."

The delectable shivers that started when his warm breath moved across my ear turned to entirely different shivers. "Why?"

"Come on, you two lovebirds," Betsy called back to us.

With my hand in Derek's firm, warm grasp, we moved to catch up with the others. The butler led the way down the long hall past a grand staircase and walls lined with tapestries, oil paintings and the many hunting trophies mounted high above them. The horned heads of bull elk, deer, and mountain goat peered down at us with their glass eyes opened wide and their mouths gaping, as if they'd died with one final bellow. At the far end of the foyer, the head of a mountain lion snarled with bared fangs at those who would dare approach.

I looked uncertainly up at Derek, trying to catch his eye. There was something about the steel set to his jaw that told me something wasn't right. Ahead of us, the foyer narrowed and the butler, Travis and Betsy disappeared around a corner.

"We can't let them out of our sight," Derek said.

A moment later, the lights went out.

I let out a cry of alarm. Derek suddenly pushed me up against the wall and covered me with his body.

I clutched at the lapels of his tuxedo jacket.

"Okay, this isn't going as planned," he said.

"What is going on?" I whispered in the pitch black of the foyer. I could only make out the faint lightness of his dress shirt. His warm breath stirred the hair at my temples.

"I meant, this date. It's not going as planned."

Why did I think that his answer required careful rephrasing?

Derek covered my hand that continued to hold tight to his jacket. "Mimi?"

"Yes."

"Do you trust me?"

"I hardly know you." Something in his tone had my knees shaking even more. "Do I need to trust you?"

"Yes. And if you don't hate me tomorrow, I swear I'll make this up to you."

"Why?" I gripped even tighter at his jacket, not wanting this warm shield to move and leave me unprotected.

"Because, despite our differences, I like you. Now follow me and don't let go."

I clutched his hand with both of my own.

Derek felt along the wall and I followed blindly. The old house smelled musty and of something exotic.

"I smell Betsy's perfume," I whispered.

"Let's follow that."

We felt our way down the hall to the corner. Derek pulled out his cell phone and it lit up. He used this as a meager light to find our way around the corner. We had only gone a few feet when we heard a muffled scream.

"That's Betsy!" I grew more frightened with every minute.

"I found a door," Derek said. "Ready?"

"No." I gripped both his hand and his upper arm. "Maybe we should get out of here and go for help."

"There's no time. We're going in. Stay behind me."

He opened the door to a parlor, illuminated by an overhead chandelier and a welcoming glow from a massive fireplace. Candles flickered from the mantle and tabletops, as well as the room's huge grand piano.

Travis and Betsy sat on a red sofa facing the fireplace. They did not turn to greet us. On a love seat nearby sat an older couple. The man wore a chef's uniform and the woman, a navy dress with white collar. Both looked frightened.

A man, wearing a black turtleneck and black slacks stood beside the fireplace. His dark hair, swept to one side, and glossed with hair gel. Dark eyes gleamed from a tanned face and his straight teeth flashed white in his smile. I stiffened in recognition.

The man who signed my moonlighting paychecks bowed slightly. "Good evening. Won't you join us?"

Derek's hand tightened on mine. "It's going to be all right. I'll get you out of this, I promise." He spoke quietly and pulled me into the room.

∽

I jumped as the door closed behind us. I hadn't even noticed the pale-faced butler standing next to the door. He'd donned a chauffeur's hat, and only then did I recognize him. He was the strange looking man I had seen outside the Columbia Tower. I stifled a scream at the sight of the gun in his hand. Derek's hand tightened over mine.

The butler, slash, chauffeur used the handgun to motion us over to the sofa. We walked carefully around to join Travis and Betsy. As we drew nearer, I saw why both sat so stiffly. Our host was equally armed, holding a handgun at his side.

I stared at my boss. "What's going on?"

"Take a seat, Genevieve," our host said.

"Who's Genevieve?" Betsy whispered.

Did I really have to explain?

Our unexpected host rested his arm casually on the mantle a few inches from where a marble bust of a Roman warrior sat. He held his head at an angle as if to better show us a comparison of his profile to the handsome bust.

"Jester," he spoke to the pale-faced butler who stepped forward. "I suspect this gentleman is wearing a weapon beneath his jacket. Please relieve him of his gun."

I was already too stunned to be surprised when Derek pulled a sidearm from a holster beneath his tuxedo jacket.

"Are you both okay?" Derek asked the older couple.

They nodded solemnly and the chef put his arm around the woman beside him.

Betsy spoke again, "Who is Genevieve?"

I sat down stiffly and Derek followed suit beside me.

Betsy leaned over to whisper, "Sorry about the lights. When he pulled a gun on us, I fell against the wall and the light switch."

"So, what do we have here?" the strip club owner began. "Is little FBI Agent out on a double date?"

"She's not FBI," Derek said.

"What is he talking about?" Betsy asked.

"I repeat," Derek said firmly. "She's not FBI. She's just a dancer in your club."

"You're a what?" Shock registered on Betsy's face.

Ignoring her, I turned to Derek. "How did you know?"

"Enough of this bull-shit drama! I don't like spies in my club and I'm going to show you what I do to them."

"He can't hurt you," Derek spoke quietly.

"Who the hell are you?" My employer pointed his gun at Derek.

"He's a police officer and he's an FBI agent so you'd best put that gun down," Betsy said, pointing at the brothers.

Derek exchanged a look with Travis. "She's right. We are law enforcement. I'm Agent Black." Derek looked at his wristwatch. "And in about two minutes, we're going to have some company. You walked right into a trap, Manilla."

Manilla looked startled. Once he got over his surprise of being recognized, he grew angry again. "You're bluffing."

Travis turned on him. "Why do you think we were at the party tonight? The FBI knew you were following one of your dancers again. As luck would have it, you followed one who lived in the States and that's what the FBI wanted. And to make our job easier, we didn't have long to wait. You appeared on our first double date."

"What?" Betsy's head whipped around to stare open-mouthed at Travis.

"He's right," Derek said. "Unless you've forgotten that one step over the border and you have no protection. You're a criminal in this country, Manilla."

"I'm a criminal in most countries, Agent Black. Do you think that stops me from coming and going as I please?" A sound outside caught his attention. "Go see who that is and scare them off," he instructed his chauffer. "This party is too big already."

When the parlor door closed behind his chauffer, Manilla pointed his gun at me. "You're coming with me."

Betsy put her hand out protectively across my body. "Over my dead body."

The gun moved to point at Betsy. "Easily arranged."

"Okay, okay." I stood up. "Just don't shoot anyone, please."

"Over here." Manilla beckoned me closer.

Lights suddenly blazed through the tall windows blinding us all, and a commanding voice from outside boomed over a speaker, "FBI. Drop your weapons!"

"Get down!" Derek ordered as he lunged for Manilla.

I dove onto the floor. The older couple fell to the floor and Travis dove over the back of the sofa dragging a startled Betsy with him.

Shouts came from outside while Derek and Manilla struggled for control of the gun. Travis stuck his head out from behind the sofa and gestured for the older couple to crawl towards him. They crawled on their hands and knees with surprising agility. Then it was my turn. Travis held his hand outstretched toward me.

Just then, Derek kicked the gun out of Manilla's hand then slammed his fist into the man's jaw, sending Manilla reeling backwards onto the floor. To my horror, the gun had slid to a stop directly in front of my nose.

When Derek went for the gun, Manilla kicked his legs out from under him. The Italian leaped to his feet and went for an equally lethal weapon. He grabbed the marble statue from the mantle before Derek had a chance to get to his feet.

My hand was on the handgun before I even realized what I was doing. I could only make it to my knees in the tight dress. "Don't!" I said, needing both hands to point the gun shakily at Manilla. Only it wasn't his heart the gun was aimed at because I couldn't raise my arms that high due to the tight constraints of my evening gown.

Manilla knew exactly where that gun was pointing. He froze in the motion of raising the statue over his head to bring down on Derek's head.

Someone kicked the door open and suddenly, people with guns poured into the room. I could only hope they were other FBI agents.

"Everyone down on the ground!"

"Mimi, drop the gun and do as they say," Derek said.

I gingerly set down the cold steel. I was shaking all over. This wasn't really happening. What kind of a blind date ends like this with me putting my hands on something I'd sworn I'd never touch? All I knew was that this night couldn't end soon enough and I hadn't even been kissed yet.

The only way to get back down onto the floor without a flat out dive like I did before was to slide onto my stomach from my kneeling position. That's when my dress seam split wide open with a loud rip, baring my side from my knees all the way up to my hip.

My humiliation was complete.

∽

"You mean he *still* hasn't called?" Betsy's voice bristled with anger

"Not a word," I said and sipped at my hot latte.

Two weeks had passed since my first experience at being patted down. It was all a blur; the ride in a black SUV back to Seattle followed by questions under florescent lights while sitting on a hard chair and sipping at bitter black coffee. I'd seen Derek only briefly through a window with half-shut blinds while he debriefed with his team. Betsy and I had huddled together for the duration of our visit to the FBI Seattle field office, using our date's tuxedo jackets to wrap around our shoulders and cover ourselves.

Rain drizzled outside our favorite Starbucks on Queen Anne Hill where Betsy and I spent many a Saturday morning, and today was no different. We were considering a matinée later.

"So has Travis called you again, other than the following day?" I asked.

"No. Remember, I told him I needed some space. He said that he really is interested in me and wants to go on a *real* date." She rolled her eyes. "I'm still miffed that those first dates were all just to get to you through me."

"Maybe you should call him." I snuggled lower in the armchair in front of the fireplace. It wasn't unusual in Seattle to have a fire blazing in the same month that purple and white pansies blossomed in the planter box at the window. Seventy-five degrees one day and fifty-two the next, a girl had to have a wardrobe to handle the temperature fluctuation. My hair was twisted up at the nape of my neck, with blond ringlets coming loose, and I wore what I considered my standard good-for-all-northwest-weather attire of slender jeans, black boots with a three-inch heel and a black T-shirt under my cropped leather jacket. Betsy, with her red curls pulled back in a ponytail, dressed similarly only her jeans were tucked into boots that covered her knees and she wore a long leather coat she'd recently found at a vintage shop.

"Maybe you should call Agent Black," she said, her smile teasing. "I'm fairly certain that man was into you."

"He got his man so he's probably off on another assignment," I said. "It bugs me, too, that it was all a ruse to get to the man they were after," I added.

"No." Betsy shook ponytail. "You can't be upset with him for the same reasons I'm upset with Travis. Yours was a blind date to begin with, so with all the chances a blind date has of being successful, which is fairly nil, a blind date trumps an FBI operation any day."

"Mimi?" The familiar voice rumbled over my shoulder.

I bolted upright in my chair, cursing mildly as coffee spilled onto my jeans.

Derek smiled as he walked around to our seating area. He held a hot drink in his hand.

"Is this a bust, again?" Betsy threw her hands up, swinging her head side to side as if expecting more agents to roll through the door.

"Sorry," Derek said. "Left my backup at headquarters."

"Oh." Betsy tried to cover her disappointment. Then she cheered up. "How's your brother?"

"Why don't you ask him?"

"Hello, ladies." Travis walked around to join us. He, too, held a hot coffee in his hand. "Nice bit of detective, work, Derek. Good guess on this Starbucks location."

I recovered from my surprise and tried not to stare at Derek. Oddly, I'd been concerned that I might forget what he looked like; the warm brown eyes, close cropped silver-blonde hair, straight nose and square jaw. I'd missed his presence...the size of him, broad shoulders and all, and that cologne of his. Wait a minute! Missed him? What was wrong with me?

"What are you doing here?" I sat back in my chair, trying for nonchalance. With one leg crossed over the other, I swung my booted foot as if I was totally relaxed.

"Looking for you," Derek said. He wasn't smiling any longer. "Care to go for a walk with me?"

My heart leaped against my chest. "Depends," I said. "Is this a regular walk or am I the bait again for some criminal type?"

He acknowledged this with a respectful nod. "Just a walk, Mimi. I promise."

"A walk sounds nice," Betsy said.

"Not you," Travis said. "You're staying here with me."

"Oh, really? Are you asking sincerely or is this all part of some detective work?"

Travis pulled up a chair and set his hot coffee next to Betsy's hot coffee.

Derek held out his hand to me. I hesitated for only a moment. I couldn't say no to a chance to be close to him again any more than I could keep from breathing air into my lungs. I needed to touch him again. I put my hand in his and he pulled me out of the chair. He didn't let go of my hand. We stood there toe to toe as if we were the only two in this particular Starbucks on this particular Saturday morning. The rain eased up and sunlight suddenly broke through the clouds.

"Hi." Derek smiled down at me.

"Hi."

"Think you could handle a real date with me?"

"What happens on a real date with you?"

He kissed me then, right in front of Travis and Betsy and everyone else in the shop who'd stopped to watch with smiles plastered upon their faces.

Derek lifted his head. I could still feel the warm, pressure of his lips on mine. I smiled, feeling halfway to being convinced this might be a good idea.

"Tell me one thing we have in common," I said.

Derek gave me a sexy as hell smile. "I'd rather show you." He took my hand and we left that Starbucks on Queen Anne Hill.

I was quite happy to go with him. Many envious gazes followed us out the door. Anyone wondering what we might discover in our search for common ground were probably dead on as to where we intended to begin.

If you enjoyed this story, please leave a review on the Amazon page or Goodreads, if you are a member.

THE LAST BLIND DATE
By Carmine Valentine
PG 13
16,093 words
Contemporary Romantic Suspense

Other Works
By Carmine Valentine

Coming in Fall of 2013
Cabin Fever
To be included in Cajunflair Publishing's
Book 4: Seasons of Love
(As yet unnamed)
An Anthology of Christmas-themed short stories

Blurb for
Cabin Fever
(Title and character names subject to change)

The plan was for Claire Goodson to do Christmas her way, alone in a cabin where she can quietly watch the snow falling in gentle patterns to the ground. No crazy family, no fiancé rushing her to the alter…Just some alone time.

That was the plan.

Claire has yet to strap on her snowshoes before diving headfirst into the spirit of the season. She generously offers to share the cabin with another Christmas loner, her handsome neighbor, Roger, whose own fiancé decides to spend the holidays elsewhere. Now she's snowed in with a man who has no idea he's slowly convincing her that she's about to marry the wrong man. Any chance he could be convinced that he's about to make the same mistake? This is the season of peace and goodwill, not heads or tails on who gets the top bunk with someone else's fiancé!

Coming soon:
Winter of the Vampire
(Paranormal Romance)

And…

Killer Regrets
(Romantic Suspense)

ABOUT THE AUTHOR

Photo by Rachel Whitney

Award winning writer **CARMINE VALENTINE** resides in Washington State. When not working her day job, she's writing romantic suspense and paranormal. She's also an online student with Arizona State University, having returned to school after twenty-some years to finally complete her Bachelor's degree. THE LAST BLIND DATE is her first published work. Please visit her website at www.carminevalentine.com to keep abreast of what's coming next.

DEDICATION

For my mom. Thank you for believing in me from the very first day I told you I wanted to be a writer, (and *that* was over twenty years ago.)

Made in the USA
Charleston, SC
20 September 2013